Oriane blinked.

'Marriage?' she whispered.

Euan flung back his head with an exasperated sigh, then glared at her. 'God's truth, woman. What did you think I was offering?'

'Well, what *was* I supposed to believe? That with all your conquests you can't find enough variety? Do you not pay them well enough these days, Sir Euan?'

She saw the colour of his eyes at last. They were dark, greeny-brown like smoky quartz, and very angry.

Juliet Landon lives in an ancient country village in the north of England with her retired scientist husband. Her keen interest in embroidery, art and history, together with a fertile imagination, make writing historical novels a favourite occupation. She finds the research particularly exciting, especially the early medieval period and the fascinating laws concerning women in particular, and their struggle for survival in a man's world.

Recent titles by the same author:

THE KNIGHT, THE KNAVE AND THE LADY
A KNIGHT IN WAITING
THE GOLDEN LURE

THE GOLDSMITH'S JEWEL

Juliet Landon

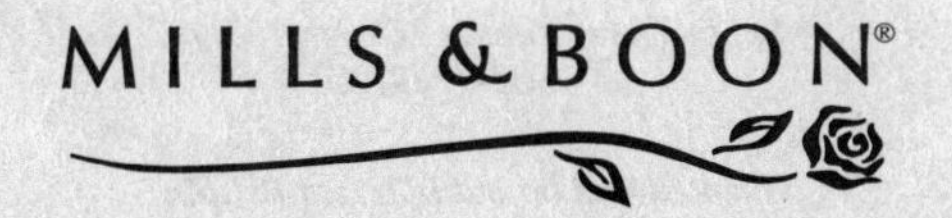

First published in Great Britain 1998
Harlequin Mills & Boon Limited,
Eton House, 18-24 Paradise Road, Richmond, Surrey TW9 1SR

ISBN 0 263 81423 8

Set in Times Roman 10½ on 12¼ pt.
04-9902-75747 C1

Printed and bound in Great Britain
by Caledonian International Book Manufacturing Ltd, Glasgow

Chapter One

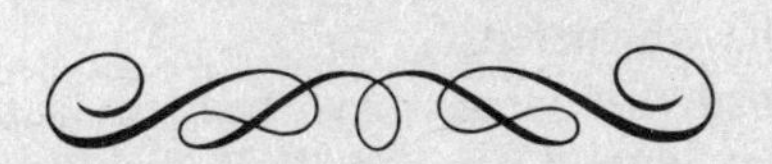

'Don't go. Please,' Leo said, plaintively, raising himself on to one elbow. 'Look...please...Oriane, leave it. We'll mend. No real harm done.'

Ignoring the repetitive plea, Oriane took issue with the tail end. 'No harm done? For pity's sake, Leo, there's a wound on your shoulder the size of a...' She searched for a suitable comparison, but nothing in the bare upper room seemed appropriate except perhaps the great red curling feather of the ridiculous hat he'd been wearing, now lying neatly on top of his folded clothes. But to say so would lessen the impact of her argument, so she rounded on him again.

'And your stepfather is in there—' she pointed to the timber-framed wall '—and like to die, and you tell me there's no real harm done? How bad does it have to be before ordinary folk like us lay complaints at his door?' She glared, hands on hips.

Leo flopped back on to the pillow with a soft thud that made him wince; his pale hair cushioned him like a halo. He frowned. 'I was not sure they *were* his men.

It was dark, wasn't it? And Father won't die. He's too strong.'

'No, it wasn't dark. You know we don't ride in the dark. You said you saw them. The blue-and-gold badges on their shoulders. You recognised it, you said, before they hit you.'

His hand flapped. 'I'm not sure. I could have mistook it,' he whispered.

Yesterday that would have been an admission to gloat about, but not now. 'Well, I'm about to find out. If I'm wrong, they'll make damn sure we know it, and if we're right they'll have to compensate us. I shall insist on it. They're not going to get away with it, Leo.'

The patient made one last try from the white linen of his pillow, his eyes closing on the effort. 'He's powerful, Oriane. I should never have said…oh, God!'

Watching him, Oriane was not sure whether her cousin's appeal to a higher authority was a sign of mental or physical anguish, nor did she dash off to demand retribution with the alacrity she had just implied. Instead, she creaked along the wooden passageway to the solar where Uncle Matthew lay, white and silent, his arms like twigs alongside his body, his legs extending like two ridges from a frail mound that rose and fell almost imperceptibly. On his temple, a red swelling the size of a duck's egg protruded from beneath a scattering of white hair and, beneath his niece's fingers, a pulse whispered through his wrist.

No doubt that Leo had thought she was being dramatic when she had spoken of his stepfather as being likely to die, but she was the one who had seen their injuries last night before they were tended, the old man unconscious, Leo nearly so. She had not exaggerated. The old man had fought hard to protect her and was about to pay for it. The least she could do was to show that she cared. Crossing her arms, she felt along her shoulders for the painful bruises that no one else had seen.

Yesterday had had all the beginnings of a blissful journey through the newly green fields and sun-dried tracks under trees heavy with showy spikes, blossom and luscious foliage. The woodlands had been carpeted with bluebells and wood-anemones beneath the horses' hooves, and their leisurely journey homewards from the wedding at Bridlington on the coast had been spread over two days, just for the pleasure of drinking in the succulent offerings of May. The sparkling sea had drawn them to stare in awed silence before turning westwards back to York, and they'd crossed the chirruping moorland, merry with the silly songs of the wedding-feast spilling out into garbled and raucous snatches. They had laughed and chuckled at nothing, still tipsy with an overindulgence of wine and ale, roasted oxen and the pet pig, capons and conies, pies and pastries.

After staying overnight at a small country inn and sharing part of the second day's journey with other travellers, Leo had become subdued, ill at ease, and Oriane had wondered if the effects of the revelry were already wearing off as they drew nearer to home. Then the companions left them, but their own party was well protected by Uncle Matthew's entire household of three adult journeymen, two well-grown apprentices, four menservants and two stout maids. At twenty years old, Leo was no weakling and Uncle Matthew was sharp, wiry and firm in the saddle. None of them had any reason to suspect, with the great white walls of York glowing ahead of them against a pink western sky, that the last forest glade to pass through would be any more infested by outlaws than the twenty others behind them. And that, Oriane supposed, was their foolish mistake. They had not been looking.

The evening breeze had rattled at the leaves above them and their horses hoofbeats had padded and clinked loudly enough to drown out the quick band of bodies that rushed them from all sides, surrounding the entire party before any of them could see what was happening. If it had been gold they were after, they had not made it immediately apparent, for most of their aggression seemed to be directed towards the women, herself in particular. Hence the bruises.

But Uncle Matthew and the men had rallied quickly after the first shock of the assault, and the outlaws with muffled faces and cloaked bodies had obviously been surprised by the strength and anger of their party. She, Oriane, had been pulled from her horse and manhandled to the ground; in defending her, Uncle Matthew had been brutally clubbed, Leo wounded by a sword and some of the others badly mauled. Even so, the attackers had been beaten off while she had been sat upon by the two women as a painful but effective way of keeping her safe.

From her inadequate viewpoint, she had heard Leo yelling at them. 'My father, you bloody idiots! My father's down! Go…for God's sake, just go!' And they had. His authority had astonished her.

They had carried Matthew le Seler the rest of the way in stunned silence, entering the city through the great stone portals of Monk Bar and along Goodramgate through the last scurrying crowds to Silver Street where the goldsmith had his home and workshop. By that time, Leo had lost so much blood that he, too, was helpless. Uncle Matthew had not regained consciousness, though at the time, Oriane had been optimistic that he would. Now, she was not so sure, and had sent one of the servants to St Leonard's Hospital to ask for the assistance of a physician.

There had been no chance to do more than poultice him with vinegar-soaked cloths, for it was still only dawn and Oriane had had no sleep. Leo had bled profusely, claiming her attention throughout the night. She nodded to Maddie, who came softly into the room, bearing a new poultice of witch hazel. 'No physician yet?' Oriane said.

The girl shook her head. 'You go down and wait for him, mistress. I'll say here and sit with the master.'

Instead of going down, Oriane tiptoed back to Leo's room. The bleeding had stopped and he was still asleep, white-faced in a pool of fair hair that had tangled like an infant's above the crown. It was fortunate that he was in no position to prevent her from making the complaint she had sworn to do, though if she had known how strong his objections, she would have kept her intentions to herself. Last night, weakened and rambling, he had told her that he recognised the badges and liveries of blue and gold. As the only badges to fit his description hereabouts were those from the Monk Bywater estate just outside York, it seemed clear that the lord of Monk Bywater should be made aware of the lawless element amongst his retainers. Too few would dare to demand justice from one as powerful as this unless they had some position in the world, and Leo was of the same mind as the few. Leave things be, he had bleated this morning, regretting his foolish chatter.

As the eighteen-year-old manager of her uncle's goldsmith's shop, Oriane was not daunted by troublesome customers and saw no reason why, if one employed unruly men, one should not be made to put the damage right. Lady Fitzhardinge of Monk Bywater was one of their customers and, if her husband was as pleasant as she, he would not deny anyone a fair hearing.

Oriane stood watching her cousin, her fingers playing idly with the pale gold hair around her fingers and allowing it to assume a natural spiral like a pointed seashell. She had seen Leo at his most charming over the last few days. Released from the immediate influence of his noisy friends, he had shown her the warmer side of his nature and a regard for her well-being which, in the twelve-month since his return from Oxford, was an exception of no mean importance. Only on the last day of their return journey had he shown something of the unease, the tension that she had come to accept as his more usual demeanour, bordering on tolerance rather than friendship.

She could understand his envy of her place in his stepfather's affections and had done her best, while he laughed off the disgrace of his expulsion from university, to assure him that he had nothing to fear by her presence in his stepfather's shop and home. Her efforts to appease Leo had largely gone unnoticed.

Uncle Matthew had little patience with his stepson's flounderings, and had made clear his displeasure at

Leo's failure to complete only two years of the seven-year course towards the priesthood. That this course had been his choice instead of Leo's did not make Matthew le Seler's disappointment any less obvious, and Leo was left to reap his stepfather's censure in the form of too-little advice, help or funds to set him straight again. It was enough, Matthew le Seler had told him, that he had a dry roof over his head.

Clearly, it was not enough and, in private, Oriane had tried, as discreetly as she was able, to tell him so. But Uncle Matthew was one of York's leading goldsmiths; he had important connections within the prestigious guild; he had wealthy and influential clients, both ecclesiastical and secular, and Oriane did not understand, he told her, how a little scandal, a wayward son, a marital indiscretion could ruin a man's name and affect his business. His own marriage, terminated two years ago by his wife's death, had been blameless, he had said, and if Leo did not begin to behave himself soon, he would have to take a firmer line with him.

The present line, Oriane would liked to have pointed out, had tied Leo unwillingly first to the Bishop of Durham's household, and then to a vocation for which no one could be less suited, despite the phenomenal cost. Eight pounds a year for board and lodging, forty shillings for clothes, two marks a year for lectures, not to mention the extras. But she kept her peace.

More recently, she had found that keeping her peace was also keeping her awake at night, worrying over the gold pieces that went missing from her uncle's safe-chest, the jewels that had disappeared from the workshop and the accounts that had been altered in the ledgers she kept so meticulously. She had tried hiding them beneath her bed each night, but it had made no difference; the gold went missing and the figures were corrected to account for it. By Leo, she was sure, who had free access to every room in the house and shop.

He must know that she knew; she was far too efficient not to know. He must also know that she was not sure enough of him to issue a challenge, nor would she risk alienating his stepfather more than he already was. Leo's obstreperous friends disturbed her by their unwelcome attentions and, if he willed, could disturb her even more. He would deny it, and so would they. She would be thought hysterical. In short, she was afraid of the repercussions, while regretting the circumstances that had pushed him this far into dishonesty. Would the assault of last evening and his father's injury bring him to his senses?

Downstairs, a door opened and closed. Voices made hushed greetings. She turned to meet the physician from St Leonard's.

He could have recommended that a mixture of pigeon's droppings and honey be applied to his patient's head, but the young and eager physician preferred a more vigorous approach designed, Oriane suspected, to demonstrate his sound classical training. Blood-letting, to be sure, was the first course of action.

'To clear the thought, to close the bladder and to temper the brain,' he said, taking his bone-handled knife from its case and wiping it carefully on the sheet. 'Prepare his arm, if you please, mistress.'

Not expecting, after that pronouncement, to see much change in her uncle's condition for some time,

Oriane held the basin under the white muscular forearm while the blood dripped sluggishly into it. As if that were not enough, she was obliged to listen to a lecture on how to keep the patient from falling into a deeper sleep.

'Tie his wrists and ankles, not too tightly, with cord. So. Now, rub the palms of his hands and the soles of his feet. You see?' The young man rubbed hard at the lifeless limbs until his face glowed and the lappets of his black cap flapped around his ears. 'We could draw blood from his nose with boar's bristles,' he said, 'but we'll see how he does with this first. It's an excess of bad blood that's causing the swelling, you see, mistress. We have to get it down.' He tapped the duck's egg on Uncle Matthew's brow. 'We might try making him sneeze and vomit with a straw in the nostril and a feather down the throat. We must get him to wake. Pinch him. Make a loud noise in his ear...a pig squealing is good...pull his hair, even. Anything to rouse him.'

Having summoned the man's help, Oriane was loath to contradict his suggestions, but neither could she bring herself to torment the poor inert body of her uncle as the physician was doing. Eventually, as the pale satin skin refused to change colour and the sunken eyelids refused to be held open, she called a sharp halt to the next assault, which would have been to wave her burnt hair beneath her uncle's nose.

'Thank you, Master Johannes, you have been more than diligent. I shall remember your advice, you may be sure. Now, allow me to help you.' Taking command of the situation, she scooped up his tools and dropped them into his leather bag, sent the bowl of dark blood downstairs and directed Master Johannes towards Leo's room where she had every expectation of a less passive resistance.

To her satisfaction, Master Johannes was as eager for Leo's sleep as he was for the goldsmith to wake. Accordingly, he left a sleeping-draught and instructions for an infusion of feverfew and wormwood for the fever he was sure would develop during the day. Which, Oriane remarked to Maddie, suited them both, for now Master Leo would know nothing of her mission.

The morning was young enough for some of the shops still to be shuttered and for a scattering of carters and waggons, washerwomen, apprentices and schoolboys to dodge round them through the sunless narrow streets. Instead of waiting for the ferryman, they crossed the river by the Ouse bridge and kept company with the shining silver water glimpsed between the houses along Skeldergate. There they joined the southern track where the nunnery of Clementhorpe lay like a contented herd across the common, warmed by the well-risen sun. The prioress was another of their customers.

Monk Bywater was hardly more than a cluster of twenty or so thatched dwellings of assorted sizes on a patch of land by the river that had been given to the monks of St Mary's Abbey in the previous century. The Fitzhardinge family, who leased it from the abbey in return for an annual rent and the usual tithes to the church, paid its priest, who conveniently doubled as their chaplain. They had also built a manor-house of grand proportions, walled and moated against incursions from the wild Scots who occasionally raided this far south. This much Oriane had learned from Uncle Matthew after Lady Fitzhardinge had called one day at the shop to order a pair of candlesticks for the manor's private chapel. There had never been any reason for Oriane to visit the place, nor did she relish the thought of doing so now in a frame of mind that bristled with outrage and a body that ached with bruises and fatigue.

The watermills were passed unnoticed; so were the heron and kingfisher. Ahead of them at the far side of the village were the stone walls of the manor, with stone rooftops rising above and blue smoke streaming like pennants from the kitchen and smithy.

Stares followed them along the track through the houses, and two tooth-gapped women called as they passed, laughing at their own curiosity. 'Going up to the manor court, then? Thou'd better get there soon, else he'll have done afore thou gets there. He don't waste no time, that one.' They cackled, nudging each other.

Oriane reined in. 'I beg your pardon? Manor court, did you say? Now? This morning?'

'Aye,' one said, more seriously. 'Started at dawn, as always. But you're not his tenants. No good you going unless you've got a complaint.'

Her companion saw a different meaning to this and doubled over in silent laughter. Then she came up, gasping. 'Aye, and the onny thing young ladies like you have to complain of with his sort is…'

'Shut up, Beth!' The other woman gave her a push that sent her reeling. 'Tek no notice, mistress. Come back another day.'

Maddie moved her horse alongside her mistress. The young groom moved to the other side, protectively. 'We'd best do as she says, mistress. It's their manor-court day and he'll not want outsiders complaining in front of everybody when he wants to get through his tenants' business. Best come back and have it out with him in private. Shall we try again tomorrow?'

Oriane compressed her lips, dug her heels into her horse and headed once more towards the gatehouse across the moat. 'Follow,' she said. 'I haven't come all this way to be told it's not convenient. It was not convenient for my relatives to be attacked by his men, either. To the devil with his manor court and his tenants. Come! Hurry!' Ignoring the attempts of the sleepy young man to hold the gates, she pushed at them with her foot and passed through at a brisk walk.

Naturally, she had expected that the monthly court would be in session within the great hall. Not for one moment had she thought it would be held, on this bright May morning, in the courtyard itself, nor that she would find herself the immediate centre of attention from the forty or so people packed silently to the left, or to the lesser group of officials seated and standing to the right, every one of whom scrutinised her from top to toe.

What they saw was enough to drop jaws and to suffer for it with digs in the ribs from sharp-eyed partners. They saw a young woman with the sun catching the pale gold crown of her hair and lighting a path down a plait that hung over one shoulder. She was seated like a goddess on a chestnut mare and looking upon them down a beautiful nose as if to avenge all wrongs. As they watched, she reached behind her neck with one hand and pulled up the white lawn veil that had dropped away during her journey, covering the thick shining hair but revealing a slim waist and perfect breasts that some could see outlined beneath the sleeveless surcoat of brown wool over a tight-fitting cream linen gown. Her movement was graceful and unhurried, as if the last thing on her mind was the spectacle she created.

The multiple fixed stare was exchanged for one glance from wide-open grey eyes that swept the courtyard in an unsmiling search. Her fine brows curved upwards, then drew together in a quick frown that suggested surprise and annoyance, but her eyes gave the game away. She had indeed come for justice. They narrowed, defensively, resting on the group of men at the table, leaving none of them in doubt that she could take them on, verbally single-handed, and win.

She was tall for a woman, slender-thighed and relaxed in the saddle, straight-backed, proud, no man's plaything. So thought the men. The women's thoughts were less generous and tinged with green. Their elbows dug again, closing slack mouths.

Without taking his eyes from the new arrivals, one of the men at the trestle-table leaned almost imperceptibly towards his neighbour. 'Anybody you know, Arnulf? Out of your class, perhaps?'

The slight hitch of Arnulf's shoulders could have been a laugh. 'Some way above,' he agreed from behind his fist. 'You deal with it.'

'Who's she looking for, d'ye think?'

'Guess, you silly bastard.'

Before Oriane's eyes came to rest on the three at

the table—steward, bailiff, receiver, she didn't know which—she had taken stock of the scene and adapted the plan she had carefully rehearsed all the way from Silver Street. To be plunged into the middle of the court without a preamble was not what she had intended. What *she* saw had to be summed up in one glance, ahead of questions.

Village folk and tenants from outlying hamlets made up the audience to the left, some sitting on the dry earth, some on logs of wood and rough benches or standing behind with children in arms. They faced the officials whose table was impressively littered with rolls of parchment, leases, bills of sale, contracts, lists and ledgers. A huge wooden box almost hid the scribe, his inkpot and quills from view.

The three officials were middle-aged and competent-looking and Oriane knew they would have been with the Fitzhardinge family for most of their working lives. They would understand the business from the inside out. She saw two of them exchange low words and struggle to conceal smiles, but she was well used to that and continued to search for one who might conceivably fit her image of the lord of the manor, the husband of Lady Faythe Fitzhardinge (who was old enough, she assumed, to be her mother). He would be white-haired and wear a full-length gown of some expensive stuff with a fur trim, and be seated in a proper chair with arms and a back. He would look dignified and important. No one here fitted that description.

Other men stood behind and to one side of the table against the stone wall of the steps leading up to the main doorway. Some, dressed in short tunics in the blue and gold livery, were holding horses ready-saddled as though waiting to ride out. The impression was heightened by a small group of well-dressed men in thigh-hugging hose and high leather boots, with soft cloaks that swung carelessly from shoulders. They were tall and well built, like soldiers, and two of them held falcons at eye level on gloved wrists. They, too, stared in silence.

The village man who stood before the table to plead his case received a roll of parchment from the scribe (who had not once looked up from his task), bowed politely, acknowledged the scattered applause from the crowd, and resumed his place among them.

The man at the centre of the table stood and addressed himself to Oriane. 'I bid you goodday, mistress. You are a tenant of my lord of Monk Bywater?' He knew she was not.

He could, Oriane thought, have stayed seated, but his gesture of respect gave her courage. 'I am not a tenant, sir, as I am sure you know. I doubt if the lord of Monk Bywater allows his own tenants to be set upon by thugs, does he? He would lose their labour and their rents. He would find that too inconvenient.' Truly, she had not meant to be so scathing so soon, but the suddenness of the scene had upset her timing and she had hoped to address herself more immediately to the lord himself.

The man, however, must have been used to such allegations, for he glanced down at his neighbour's face before returning to hers. 'Your name, mistress?'

'Oriane of York, niece of Matthew le Seler the goldsmith who was set upon last evening by men bearing the blue and gold badge of Fitzhardinge.'

The crowd became perfectly still, settling into their

benches for a development that could be far more entertaining than anything they would produce that day.

Her inquisitor began a half-glance over his shoulder, decided against it and pulled in his top lip instead, holding it for a second with his teeth. 'I fear, mistress, that this court is for manorial business only. Any complaints and supplications must be dealt with...'

Oriane had not waited for the rest of his dismissal, nor for her groom to offer his aid. She dismounted with impressive agility and grace before the man had time to finish, confronting him in two strides, face to face as '...on another occasion,' limped from his lips.

'No, sir. I think not!' she snapped. 'On *this* occasion, if you please.'

The glance behind him, which had been halted, now materialised at a second try, together with a small step backwards as if to make way at the table. But no one came forward or even acknowledged his signal, and the unfortunate man was obliged to resume his position. He drew a deep breath.

It was wasted. Oriane did not intend to be dismissed or waste precious time on courteous fencing. 'Matthew le Seler,' she said, making him flinch with the full force of her eyes, and speaking loud enough for all to hear, 'lies unconscious, still. I doubt if he will recover. His twenty-year-old son lies badly wounded. Whether your master admits to the cowardly attack by his men, whether he punishes them or not, is his affair. But for my uncle's honour, I demand immediate compensation for that disgraceful assault.'

The steward was not easily dismayed, but this was outside his province. Fees and fines, amercements and punishments, boon-work and boundaries he could handle in his sleep, but women of this calibre, with wealthy uncles and claims of assault by the lord's own men, well—he shifted uncomfortably—this was a different kettle of fish. 'Er…' he coughed, then felt the longed-for movement at his back. He stepped aside, thankfully.

A tall man, who until this moment had been lounging in apparent uninterest against the wall of the steps, pushed himself away from the cold stone, handed his goshawk carefully to the falconer and pulled impatiently at his leather gauntlet, slapping it hard on to a pile of parchment rolls. He stepped into the space vacated by the steward, flattened his hands on the table and leaned towards Oriane, hunching his shoulders to lower his head to her level. The table was a long way down.

Unlike her, he did not intend his voice to carry, but spoke clearly and slowly, as if to a child. 'How do *you* know what happened?' he said.

In the same patronising tone, she answered, 'I was there.'

She had expected disbelief, of course, and was prepared for a fight every inch of the way but, whoever this man was, she was far from sure he had any right to question her or to expect her co-operation. Perhaps he was a notary trained in law, a friend of the family, or one of their retainers who saw himself and his friends being blamed for the incident. In return for services, such men were paid and kept well by their lord, but it was not unknown for some to supplement their earnings with a little lawlessness in the summer months.

He looked like a soldier, come to think of it: massive shoulders, long, strong arms and legs that bulged with muscle, narrow buttocks barely covered by the fashionable tunic of cut velvet, the brown hands and well-developed wrists of a swordsman. His eyes never left her face and, despite her resolution, Oriane found it difficult not to quail under their silent invasion for, while hers were wide open in anger, his were so narrowed that she could not even guess at their colour. His head was untidily thatched with straight dark hair that fell in spikes over his brow and met above his ears, and he had a close beard that no more than outlined his jaw and mouth, underscoring the narrow buttress of a nose with a trim crescent moustache.

By his stance, she knew he meant to intimidate her, but saw him blink at her answer. He straightened and folded his arms across his chest, not at waist height, where a woman's would be, but high up, widening himself. 'And you saw the blue-and-gold Fitzhardinge badge, did you? Personally?'

It was the question she had known would come. So soon. She could not lie. 'No. Not personally. But my cousin sw…'

'What time of the day did this…incident…occur?'

'It was sunset.'

'And which way were you facing? Towards the sunset, or away from it?'

She resented the simplicity of his questions and knew exactly where they were leading. The man must be a lawyer. 'West,' she said. 'We were on our way home from the east coast. We were…'

'Ah! So you were dazzled by the low sun.'

'We were *not* dazzled! We were in woodland at the

t—' A mistake. A foolish mistake. Why had she given that away?

His head jerked back and his white teeth showed, briefly. 'Woodland. Even better. You were in dark woodland, facing the sun, and *you* did not see the badge of which you complain. Personally. But you had it from a wounded man that it was of blue and gold, a man who will be quite anxious to lay the blame at somebody's door, anybody's door, and thinks that the Fitzhardinge door will do quite well since it's not too far away. So he sends his cousin here, first thing, to...'

'He did *not* send me here! He forbade me to come, but I came for my uncle's sake because he's at death's door.' Oriane's fists, now clenching at her skirts, shook with anger. Everything she had prepared demolished so easily.

'Death's door? How do you know that? Have you had the word of a cirurgeon?'

At last, she was on safer ground. 'At dawn this morning. Master Johannes from St Leonard's Hospital. He came—'

'Hah!' His great chest heaved. '*That* whelp! Don't tell me; he bled him dry and then told you thirty-nine ways of keeping him awake. Eh? Well, if your uncle's survived Master Johannes, he'll survive anything, believe me. Go home and tend him, woman. You belong at his bedside, not here.'

'And you are worse than insolent, sir, and have no right to question me thus. I came to see the lord of Monk Bywater, Lady Fitzhardinge's husband, not one of his stableboys. I expect to get a fair hearing from him, and if his men are to blame...'

The man dropped his arms and grabbed at his gauntlet, barely looking at her. 'If his men are to blame, Mistress Whatever of York, this will be the third time in as many days he'll have to hang them for this nonsense. It's going to be an exceptionally busy week for them, you'll agree. Go home and get your facts straight, for all our sakes.' Without giving her another chance to reply he turned away, leaving her helpless and raging to face the three officials. She saw the pity on their faces.

A woman moved towards him, one who had been standing out of sight during the verbal warfare and who now spoke to him quietly. He halted and listened, bowing his head to hear her, then spoke, picked the hand off his arm and kissed it. In the next moment, he was in the saddle and leaping away towards the entrance of the courtyard followed by the others who had been near him. The gates closed and swallowed them.

Yesterday, Oriane had travelled far. She had been pulled from her horse and badly bruised. She had had no sleep and little to eat. And now this. She swayed and felt a hand on each elbow and, without seeing a thing, allowed herself to be led to one side and seated. A goblet shook in her hands, spilling liquid on to her surcoat. 'It doesn't matter,' she whispered. 'Really. I came to see the lord of Monk—' She stepped into an ice-cold black tunnel and fell headlong into its embrace.

Chapter Two

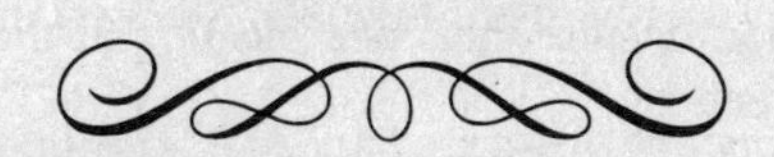

She had always had the utmost contempt for women who swooned. It was weak, foolish, pity-seeking and, much worse, showed a total lack of control. She was now able to add another epithet. It was vastly humiliating, especially before an audience.

Oriane knew that no man in his right mind would instantly admit that his employees were out of control. She had expected no admission of guilt, only a courteous reception and an assurance that her complaint would be examined. Her swooning all over the place would surely have made it look as though she could not bear to be thwarted, as if that…that *creature* had affected her. On the contrary, he had been the one to leave the contest. Her anger with herself was boundless.

She felt cold. And hot. 'I must see the lord of Monk Bywater,' she said, willing her legs to respond.

'Yes, dear. So you shall as soon as you've got your legs back.' The woman was tenacious, one must allow her that, Lady Faythe thought.

So, they knew her legs were missing. Without them,

it was not far to walk along a passageway and down the side of the kitchen garden wall to the small enclosed pleasance where a seat in the sun faced the well-kept plots and pathways, the orchard and the river beyond. There, with Maddie on one side of her and Lady Faythe on the other, Oriane made an effort to reverse the impression she was sure her hostess would have of her, despite their one meeting at the shop on Silver Street.

Maddie, bless her heart, did her part. 'She's had no sleep, my lady,' she said, putting a drink into Oriane's hands.

Lady Faythe Fitzhardinge, already sympathetic, received from Maddie an outline of events that had caused Oriane's weakness, having been drawn to the courtyard by raised voices and so witnessing only the last few moments of the hostilities. For a woman approaching fifty, whose high-cheeked face and skin like a ripe apricot was the envy of her women, Lady Faythe was ageless in other ways than beauty. She was petite, still slender and unwrinkled except when she smiled, which she did often, and her hair was still dark, profuse and glossy, with silver strands one could easily have counted. Even her elegance was, like Oriane's, youthful.

With the events of last evening now clearer in her mind, Lady Faythe sought the cause of the argument. 'The insignia?' she said. 'You were able to identify the badges?'

'My cousin did, my lady, though he admits he may be mistaken.'

The older woman placed a warm hand over Oriane's and held it. 'Then that is more than likely to be the case. No outlaws, unless they wished to plant the blame on someone else, would wear badges, would they? My son and his men only returned from France three days ago, my dear, while you were away at your wedding in Bridlington, and they've certainly had neither time, nor energy, nor motive to go raiding York's citizens since then. Besides, none of them are hooligans. The blue and gold are, you see, Euan's colours. My husband's are red, blue and gold. That's why he told you to be more sure of the facts, though I cannot approve of his rudeness.'

'Your son? Fitzhardinge...that was your *son*?'

Lady Faythe's smile was both proud and rueful. 'That was Euan, our son. He's war-weary and still a little short-tempered. I hope you'll overlook his soldier's ways. He usually keeps his forcefulness for the battlefield, I'm told.'

'It *was* a battlefield,' Oriane said, not entirely accepting the well-meant reasoning. 'Why didn't he explain? He knew I wished to see his father.'

'Perhaps, my dear, because my husband is ailing and still asleep at this hour of the day. That's partly why Euan has returned—to take up his father's duties. In all but name, Euan is now the effective lord of Monk Bywater.'

'I'm sorry.' Oriane paused out of respect. 'Then that is the only redress my uncle will receive. My cousin was right. I should not have come.'

'Until new evidence comes to light, my dear, we shall have to wait.'

'It isn't likely, is it, my lady?' Oriane's natural optimism had sunk almost out of sight now at the new humiliation of knowing that her public tongue-lashing had been administered by none other than the lord's own son. Not the stableboy but a bad-tempered war veteran with a soldier's cunning. And what of her mistake? Was it so very unforgivable to upset a manor court for the sake of her uncle and cousin? Could the man not have taken her aside to receive her complaint himself? In private?

'It *is* likely, Mistress Oriane, in view of the fact that your complaint is the third of this nature to have reached us this week. Even before Euan returned, the first complaint was already waiting for him. So you see, it could not possibly have been his men, nor were they ours. That's why he's so angry to hear it yet again. He will investigate. I will intercede for you, for it was exceptionally courageous of you to come so promptly to your uncle's defence when you have suffered so.'

'My timing was sorely amiss, lady. I have never passed out before.' Her hand was squeezed and released.

'Your uncle surely belongs to the Goldsmith's Guild? They will help?'

'They will help, yes. My uncle is well respected and they take good care of their members. But they cannot arrest outlaws until they can find them, my lady.'

Lady Faythe was silent for some time while the sound of distant applause and cheering floated over the rooftops from the courtyard. A popular judgement in someone's favour; permission to marry; a grant of land. Her next question was gentle. 'You have no parents of your own, mistress?'

'My father, Mark of Scepeton, and Matthew le Seler are brothers. My father is the elder; he lives and works in the dales as a wool-merchant. My mother died when I was thirteen, and my father sent me to live in York with my aunt and uncle. They thought I'd be better off in a woman's household with a business to learn. And indeed I am, my lady, though I miss my father and brothers.'

'How old?'

'Fifteen. Twins. Even my father gets their names wrong.'

'And your aunt?'

'She died two years ago. I've managed the business since then. Leo, her son by a former marriage, was sent to Oxford, but—' she stopped, abruptly.

Lady Fitzhardinge was quick to understand. 'And now he's back home again—well, at least he discovered which direction not to follow before it took him too far. I pray he recovers soon.'

She could not have known how ambiguous the sentiment was. Even before she had finished speaking, Oriane wondered whether she should confide in her about Leo's other problem which she saw as being far more serious than the wound. It was only a passing thought and disappeared as quickly as it had come.

At any other time and in other circumstances, she would like to have talked of a great many things, for she saw in the older woman much that she had missed since her mother and aunt had left her without female support on the very edge of womanhood. She had had more than a passing interest in the attractions of courtship and marriage, but living for two years with a lone uncle whose thoughts on the joys of love appeared to have flickered and died long before his wife did, did not make it easy for her to welcome any interested young suitor either to the shop or home. Uncle Matthew's eagle eye at the small window between the shop and the place where he worked ensured that no one lingered without good reason, and any protest from Oriane was invariably met with, 'I don't like the look of that young scallywag,' or, 'I don't trust his face.'

Leo's friends were never turned away even when they frequented the hall so often that Oriane was obliged to keep to her own room for some privacy. They were loud and foolish, and she had reluctantly come to the conclusion that her uncle was committed to preventing her marriage, presumably to keep her tied to the business. Leo, thrust into another direction, had been given no chance to take an interest in it.

A mother, she thought, would have solved the problem in no time, yet over the past half-year Oriane had given serious thought to rejoining her father at Scepeton, even though she had enjoyed living in York until Leo's arrival. The problem robbed her of much sleep. Now, it looked as though it might solve itself for, if Uncle Matthew did not recover, the question of staying would not arise. And if that was a development about which it was too soon to speculate, she did, just the same.

Lady Fitzhardinge's aim was to keep her lovely young guest in conversation until her strength had returned. For her part, it was the son's return that concerned Oriane most and her decision to leave could not be overturned. Thanking the kindly woman for her care and apologising for the inconvenience of her unplanned arrival, she promised to keep her informed of the uncle's and cousin's progress. She left, thankfully, before the hawking party was in sight, but her relief was short-lived—the morning, in which she believed that no worse could befall her, had only just begun.

And, as if her lesson in tolerance had not fully been rammed home, she was to discover to her mortification that it needed more than sheer willpower and fortitude to keep one in the saddle for two miles so soon after a fainting fit. Thousands of others before her must have made the same discovery but failed to pass it on.

The midday sun was almost at its height, the track was hard and rough, and before long Oriane began to see two of everything, particularly the horse's ears. The chestnut mare felt the reins slacken, dropped her head and stopped, and Oriane, seeing the cold black tunnel rush towards her once more and feeling that her need to be sick might coincide with it, flopped forward over the high pommel of the saddle, panting, shivering, and fighting to stay aboard. A numbness crept insidiously up her arms and, without knowing it, her plea to remain upright was spoken out loud. Nor did she hear the hoofbeats alongside.

'My god, she's going to come a cropper,' a deep voice said. 'Here, lad! Hold the mare while I take her on mine. Come on, lass, over here. That's it. What?' He spoke to someone over his shoulder, turning the horse with his legs. 'Yes. Passed out. Worn out by her own spleen, by the look o' things. You go on and I'll join you when I've taken her home. Won't be long.'

Dimly, Oriane was aware of floating, of being angry again, of blackness and tears forcing themselves between her eyelids. She was held painfully close in a grip that jammed her into a narrow space, but the rest was a mystery until she came to her senses with the hollow echo of hooves through the Skeldergate postern in the city wall. Then she was aware of the dazzle of the river through her eyelids and the quick shadow of houses, and knew that she was again in York.

'Ah, you're awake,' the deep voice said.

'I'm going to be sick,' she whispered.

'What?'

She could not raise her voice, but Maddie said it for her, and Oriane's mad world was tipped upside down with the track for sky as she was supported, retching noisily, over the side, and narrowly missing an elegant boot.

'That's enough,' the voice told her, not unkindly. 'Come on, it's only ale. You can hold the rest till you're home.' She was brought upright again.

Vaguely, and to the rhythm of giant hammer-blows in her head, she deduced that she must have done something of exceptional wickedness to be subjected to such misery, with this creature to witness it. What it could be she had no inkling, nor did she expect to live to find out, but she would rather have died in her own bed than in this man's arms.

She did not die in his arms nor indeed anywhere else, though in the next few hours there were times when she thought it might have been all for the best. At last, lying on her bed too worn to move, she was able to wonder why it mattered so much that the man had actually entered her room and laid her here and why it was that the imprint of his hands and arms beneath her body could still be felt so clearly. Unable completely to accept that the circumstances of her visit to Monk Bywater had not been in her favour from the start, the only recourse left was to blame first him and then herself. In spite of her protests about being able to walk, he had turned a deaf ear and carried her through a shop full of customers, through the hall full of gawping servants, up the staircase to her room where he had deposited her on the bed and ordered Maddie not to allow 'that idiot from St Leonard's' to see her but to send for Father Petrus from St Mary's Abbey, if need be. They were to mention his name.

That was not helpful, nor was it chivalrous; it was done specifically to take insolence to its limits. She drew up her knees and curled into a ball.

'Mistress Oriane! Wake up! I think you should come.'

'I'm awake, Maddie. What is it?'

'The master. He's...'

'He's what? Not...?' Oriane rolled and leapt to her feet, purposely not registering the lightness in her head.

'No, I don't think so. Better come and look.'

The solar, which was also Uncle Matthew's room, occupied the largest space above the shop that fronted on to the busy Silver Street. Doubling, as all solars did, as the main family room, it held a chair for the master's use, a large iron-bound chest and two smaller ones, two stools and a small table. The main feature, apart from the great bed, were the tapestries that covered two walls from beamed ceiling to floor, still bright with gaudy scenes of hunts and hawking, pastimes in which the master had never shown the slightest interest except when the results reached his kitchen.

Within the white-curtained bed, the shallow undulations of Matthew le Seler's body had not responded by the smallest sign to the physician's suggestions, and now his breathing had become so shallow that Oriane, who had seen death only three times before, knew that he was further than ever from recovery.

'I should not have slept,' she said, taking his cold and heavy hand between hers. 'I should have stayed with him. Oh, Maddie.'

'Nay, mistress. It would have made no difference. Let me send for the man from St Mary's. What's his name?'

'Father Petrus. And there's no need to mention that man's name. Uncle Matthew knows him well enough; they've been friends for years. Send Bec. Ask Simon to excuse him. Quickly.'

The three journeymen, Simon, Brian and Ephraim had all served their seven-year apprenticeship and had worked as master-craftsmen in Matthew le Seler's workshop ever since, smithing in harmony and living on the premises as one large family. The two seventeen-year-old apprentices, Bec and Davy, had come to look upon their master as a second father. One of the house-servants had taken Oriane's place behind the counter for that morning. An efficient and trusted man who took a pride from assisting in the shop, Gerard had been with her uncle from his earliest days, a family friend in most respects. There was not one of them who would not grieve at the passing of Matthew le Seler.

The hospital of St Leonard and the abbey of St

Mary both lay to the east of the minster, side by side, the hospital inside the city walls and the abbey outside but in its own extensive and highly protected environment. The almoner here was used to requests for visits to the sick and would usually send a servant to discover the problem and suggest a remedy. Matthew le Seler was, however, known to the abbey's inmates through long association, mostly because of the commissions he undertook and the special care and interest he gave to them.

Acknowledging his close bond, it was Father Petrus the infirmarer himself who answered Oriane's request without a moment's delay, taking strides with which the short-legged Bec could scarcely keep up, throwing over his narrow habit-clad shoulders questions that Bec could not answer concerning the reason for Oriane's procrastination. Why had she not sent for him at once?

At the goldsmith's house, the same question was put to Oriane herself.

'I suppose because I didn't want to believe his injury might be serious, Father. A sleep, then I thought he'd wake.'

'Tch!' The lean legs took two of the wooden stairs at a time. 'How old is he now, Mistress Oriane? Forty-five-ish?'

'My father's forty-five; Uncle Matthew's a year or two less.'

'Still, a blow over the head's not funny at our age, and if he's not regained his wits since last evening, it's serious. Ah, here we are, my old friend.' He picked up a limp hand, his fingers closing about the pulse, his large blue eyes watching the white face inside the close-fitting cap that looked as though it had been chiselled, with the pillow, from marble.

He replaced the hand on the sheet and sat on the bed, gently reaching out to lift one eyelid, then brushing the hair back to reveal the shining swelling on the forehead. He sighed. 'Who did this?' he said.

Oriane told him briefly, omitting to lay the blame on the Fitzhardinges for she was now no longer so sure of her ground, and when Father Petrus asked her to sit, she knew what he was about to say.

'I think you will have to prepare yourself to lose your uncle,' he said. 'He may continue in this state for days, even weeks, but I doubt it. Even if he regains his senses, he will probably be unable to speak or work and your care of him will be…intimate…and constant. Whatever the Lord wills, you must accept. I shall come again this evening. Shall we say a prayer for him?'

Together, they knelt at his bedside, then the priest went through to the small room where Leo was sitting up against the pillows, his arm and shoulder strapped with linen bandages. He closed the door behind him.

It was with some sense of guilt that Oriane did what she could to remedy her morning's shortcomings and put aside any weakness to which she might otherwise have submitted. It would not do for all three of them to be out of action, and the two men's wounds were indisputable. To give him his due, the kindly infirmarer had asked about her health too, concerned by her lack of colour, but she had assured him that she was well enough and then set about proving it to herself and the rest of the household.

On this first day after the holiday, the sound of hammers and chisels, the roar of the furnace, the clack of the shop-door and the drone of voices could not be entirely subdued, even for the sick, but straw had been scattered on the street outside to muffle the noise and to remind passers-by that whispers would be appropriate.

Leo was feverish and fretful, his colour heightened and his brow beaded with sweat. His appetite was for liquids, preferably his stepfather's best. Weak ale was the only liquid with which she could wet her uncle's lips from time to time, and Oriane's own meal of chicken broth had been meant for Leo, but which he had refused.

As the evening drew to a close and the shutters were fastened across the shop-front, her last task as manager-housekeeper was to remove the most precious materials and objects from the shop and place them in the great chest in Uncle Matthew's room for safekeeping. The gold coins which they melted down, the money from the shop, the jewels waiting to be set and the jewellery for sale was collected by herself and Gerard, taken upstairs and locked away overnight. Since the great chest had only one key which the master himself kept by him, Oriane took it upon herself to keep it with her, telling Gerard of her intention. He agreed, saying that Master Matthew ought by now to have thought about buying a chest with a multiple lock, for safety.

Out of loyalty, Oriane would not ask him what was behind that remark, but the knowledge that the key would be in her safekeeping seemed to reassure them that whatever was placed in the chest would still be there in the morning. But there was something else of great value in the chest which had not been removed on this day as it was on other work days. While Simon specialised in engraving, Ephraim in enamelling and Brian in the setting of gemstones, Matthew le Seler's main task for the last two years had been to craft a reliquary of gold and precious stones to hold a bone from the finger of one of the great northern saints who had died in the seventh century, Benedict Biscop. The casket was to be Matthew's life-gift to St Mary's Abbey and, apart from another day or two's work, was finished.

On occasion, Oriane had watched him at work, marvelling at his skill and dedication, and sometimes wondering whether this beautiful object was more a symbol of something from his past than a gift to his beloved abbey, for he had only begun it after his wife's death. Now they would never know its true significance.

As he had promised, Father Petrus came at nightfall; so convinced was he that his friend of many years would not last through the night that he administered the last rites, speaking Matthew's responses himself.

'Go to bed, young lady,' he told Oriane. 'There's nothing more you can do. He'll go peacefully now.' He removed the long stole from his shoulders and rolled it over his hand. 'Perhaps one of the servants...?'

Oriane thanked him but did not ask one of the servants to sit with their master. She had, after all, slept for an hour that morning and had no heart to leave him to die while she was abed. So she left the key to the chest under her pillow, with Maddie, took a long draught of the ale at her bedside and, after doing the nightly rounds of the house and workshop, took a last look at Leo's sleeping form and went to take up her vigil.

With a masochistic eagerness, she pulled forward the events of the morning, ready to suffer again the man's scathing words, his contempt and then his insufferable closeness, his cruel grip. From the low stool, she leaned on to the bed and pulled a woollen shawl around her shoulders, wincing as her fingers passed over her bruised arms. An overwhelming softness misted her thoughts as she tried again to line them up for inspection. It was no use. Her head fell forward and her breathing relaxed into the even rhythm of sleep.

It was the noise of the two apprentices clattering forgetfully down the wooden steps from the attic that woke her, gradually. Her mind was slow to clear; where was Maddie? Why had she not called her? Her hand moved and touched the cold one of Uncle Matthew and then she understood that she had not moved from his side, even though the sun sneaked through the cracks in the shutters and her limbs were set in stone.

Staggering, she let in the early light and returned to the bed. A curl of black and white fur lay fast asleep on top of the mound and when Oriane lifted her off, still purring, the cat stretched, stalked off towards the half-open door and turned back to look. Oriane stood with her hands over her face. Before her lay the lifeless body of her uncle, cold except for the warm circle on his chest. Taking his hand in her own, she held it for some moments, kissed it, and laid it carefully back on the covers.

Like her uncle's, her room was still shuttered, and Maddie, who should have been astir an hour ago, fast asleep. In Leo's room it was the same except that he had the excuse of the sleeping-draught that Master Johannes had left. Even so, he must be told before anyone else.

His noisy reaction was not entirely unexpected, making much of the fact that his stepfather's death had only just been discovered and that he should have been told as soon as it occurred. That Oriane had been too exhausted to stay awake had not, apparently, crossed his mind, or that it would have been impossible to wake him, anyway, or that it would have been difficult to define the moment of Uncle Matthew's death, in the circumstances.

Oriane deeply regretted her lapse into sleep but countered her cousin's disapproval. 'But I'm telling you now, Leo, before anyone else. What could anyone have done? We all expected it, even you, and Father Petrus said—'

'Father Petrus! You'd have done better to take Master Johannes's advice. At least he tried to revive him. But you didn't want that, did you?' He knelt awkwardly by his stepfather's side and sobbed loudly into his hands. 'And you didn't even allow me the chance to say farewell,' he cried. 'You take too much upon yourself, cousin, indeed you do. I'm excluded even to the very last, am I not?'

'You were soundly asleep too, Leo, and your father never once…' She looked heavenwards and, leaving father and son together, went to rouse Maddie. She knew that whatever she had done would be misinterpreted by Leo, as he had most things since his arrival. But his carefully wounding remark had gone deep, for Master Johannes's advice had been disregarded for Uncle Matthew's sake, not for her own, and what she had done had been for his dignity alone. She was hurt that Leo would not see it that way. She also had a pounding headache.

She sent Maddie to fetch a tub and hot water, a pot of lye with which to wash her hair, and clean clothes, purposely giving Leo time to go downstairs and announce his father's death himself, without her support. That he would misinterpret that, too, was taken for granted.

There was no question of opening the shop that day, nor indeed until after the funeral. With very little persuasion, Leo returned to his bed and Oriane designated Gerard to see to his every need. There was much to be done, black curtains to hang and mourning clothes to arrange, the transfer of the body to St Mary's Abbey to organise, the guild-master and friends to notify. They would pour in to offer to help and to pay respects as soon as it became known. A messenger was sent to Scepeton to tell her father of his brother's death and Leo was left alone to harbour whatever grievances came more naturally to him than breathing these days.

Father Petrus and Father William, the abbot, took a short family service in the solar before conducting the body away, assuring the family that their instructions for month-minds, obits and other masses would be followed to the letter. Not only that, but the abbey would accept his body for burial where he would be amongst friends.

Another morning caller was a servant wearing the blue-and-gold livery of the Fitzhardinges to discover 'for his mistress' how Master le Seler did. Remembering Lady Fitzhardinge's kindness, Oriane framed her reply accordingly. 'Give your mistress my thanks and tell her that my uncle passed away during the night.'

The young man bowed, wishing he had more questions to ask. 'And you, mistress? I'm to enquire about your health.'

'I am fully recovered, I thank you. My cousin is the one who was wounded.' Later, when she had time to recall the incident, she remembered how the lord of Monk Bywater's livery was *red*, blue and gold.

It was the three journeymen's suggestion that, for all those who would come to pay their respects before the funeral, a selection of the master's finest pieces should be displayed in the solar, particularly the reliquary on which he had been working when he died. What could be a more fitting tribute than to exhibit his skills before his masterpiece was taken to its final resting-place in the abbey?

With the key still warm from Maddie's pillow, Gerard unlocked the chest and lifted the casket on to the table by the window where it shone in the sunshine with breathtaking beauty, reflecting light from its gold and enamelled surfaces, from the rubies, pearls, amethysts and garnets. The gabled top was like a roof of engraved golden tiles studded with opals and moonstones, and the small side-panels of beaten gold were set into decorated arches behind which the saint's bone would be contained in another smaller casket. The whole rested on a deep base supported by the gold and enamelled symbols of the four evangelists, the borders embedded with jewels.

A sound from Gerard made Oriane turn. He was looking into the chest. 'Mistress?' he said. 'Did you need the money for something?'

Too astounded to speak, Oriane knew what he referred to and understood his reasoning. Last night, together, they had placed five bags of gold coins, some of foreign currency for melting, others from purchases, the men's materials, the loose jewels and the most costly contents of the shop into the chest and locked it. Now, all the bags of gold coins were missing; the rest was where they had placed it. And she had taken the key for safety.

Chapter Three

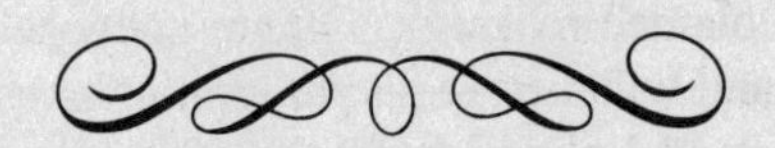

'Mistress?' Gerard repeated.

Oriane could see from the expression on his round polished face that the answer was already firmly established in his mind. She had had the key, therefore she must have removed the money. She had been here in the solar all night, alone with her uncle, despite offers to relieve her. Leo had been sedated. What else was there to say?

'Gerard…I…I don't know. Really. I don't know.'

He made a gesture of impatience, looking away and half-turning in embarrassment for them both. 'Mistress—' the word became a chastisement '—if you needed—'

'Gerard, if I needed money, I would say so!' she blurted out. 'I would not take it from the chest in the middle of the night while my uncle was dying.' Her voice was too loud. Too strident. They both looked towards the door.

In contrast, Gerard's voice was wearily quiet. 'You had the key,' he said.

'Yes, I know.' What she also knew, but would not

say so, was that there had been other times during the last six weeks when gold had disappeared from the shop and workroom, but in smaller quantities than this, where only she would be able to tell by weighing it that some was missing. Everything was weighed in and weighed out again: she was the one to record the details. This, she was certain, was a deliberate attempt to lay the blame on her, though how anyone—Leo, of course, that devil Leo—could have woken from a deep sleep to take a key from beneath Maddie's head was more than she could explain. Nor was there any point in trying, without proof. Any accusation would be denied, countered, and thrown back at her, especially as she had kept a silence about every other occasion.

'Gerard, please, *please* say nothing of this,' she said. 'Wherever the gold is, I'll find and replace it. Whatever you believe, I'm not a thief, you must know that. But I cannot lay the blame on anyone without proof and that is something which will be difficult to find. Please...say nothing.'

Gerard looked at the reliquary and Oriane knew that he would never fully accept her innocence. He had all the proof he needed except the five bags of gold. 'Did your uncle make a will?' he said.

The very nature of the question, its delivery and reception, its answer and the deliberation that followed was an indication that already their mistress-servant relationship had begun to founder, and that, at a time when she needed every ounce of support she could get, was something for which she would never forgive her resentful cousin. He was out to damage her. Well then, if this was war, she would have to fight.

This assertiveness was not easy to sustain over a

strong undercurrent of insecurity, and it was only the warming thought that her father and brothers would be arriving some time tomorrow that gave her any comfort. While her uncle had been alive, it had always seemed that Leo's pilfering was his responsibility rather than hers. He had been unshakeable in his trust of her and, if she had at any time denounced Leo to him and shown him the evidence, he would have believed her and turned his stepson out.

Who Leo's natural father was had never been made clear to her, only that Leo had been two years old when his mother married Matthew le Seler, but anyone could tell that they had little in common. Leo looked like his mother, blond and sharp-faced, but behaved like neither parent. Despite the reputation that preceded him from Oxford, Oriane had never been happy to exclude him from his father's good graces at her own expense and had believed that, in time, Leo would settle down and all this would be forgotten. Neither of them could have foreseen that this catastrophe would happen, though why Leo could not simply have suggested that she leave instead of attempting to disgrace her like this was hard to understand. She would tell her father, get his support, return with him to Scepeton, forget the whole dreadful nightmare and hope that Gerard would keep his suspicions to himself.

Gerard had not, however, promised to remain silent and his seemingly innocent query about her uncle's will raised some questions, the first of which must be about the existence of one at all. It was the accepted custom, Oriane knew, for a father to leave the bulk of his property to his eldest son and make generous provision for his wife, but this was by no means universal nor obligatory. If the father had a better idea about who would best continue his business, whatever it was, he could leave it to them instead, or to a younger son, to illegitimate offspring, or to a niece.

Oriane was determined not to mention it. It was Leo's affair, not hers.

Towards the end of the day, when the guild-masters had been to assure her of help with the funeral, when the late master's friends had been to offer support, the evening meal was laid on the table and a tray prepared for Leo. Before it could be carried up to him, he descended, part-dressed in shirt and hose and with one arm suspended in a sling. With one hand he scooped up a jug of ale and a beaker, kicked open the door to the workshop where Davy and Bec had just finished clearing out the cooled furnace and limped through to the shop beyond. His immediate commands were for some light, the shop being shuttered and dark.

Half a noisy hour later, Leo appeared at the doorway to the hall where the household, including the master's niece, was seated at the long table eating roasted chickens with herb stuffing-balls and last year's apples baked in honey. Well aware of the reason for Leo's activity in the shop, the servants were subdued, and Gerard, who might at one time have gone to see if he could assist his new master, kept his eyes on his piled-up bread platter and said nothing.

Master Leo had two ledgers under his arm. 'Where is my father's will, mistress?' he said, looking directly at Oriane.

She laid down her knife. 'I know nothing of your father's will, Leo. If he made one, he didn't mention it to me. It's none of my affair. You've searched his room, I take it?'

'It's not in his room,' he said, without moving.

'And the shop? Gerard knows where your father kept everything.'

'It's not in the shop. I've just looked.'

'Then I'm afraid I cannot help you.'

'I think you can.'

Except for Gerard, all had stopped eating, leaning back and watching the two protagonists alternately as if to judge which one to back, wishing that their late master's son had chosen a more private venue to make his request.

Oriane had paled. She said, 'You think I am lying? Why should I keep such a thing secret? Surely it's in both our interests to carry out the wishes of Master Matthew as quickly as possible? Whatever he had willed I shall be happy to accept.'

'Oh, yes!' Leo came further into the hall, gathering a wad of rushes around his toes as he walked and falling heavily on to a stool. 'I'll wager anything on that, cousin. You'll be happy to accept the whole bloody business, won't you, eh? And leave me to go and hang. Well—'

'*Well*, if you are saying what I think you're saying, Leo,' Oriane's loud interruption cut him off, 'it would hardly make any sense for me to hide your stepfather's will, would it? If you have some strangely warped reason of your own for believing that he may have favoured me instead of you, then why would I not be waving it beneath your nose by now? If I knew where it was. And now, perhaps you'll either join us in our meal or allow us to continue in peace without you.

Your late father would never have condoned the airing of such private matters before the servants.'

Leo lurched forward, slamming the two ledgers on to the table. 'Not so easy, mistress! Don't think to silence me with that, and don't think I haven't seen how things were being handled in the last year. What are those, then? Eh?' He patted the ledgers, leaning forward, his face glistening with the sweat of wound-fever.

'They're ledgers,' Oriane said. 'Account books.' From the corner of her eye she saw Gerard pause, his hand halfway to his mouth. Mentally, she kicked herself for not having had the foresight to see that this might happen. The accounts containing all the transactions, purchases and sales of metals, jewels, materials, tools and fuel, of commissions and specifications, of debts and payments, cash and installment terms, all were contained here, including the alterations in another hand made to look like hers. How he had managed to do this without being seen was something of an enigma, but never had she thought he would have the audacity to bring his own deviousness out into the open like this and challenge her before them all. Leo was unwell and part-drunk, his caution scattered to the winds. He was likely to say anything now and she could not allow the servants to hear it. She stood and walked round the table, passing him. 'Come into the workshop, if you please, Leo. We shall do better to continue this conversation without an audience.'

He had no choice but to follow her, albeit unwillingly.

Oriane held the door for him and closed it, noting

his anger as the books were once more slammed on to the bench. He would have preferred witnesses.

'Right,' he said. 'Ledgers. So you know all about the alterations where payments have been made to show how metals received were less than the amounts ordered and where bills have been submitted to customers with the amounts stepped up from the agreed price?'

'Yes, Leo, I've seen all of that. I see them most days.'

Leo hitched himself up sideways on to the bench. 'Well, well. And did my stepfather, who made the very seal that stamps these transactions, know of all the times these accounts have been falsified? Did *he* count the takings each day, or were you the only one? He trusted you, of course.' His eyes protruded, glittering and pale, his hair damp on his forehead. 'Didn't he?' He poked his head forward.

She should have been intimidated, but she was not. Pained. Angry. Impatient with the charade. All of those. 'That's enough!' she scolded as if to a bad-mannered child. 'How could you have discovered all that in half an hour unless you yourself were responsible? Don't take me for a fool, Leo. Yes, my uncle did trust me, and so should you, cousin, for I've covered up months of your petty thieving, as you well know. Did you particularly want to know how much I know of it? The gold pieces, the jewels, plate, and...yes...copies of bills and receipts falsified to account for the discrepancies, weights altered, specifications changed. I'm not blind, Leo. I saw them. What I ought to have done is to tell your father instead of trying to protect you.'

He opened his mouth to speak, innocence still finding a way through her exposition. But Oriane cut him off again.

'How *dare* you suggest that I am dishonest? To make alterations in my own hand when I could easily have stolen without a single alteration, if I'd wanted to. I'm the only one to make entries in those ledgers—' she shook a finger at the books '—and until you began meddling, there was not one mistake. Not one! Now they're full of them. Explain that!' She was sure that the next thing to be brought into the argument would be the five missing bags of gold, but perhaps he was saving that for an encore.

'Nay, I can't explain it except to say that you're as cunning a woman as ever I met. Only you would turn the truth around so and accuse me of stealing from my own father, God rest his soul. What do I know of weights and measures and exchange-rates? And if I'd needed money as badly as you seem to believe I do, I'd find an easier way than *that*—' he slapped the leather-bound books '—to do it, believe me. I would not have known of this had I not been searching for his will, nor would I have shamed you before the servants, Oriane, but I cannot keep such a thing to myself without giving you time to think what to do about it. If you return the money to me, I shall be prepared to reconsider, otherwise I have no choice but to bring a prosecution.'

Oriane had difficulty believing that she was not in the middle of a nightmare. 'Leo, I believe you are unwell. Let one of the servants take you back to bed.' She did her best to return him to some kind of sanity, even softening her voice to reassure him. 'Your father's death has shocked you, or you could not have said that. I strove to keep silent for your sake so as not to anger your father against you. You must believe that. I was never a contender for his esteem, nor would I ever have done anything to turn him from you. Let us talk of this when we are both calm and refreshed. My father will be here tomorrow; I will acquaint him with the facts and see what he suggests.'

At the back of her mind was the thought that that might be the last thing Leo would want in case her father proved Leo's guilt. But whether Leo was too stupid or too ill to see that, it made little difference to his determination, and the implications passed him by.

'Whatever he suggests, Oriane, is immaterial to me, though you might consider that the shame you will be asking him to share with you will be considerable. Better by far that you should find some way of repaying the money. Think on it.' He slid off the table and picked up the ledgers with his good arm. 'I hope you sleep as peacefully as you did last night.' He waited for her to open the door for him, then turned. 'And you may also make an effort to remember where my father put his will.'

For the servants' sake, Oriane put on a show of mild exasperation, explaining that Leo's fever was causing him to imagine problems and that another night's sleep would bring back his usual self again. Which was something of a vain hope and unlikely to pull the wool over anyone's eyes: Leo was already being his usual unfortunate self.

What surprised Oriane most was that her cousin should have drawn attention to something about which she had expected he would keep quiet. The risk was great that his duplicity would be exposed, yet he apparently felt confident enough to lay it at her door. She had suffered his disapproval during the last year, but never such outright animosity. His talk of repaying the money missing from the shop was ludicrous, a development that had never occurred to her except as a sudden future repentance on his part; never for her to undertake. It was as though he believed it himself.

Unaccountably, the scene at Monk Bywater Manor imprinted itself upon a pile of sheets Oriane had just removed from the linen chest, perhaps invoked by the smell of lavender and rosemary, when that man, with a quick volley of well-aimed questions, had shot down her accusations and stifled her demand for compensation as if it had never been uttered. Had he been there at her side just now, her cousin's tail would have been tucked firmly between his legs as he staggered upstairs, and probably knotted around his neck, too. More recollections of that morning were too unpleasant to entertain and so she halted their flow, but not before inflicting upon herself once more the sensation of his hard chest upon her cheek.

There was no place for shame as she anticipated as never before the arrival of her father and brothers who would, she knew, support her and demand that Leo come to his senses.

During her restless night she counted the bells and imagined the unhurried calmness of the many monks and nuns throughout the city and counted her blessings that Leo had not thought fit to include the missing gold bags amongst his accusations.

In the morning she delved to the bottom of every chest in the house, except those in Leo's room, whilst the servants assumed she was searching for the master's will. Unfortunately, the gold remained hidden.

The commotion in the courtyard at the rear of the house convinced Oriane, before anyone came to tell her, that the guests had arrived at last. Dropping the black rosettes that she had been sewing, she hurried outside to meet them, colliding with a man who entered at that moment and who took full advantage of the smile of welcome she had prepared. Before it could change to annoyance, she was taken up in an embrace more like a bear's than a man's and kissed full on the lips by a wet mouth that writhed like mating slugs.

Her legs, the only part of her able to move, doubled up into a vicious knee-jerk that her brothers had taught her, connecting with the man's groin and making him release his hold on her in the same instant in a screech of agony, leaving her to stagger backwards with the force of it into the chest of his comrade. She was caught, and held, not around her waist but higher up by two large interfering hands, to face another tormentor who leered at her in pained surprise.

'Why, Mistress Oriane! What an enthusiastic welcome. Is there a kiss for me, too?' He laughed at his companion's doubled-up form and red face, shook off the young groom who had come to Oriane's aid and sent him hurtling into the stable door.

Infuriated by this mauling, Oriane bent her head and released herself by biting hard into the thumb over her breast, feeling the bone grate beneath her teeth and the sudden slackening of his hands. Then, almost in the same movement, she threw the back of her hand across the cheek of the advancing man, seeing his head swing sideways with the force and his grin distort into an ugly grimace.

His high-crowned beaver hat stayed firmly on his head, his long piked hose over his shoes pointed aggressively towards her and his hands opened, ready to catch. Leo's friends, always on the lookout for a moment alone with her, had never engineered it until now.

She found her voice, but it had little power behind it. 'Keep back! You dishonour my uncle's house with this disgraceful behaviour while we are in mourning. If you've come to see Master Leo...'

The man's eyes opened wide. 'Eh? In mourning? The old man's snuffed it, has he? Well...that wasn't the general idea, was it, lads? Never mind, friend Leo and his shoulder-wound can wait while you and I...' He moved slowly towards her, but there were now two injured men at her back whose bulk purposely prevented any of the hall servants coming to her aid.

She screamed, but it was knocked out of her by a sudden punch into her back and a hand that covered her nose and mouth, a hand over which lashless eyes stared closely into hers. 'Shut up, bitch! We'll not miss you so easy in broad daylight, I think.' He withdrew the hand that reeked of horse-sweat and clamped his mouth over hers, but missed her lips as she twisted away. Forced against his cheek with her mouth free, she yelled loudly into his ear.

The effect of this astonished her; his arms were wrenched away with a sudden violence, his head snapped back, open-mouthed, and the rest of him flew across the cobbled yard in a backward dive that would have graced a cat for elegance. Except that he landed on his back. What happened next was even more astonishing, for the two injured men followed their friend in a manner almost as spectacular, ending in a scrabble of hands and knees over the cobbles.

A fourth figure, tall and neatly bearded, stood by to watch them rise. 'Get them out of here, Tomas,' he said.

One of them mouthed, aggressively, but changed his mind at Tomas's persuasive manner. In any other circumstances, Oriane would have allowed herself to be comforted by Maddie, or even wept a little at the sheer fright of having three grown men molest her, and even now could scarcely keep her eyes from burning with hot angry tears while her voice was inhibited by uncontrollable gasps. To Fitzhardinge's enquiries she could only nod, and pant, hold her arms across herself and push the hair away that had come loose during her struggles. In truth, she would rather anyone—yes, anyone—had intervened to save her at that moment than this man who must now be convinced that she was well practised in the art of helplessness.

Irritably, she shrugged Maddie off, discovering a lower register for her voice and a way of easing it out between breaths. 'Yes, of course…I'm all right…it's nothing, nothing at all. Go inside and prepare some…er, wine for these…er, guests.' She placed her fingertips to her chin and looked at the smear of blood on her fingers, frowning.

'It's yours, mistress, not theirs. Just a scratch,' Fitzhardinge said.

She nodded. 'Yes, of course. I am…most grateful to you…once again…for…for, er…'

'For saving you?'

'For getting rid of those...' The words eluded her.

'Unwanted guests? They obviously thought they were welcome.'

'I am expecting my father at any moment. I thought the noise in the yard was their arrival.' From his feet, her eyes were lured upwards from the pointed toes, tight-fitting dark red hose that showed every bulge of muscled calves and thighs and on up to a disgracefully short tunic of green Flemish siskin. His hips were so narrow that she could see no reason for the wide gold-linked belt not to fall off, in contrast to the shoulders swathed in the lower edges of a red hood, its deeply dagged border lined with green.

Against her will, her examination continued briefly to take in the darkly frowning face and the narrowed eyes, the shining straight hair that looked as though the last person to cut it had used a blunt dagger. In fact, it had been the army physician. His neck was thick and muscular and, at that, her eyes withdrew, having taken a mere four seconds.

'Your father?' he said. 'Then I will not detain you, mistress. I came merely at my lady mother's command to see if there is any duty the Fitzhardinges can perform.' His tone was businesslike and uninvolved.

It was a formality, she knew; he was making that quite clear. At the command of his mother. He could hardly ignore that, could he? 'I thank you again, sir, but you have already performed two extremely unpleasant duties that I would never have wished upon anyone, least of all a complete stranger.' She gave the word 'complete' some emphasis. 'You must be thinking that—'

He cut her off, rudely. 'Yes, well, never mind what I must be thinking.'

'I assure you, I don't...'

'You don't plan to be in difficulties day after day, do you?'

'I could not have known...'

'No, you could not have known that I would appear just now. But I feel I should warn you, mistress—'

'You may be sure, sir—'

'—that such things often happen in threes, like breakages.'

She could not tell if he was laughing at her, but his cheek moved and his mouth parted above the black beard as if he had more to say on the subject but had thought better of it. She was in no mood for jests. 'You may be sure, sir, that I shall take your warning very seriously indeed, and I willingly discharge you from all further duties. Please thank your lady mother for me and explain that you have more than fulfilled her...command...was it?' She observed the movement of eyebrows that passed between his two waiting friends and knew that she had scored.

From the other side of the high courtyard gates came a medley of sounds that could have been any passer-by, but Fitzhardinge's head turned towards it seconds before the double gates swung open and the hoofbeats changed to a hard clatter.

'Father...thank God!' Oriane whispered.

Something like a sob tangled into the words which, though whispered, escaped with such intensity that the man stayed by her side and, when she swayed unsteadily to take her first step forward, placed a hand beneath her elbow and felt her lean on it without realising that it was there. By that time it was too late for him to depart, for the gate and courtyard were jammed with horses and pack-mules, servants and grooms, hounds and baggages, and the Fitzhardinge trio was swallowed up in the general bustle of arrivals and greetings, unable to get out even if they had wanted to.

As it transpired, the blockade was a useful device which gave him the opportunity to watch the way she conducted herself when she was not scolding and arguing, fainting or being manhandled. If she could manage this throng after that roughing-up, however welcome her guests, then he would be convinced of the pluck his mother had admired in her. That she had been shaken he had no doubt, nor that she had inflicted some damage of her own, and he wondered how many times that nasty bunch had tried it on and whether that, and that alone, was the reason for the deep relief at her father's appearance.

It was not difficult to identify the father: that would be him on the big bay gelding leaping down in a welter of black-scarlet and cameline, a tall strong-limbed man with a handsome head of snow-white hair and an outdoor face wide open with happiness, despite the bad news that had brought him here. His arms were wide, too, and Fitzhardinge watched with interest the way Oriane of York bent into the soft folds of her father's knee-length gown without reserve and threw her arms about his neck. Then the embrace was rocked and laughed apart, their pleasure unfeigned and mutual.

They spoke, almost nose to nose, intimate words that made her drop her head when he touched her chin and, from him, a bellow of laughter that, had he known the truth, was almost insensitive. She did not flinch but brushed it off to greet her twin brothers and to perform with them a triangular hug that would have injured a weakling. Again, she laughed, ruffling their corn-coloured hair, darker than hers, exclaiming at their new height and lissome grace.

Ready to move into centre stage, her father was handing forward a lady of mature years and here Fitzhardinge was at a loss, for his mother had made no reference to a stepmother. Well, if she was not one yet, it looked as though she soon would be, for on the man's face he had glimpsed the quickly veiled expression of lust and its enticing counterpart from cleverly painted eyes.

Of medium height, the woman's impressively rounded proportions were revealed for all to see in an expanse of fine golden skin across neck and shoulders. Her mid-blue surcoat was cut away deeply at each side to leave only a narrow fur-edged panel attached to the skirt at front and back that hid no detail of the figure-hugging wine-coloured silk kirtle beneath, the fullness of each breast, the fleshy hips low-girdled with enamelled silver.

With an outward composure that concealed her dismay most successfully, Oriane waited for the introduction, all the more disconcerting for being without warning and in public. Her father had never been happy to be celibate, she knew; this had to happen some time. But not now. Of all times, not now.

'My dear, this is my daughter, Oriane. Sweetheart, Mistress Katherine Cherry.'

For the briefest moment, she thought her father might be jesting, as they often had in private with names. She saw the boys' faces over her father's shoulders and willed her face to stay on course, inclining her head in a curtsy towards the glossy black one and rising again, holding on to what grace she could muster after the sudden and unwelcome discovery that her father's affection was to be shared from now on with a stranger. The implications flooded in, swamping any greeting she ought to have made.

Unnoticing, her father continued, 'And Mistress Cherry's daughter, Jane.'

A plump girl of some sixteen years came forward from behind her mother with an anxious sidelong glance, and made an unsteady curtsy that Oriane put down to too many hours in the saddle. Whatever efforts Mistress Cherry had made with her daughter, they had failed, so far.

Her father's two massive wolfhounds created a diversion, almost knocking the poor lass over in their search for new smells and Uncle Matthew's cat that clung to Oriane's legs, hissing with flattened ears. Oriane stooped to pick it up and offered it to Jane, placing it gently into her arms with a smile and a request to protect it, which was easier by far than making polite conversation with her mother.

Fighting the intransigence that had already found a foothold in her mind, Oriane prepared to lead them into the hall while mentally scanning ahead to see that all was ready for them. Refreshments. She had asked Maddie to…ah!

The Fitzhardinge man.

The recollection made her turn to look towards the corner of the courtyard where Fitzhardinge's friends still held the horses. She hoped they would have gone by now. Instead, the man in question stood watching her in open regard, relaxed and waiting for her attention as if he had willed her to notice him.

Whether it was because she was unsettled by the ill-timed appearance of a woman in her father's company or because the earlier incident had shaken her more than she was able to admit just then, the idea of maintaining her declaration of dismissal from duties began to seem a little premature. A diversion was called for, a breathing space, a time to gather her thoughts. Anything rather than a pretence at equanimity. She had not realised how she had stared back at him until her father said, 'A friend of yours, love?'

Leisurely, as if he had heard, Fitzhardinge came forward to be introduced and, although neither of them had any reason to like each other, he was prepared to help her out yet again. Like breakages. In threes.

No, not a friend. 'Sir Euan Fitzhardinge of Monk Bywater, Father,' Oriane said, unable to fault the courtly bow that followed.

'A Fitzhardinge! Well, that's a name I know well enough. I followed your father into mischief often, young man, in our heydays.' The introduction sparked into life at the first words, then towards the two friends who were brought forward and presented as Sir Tomas Vittorini and Sir Geffrey d'Azure, both of whom Oriane recognised as the soldierly companions of her first encounter.

Eagerly, Mistress Cherry moved forward into the circle and Oriane eased herself backwards, glad of the short respite that had been provided so punctually and falling into the sturdy company of her brothers like a stranded fish into water.

'Who's that?' she whispered, frowning. 'Future stepmother, is it?'

Though equally troubled by the flamboyant appendage, the twins found her more amusing than their sister did. Paul laughed, eyeing the group. 'Looks like it.'

'He daren't let her out of his sight. That's why...'

'...he brought her. With a name like that I'm...'

'...not surprised.' They squeaked into a suppressed giggle, then dug each other in the ribs. 'Shut up!' Patrick snorted. 'It's true, Orrie. He's going to marry her. Loads of money.'

'And connections all over the place.'

'He's trying to impress her with his...' Another bout of boyish sniggers.

'What d'ye mean? The goldsmith's business?' Oriane said.

'Everything. And now the Fitzhardinge here. You don't come much better connected than that, do you?'

'Does he want to marry you, Orrie? Is that why he's here?'

'Why *is* he here?'

Oriane compressed her lips. 'Tch! I don't know why he's here. He's only one step removed from a complete stranger, and marriage to anyone at this moment is the very last thing on my mind.' That, at least, was true. What *was* on her mind was the complete destruction of all her comfortable hopes of support against Leo's accusations, for she could hardly involve her father in a potential scandal when gilt-edged connections as pure as snow were what he required for his future happiness. If he had come alone, it might have been different. Now, help was out of the question, for if she mentioned it to him, he would risk everything to clear her name.

Leo stood in the doorway, reminding them what they were about, and saw that Oriane was thanking the young groom who had tried to protect her.

Chapter Four

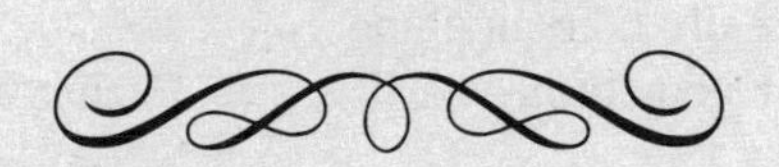

Leo was not to learn what Oriane had been protected from until some considerable time later, and then his chagrin was not that she had been abused by his friends but that they had been sent so rudely packing without seeing him. Which did not endear him to the powerfully built and expensively dressed member of the Fitzhardinge family who attended the funeral with his lovely and distinctive mother.

Nevertheless, Leo was obliged to be civil when Fitzhardinge enquired about his injury and to respond politely when the man confirmed that he had every intention of discovering who the culprits were if only to quash, once and for all, rumours that they were his own men.

'Believe me, Master le Seler,' he said with impressive sternness, 'I shall not be satisfied until I've found out who they are and how they come to be wearing my men's cast-off cloaks.'

Master le Seler was bound to be concerned by this assurance while realising how dangerous it might be to voice a grudge about the treatment of his friends on the previous day.

Mark of Scepeton, Oriane's father, was of the same mind as Fitzhardinge. 'Matthew's fellow guild-members have expressed the same intention,' he said. 'We're to have another talk about it later on. Got to stamp out this kind of thing, you know, even if they didn't actually take anything.'

'Except your brother's life, sir,' Fitzhardinge said, solemnly.

'Well, yes. Of course.' Caught with such ease on the wrong foot, he turned to the nearest of his sons. 'Patrick!' he said, snappily.

'Yes, Father?' Patrick replied.

'You'll walk behind me with your sister and Paul.'

'Yes, Father,' he said, staring at his brother innocently.

Like any normal fifteen-year-olds, the twins were impressed not only by the Fitzhardinge name, of which they had heard, but by the man's obvious presence which helped to amplify what they already knew of his bravery in battle, his leadership and tactical skills, of his wounds which were healing. What else they heard during that long funeral day from others who knew him was not of the same order, though equally fascinating, and whilst this was perhaps not the kind of thing that should have been related to a woman, their sister was somehow exempt from that species and, anyway, had said that she couldn't bear the man. She had barely greeted him with civility.

Naturally, she did not want to hear it, but listened, just the same, telling herself that it was no surprise his energy overflowed into that kind of thing if all he had to do was sit on a horse and give orders. Two or three women a night? What of it? He must have paid them well.

Her dislike of the Fitzhardinge man grew in almost direct proportion to her fondness for Lady Faythe, his mother. It was strange how many times during the long and tedious day, during the funeral procession and the service, the mass and committal, the feast afterwards in the hall, that Oriane recalled Lady Faythe's insistence that she had only to send a message and help would come. She had placed a hand on her arm. 'Anything,' she had said.

Oriane had thanked her and pushed her most pressing need for help to one side, knowing how such offers are made in all sincerity but are not always easy to fulfill. No one could share her problem, not even her father.

The same instant affinity had not developed in the context of Mistress Cherry, her father's new lady, for the same background of personal choice did not apply in her case. Their relationship was about to be foisted upon everyone and somehow the need to make an immediate impression became all the more pressing. In her unquiet state, it did not occur to Oriane that Mistress Katherine Cherry was not nearly so confident amongst her forthcoming new family as she appeared to be, nor that yesterday, in trying to impress, she had greatly overdone things in a seductive gown to which her daughter Jane, discomfited by her mother's apparent vulgarity, had overreacted by making no effort at all. As in many relationships, what appeared to be obvious on the outside was often far from the truth, and the distorted impression that Oriane received from the showy Mistress Cherry and her quiet ungainly daughter was given no time or space to adjust to anything like reality.

Again, to convince her future relations of her self-assurance, of her ease in the company of wealthy and well- connected strangers, Mistress Cherry's attitude to Oriane and her brothers, especially when others were near, was intentionally motherly and over-solicitous. Had she stopped to think of the five years of motherless independence and Oriane's successful occupation in York, she would have seen that simple friendship would have been preferable to any attempt to take her in hand. To Oriane's mind, it was daughter Jane who required the extra attention, not herself.

'If she tells me one more time that I would look well in red,' Oriane growled quietly to Maddie, 'I shall be rude to her.'

A man's voice behind her was fruity with laughter. 'Whoever she is, mistress, I'd be tempted to agree with her. Now, you may be rude to me instead. I deserve it for that.' Sir Tomas Vittorini bore the dark Italianate good looks of his ancestors and a splendidly scimitar-like nose that would have looked too large on most men. But not on him; his frame and strong face were well able to support it, with a genial personality to which only one who truly meant to wound could have been rude. Which, for an odd fraction of time, could have included Oriane before she collected herself.

She expelled the air from her lungs and dropped her violet-grey clad shoulders.

His face widened with an appreciative smile. 'That's better, Mistress Oriane. Now you are in control. May I call you that, or must I be formal?'

She could not contain the impulse. 'Mistress Whatever of York will do quite well,' she said, but softened it with a gentle expression.

'I beg leave to differ,' he said. 'It will not do at all.' Without looking at the one to whom they obliquely referred, he told her, straight-faced, 'You must not mind his manner, mistress.'

'I do not mind his manner, Sir Tomas. I give it no thought at all.'

With women, Sir Tomas knew better than to insist, but he was nothing if not loyal and his regard for this woman was well beyond any, so far, except the man's own mother. 'Then will you allow me to say this much for him before we close the subject completely? We were in the middle of a successful campaign when Fitzhardinge was wounded. Then he had an urgent summons from home to say that his father was weakening. Can you have any idea how frustrating it is for a man to be stopped at such a moment and brought back to take on the responsibilities of an estate, to learn the managing, to—?'

'Spare me any more, Sir Tomas, or my heart will burst from the sheer pity of it,' Oriane said, her voice rasping with contempt. 'No, as a mere woman I could have no idea. Nor could a man have any conception of how it is for women to live in a world in which they are bound to come second, third, even fourth.'

'But surely, mistress, that is how it must be.'

'There are plenty of women who would agree with you because they prefer not to think for themselves, but I am not one of them. Don't speak to me of pity for men, sir, I beg you, or I shall have to leave you to your own company.'

Tomas's gallantry was as much a part of him as his magnificent nose, and the notion of ruffling the lady's feathers just for the pleasure it gave, as Fitzhardinge could, was unthinkable to him. He smiled and ran a strong elegant hand around his bearded chin.

'Mistress Oriane, that would be a punishment I should never recover from. Shall we speak of your brothers instead? They are fine, mannerly lads. I believe you must have missed them.'

Relieved to move away from conflict and unsure why on earth she had chosen to labour the point just now instead of letting it pass, she followed his lead and talked of Patrick and Paul, of their longing to be soldiers and their fear that their father would never find anyone he could trust to take and train them. And through the man's clever diversion of hostility, Oriane's spirits were calmed so that, later, when Lady Fitzhardinge asked if she planned to return home with her father, she was able to answer with composure that he expected her to stay here in York until her uncle's affairs were settled. She did not know how long.

Oriane was under no delusions about why her father should have made this assumption. Made with such conviction, it had the nature of a decision which he and Mistress Cherry had formed between them without consulting her. A managerial stepdaughter was the last thing a new bride would want, nor would Oriane plead to be allowed back home if they had planned otherwise. It seemed as if this spate of setbacks was more like an endless stream than breakages that went in threes, and, when Leo approached her at the end of the day, she was sure he had made the decision to acquaint her father with details of the thefts, after all.

'Your father,' Leo said, 'has been helping me to look for my stepfather's will. You must have some idea, Oriane.'

She looked up at the patterned framework of rafters that lined the roof of the hall, lit on one side by the low sun from across the kitchen garden. 'Leo, Uncle Matthew didn't confide in me to that extent, I've told you. Not where his personal affairs were concerned. What's that?'

A key, small and golden, lay on his outstretched hand, glinting in the sunlight. While the next words formed inside her head, something warned her not to say them, for if it was indeed hers, as she believed, then Leo must have taken it from the pouch that hung from her girdle. If it was not, she must not let him know that she carried one exactly like it.

'I found this in my father's room, in a casket. I wondered if you knew what it unlocks.'

'May I look?' She knew, without the pretence of closer examination, that it was of solid gold, a mere inch-and-a-half long, its head in the form of a three-leaved clover. 'It is possible,' she said, feeling her way with the words, 'that it could fit the reliquary. I don't know if any of it unlocks, but that's all I can suggest.'

'You may be right. It had not occurred to me.' He turned to go, but stopped as she spoke his name.

'Leo, have you decided what to do about the thefts?'

He waited until a servant had passed through and disappeared into the kitchen yard. 'I didn't want to broach the subject with your father today, but I can do so tomorrow, if that is what you wish. Or you can tell him yourself. He will be put out, I dare say, but I cannot help that. He's been invited to take the twins to Monk Bywater, you know.'

Her brows drew together. 'Tomorrow? Whatever for?'

He shrugged and pulled his fair brows into his hair. 'Sounds as though your new friends might like them to train there. So your visit was not in vain, was it?'

Oriane could not let him think along those lines. 'They are not my new friends, Leo. I like Lady Fitzhardinge, but not her son. If the boys are taken on, my father will be pleased, but it was none of my doing. Another connection for Mistress Cherry to gloat about, certainly.'

'Aye, she's rammed her connections down my throat ever since they arrived. As if I care.'

There was a silence of agreement between them as the air warmed by a degree or two. Oriane took advantage. 'Say nothing to spoil my father's happiness, Leo, about the thefts. I still hope we may be able to talk it over, privately. Please believe me, I bear you no ill will. Surely we can come to some understanding.'

He stood for another moment, looking down at the key in his open hand, then closed it quickly, curling his fingers up with a snap as though a decision had been reached. He nodded once, then left his cousin to her thoughts.

Her thoughts, already racing, separated. The key given to Oriane by her uncle after the death of his wife had never been used, nor had she ever been told by him which part of the reliquary it unlocked. Quickly she pulled her soft leather pouch on to her knee and eased open the thongs, delving a hand to the bottom and closing her fingers around the key. So, Leo's was a duplicate. It had never once crossed her mind that the will might be in the reliquary. Privacy was a rare commodity at the best of times, and Leo would have to wait until the guests had left the house completely before going to the reliquary still on display in the solar, for they slept there at night and chatted there by day.

The possibility of the boys' placement as squires with the Fitzhardinges was undoubtedly the best opportunity they could have wished for, but it placed upon Oriane an even greater pressure not to become involved in the scandal that Leo seemed bent on nurturing. If her father took such care to seek out the best for his sons, so their patron would do likewise, and a sister condemned as a thief would spell the end of their hopes of becoming knights in seven years' time. Nor would it impress her father's future wife or help to secure an honest husband for the dowdy Jane.

If not for the invitation to visit Monk Bywater Manor, the guests would have departed on the day after the funeral, and though it must have been unprofitable to speculate about what might (or might not) have happened otherwise, it was certain that the extra day affected the course of events, for the absence of guests in the daytime gave Leo the chance to use his key on the reliquary.

Oriane had declined the invitation to go to Monk Bywater, and it was quite by accident that she was in her room alone and trying quietly to tidy up the mess left by Mistress Cherry and her lumpy daughter when she heard sounds coming from the solar that was supposed to be empty.

The cat which had been lying on Uncle Matthew's bed had left the room when Leo entered it, pushing the door open with one paw and sliding through the space. Through the gap above and below the hinges, Oriane could see clearly how Leo had found a tiny keyhole in the base of the reliquary, almost hidden by jewels. His key fitted, his fingers slid beneath and, with fingers and key together, he slid forward a drawer from within the base. Then, with a half-glance at the door, he removed a thin wad of papers, tied once round with a ribbon, which fitted the drawer so exactly that Oriane suspected the measurements of the drawer had been planned for that purpose.

She stilled her breathing and held herself rigidly against the door-frame.

Pulling the ribbon undone with his teeth, Leo read in silence, page after page, with little to indicate its contents except an audible blow down his nostrils, like a seal.

At this point, Oriane was prepared to move away; he had found what he was looking for. But had he? Before she could turn with the required amount of stealth, she saw him tap the papers together, leaving the ribbon untied, replace them in the drawer and lock it, placing the key in the pouch at his belt. Which meant, she supposed in the peace of her room, either that those papers were not the will or that Leo didn't want anyone to know that he had found it. And if that was so, perhaps he didn't like what he had discovered, after all.

In her mind she saw that there would be no difficulty in finding out, using her own key, and there the matter rested for the time being, during which the party returned in high spirits with the news that her father had been invited to leave the twins at Monk Bywater in Fitzhardinge's care and that they could go tomorrow when their father left.

They were ecstatic, all the more so because it would bring them nearer to Oriane and York's civilisation, they said, but she would have to make more effort to visit Monk Bywater Manor than she had today. Her absence had been remarked upon.

'Who by?' The question was as idle as she could make it.

'Lady Fitzhardinge, for one. Sir Geffrey and Sir Tomas.'

'I see.' The name she had thought to hear was missing, which in itself was significant. She had not spoken to him yesterday. He would not have missed her. They were evenly matched.

After supper that evening, Oriane's father took his daughter quietly to one side and asked how she felt about his intended bride: did Oriane believe that Mistress Cherry would make him a good wife? Did she do him credit?

Obediently, because there was no use doing otherwise, Oriane told him what he wanted to hear about the excellence of Mistress Cherry and of her own delight in his obvious happiness while her heart seethed with bitterness that he had offered her not the smallest chance to discuss her situation with him. His assumption that she would manage her own affairs turned the resentment she harboured for the two usurpers towards him, too. And for that reason as much as for anything else, she was almost relieved to see them go the following morning, albeit with a nagging guilt at her relief.

Paradoxically, the parting with her two brothers, who were to live only two miles away, was damp with tears which changed to laughter at the disclosure of a remark that Fitzhardinge had made in their hearing yesterday. He had, apparently, offered the opinion to Sir Geffrey d'Azure that if one of *them* had been wounded in the shoulder, as Leo le Seler had, they'd have been back in the bloody saddle by now with a lance tucked under an arm. While this had the desired effect of stemming more tears, its callousness lay heavily upon her as she waved them away.

By this time, the shop and workshop at the front of the house were coming alive with industry that picked up where it had left off with the last dying breath of the small furnace. Tools were arranged and shelves were dusted and requests were made for the goods and materials to be resurrected. Would someone, Master Gerard, Mistress Oriane, please go up to the solar and open the chest and send down the necessary items?

In the solar, arranging a deep blue velvet cloak over his bandaged shoulder, was Master Leo, whose eyes were not in the least impaired. And Master Gerard, cynical of Oriane's assurances that the five missing bags of gold would be found and replaced, felt it his duty to explain, when it was seen by his late employer's son that the chest had already been entered and that Mistress Oriane still had the key. Predictably, Leo pretended that this was the first he knew of it.

The goldsmith's garden beyond the courtyard was long and narrow and of no great beauty, being full of green growing things for the kitchen and still-room where Maddie, and sometimes Oriane herself, would prepare medicines and potions, unguents and soap and stuff to keep flies away. Rarely did Oriane sit in the sunshine with her back against the wall and do nothing. But this day was an exception. This day was to be exceptional in many ways.

Ladies did not usually receive their guests in the kitchen garden but in the solar, where tiny almond biscuits and sweetmeats would be served with sweet and spicy hippocras. But because Maddie could not find her mistress when Lady Faythe Fitzhardinge came to call, and because this determined lady had more than an inkling that something was wrong, she followed the maid up the garden path to where Oriane sat with the cat on her lap. Tipped off as the knees became vertical, the creature blinked with exquisite slowness and strolled away with its tail in the air.

'Now don't scold your maid,' Lady Fitzhardinge called, lifting her silver-grey skirts and stepping over the heads of fallen marigolds. 'Do you crystallise these things? She didn't bring me here; I insisted. You did not accept my invitation to Monk Bywater yesterday and you are not in the shop today, so what's to do?' Her voice lowered to a confidential level and she closed a hand over Oriane's arm, drawing her down again to the bench by her side. 'There's something wrong, isn't there? Have they banished you for some misdemeanour?' She meant the question to bring a smile, but it didn't.

'Yes, my lady,' Oriane said.

'What!' An exclamation rather than a question.

'I've been forbidden to enter either the shop or the workshop.'

The hand remained on her arm and the pause lasted long enough for them to hear the distant call of servants and an apprentice shouting about his master's fine silver buckles next door. 'Can you tell me?' Lady Faythe whispered, acutely alert. 'Who by? Your cousin?'

Of course Oriane should not have spoken of it, but her reply slipped out as though it needed the quality of sound to verify it. Now, it was too late to recant and, of all the women she knew, this was the only one to suspect that the bright and efficient manager who ran the goldsmith's business needed help, rather than praise for her competence. 'Yes,' she said to the hand over her arm.

It squeezed, gently. 'This cousin, Leo—you don't get on?'

Trying to frame a reply that did not sound self-pitying was difficult, but she tried. 'He's…he's afraid, I think, that his stepfather held me in more affection than he did him. Some gold has gone missing from the chest in the solar where I put it, and Leo believes that I took it. Stole it.'

'He says so?'

'Yes. I know full well that I didn't and he knows that I believe he's the one responsible for its disappearance, but he ordered a servant to search and it was found in my clothes-chest, so he's proved himself right. To himself, anyway.'

'And he's forbidden you…?'

'To go near any of the business. Before my father's

visit, Leo accused me of embezzlement, of falsifying accounts, which anyone in their right mind would know I'd not do. It only happened since he came home from Oxford. It makes no sense, my lady.'

'You told your father of the accusations?'

Oriane shook her head, turning to her friend with sadness. 'You saw him, my lady. How could I speak of such things at a time like that when he had the sadness of his brother on his mind? And you saw how he was all out to impress his new lady and find a match for her daughter. The last thing he needs is a thief in the family.'

'But surely he'll find out about this one way or another? He'll have to pay for the trial. How can you hope to keep it quiet? Would he not have been glad to help you, if he'd known of it?'

'Until now, I had hopes of being able to solve the original problem by some private agreement with Leo, never thinking for a moment he'd want to foist it on to me. I thought I could make him understand that, now he'll inherit, he's entitled to take whatever money he needs without being secretive about it. His debts are more or less wiped clean. But now…'

'But now he's insisting it was not him, but you.'

'Yes. I never thought he'd go this far. And now he's determined to send for the sheriff's men and have me charged with common theft. I don't understand it, my lady. Now my father's happiness will be ruined, and my brothers', and I shall no doubt be condemned for lack of any defence.'

'He wants to get rid of you, obviously. And the will?'

'I believe he's found it, but is pretending not to have done.'

'Because it's in your favour, perhaps?'

'I have no way of knowing that until I can see it for myself.' She told the older woman of the key and of what she had seen earlier and, to that remarkable lady who could see things from a healthy distance, there appeared to be no reason why they should not go and take a look together.

'Your cousin's out,' she said. 'I saw him go.'

The reliquary was still in the solar, as were the almond biscuits and the Venetian goblets of sweet spicy hippocras and so was the key carried in Oriane's pouch. Unfortunately, try as they may, it would not unlock the drawer as Leo's had done.

Being a lady of great resourcefulness, Lady Fitzhardinge took matters into her own hands because she could see how events, coming so fast one after the other, had begun to numb poor Oriane's brain to the point where she was unable to think about what to do or how to do it. 'All right. It's the wrong key. Don't let's waste anymore time on that. Send for your maid, then go with her to your room and pack everything that you own, quickly, before your cousin returns. You must get out of this place immediately.'

Oriane tried to make some sense of this. 'Lady…my father…'

'No, dear, not your father. You're coming with me back to Monk Bywater. Now, hurry! I'm going down to get a servant to saddle a horse and we'll take your Maddie with us. Don't look like that…your cousin can have it back tomorrow. If we can't sort him out between us, then my name's not Faythe. But you're not staying here, that much I do know.'

Oriane was in no mind to protest at any scheme that offered a way out of this terrible nightmare, even one that took her within range of that man. And in a most unusually dazed state of disordered thinking, she allowed herself to be swept through hasty and astonished farewells to the few who actually witnessed her departure, aware that she was being presented with yet another of the Fitzhardinges' well-known breathing-spaces. Also, that she was heading towards her brothers, which seemed less strange than other alternatives. Other than their progress through York's narrow and dirtily bustling streets, than the desire to avoid any sight of Leo, than the strange comfort of being padded behind by Maddie and their baggage, Oriane had no perceptions, succumbing to a dreamlike unreality and saying little to anyone.

On her nimble grey mare, Lady Fitzhardinge said just as little but thought with a great deal more clarity. Behind and before them, her liveried escort cleared the way between ale-wives and pedlars, friars and pilgrims and, at her command, led them through ginnels between houses and on detours of marvellous ingenuity to reach the ferry by the city wall at Skeldergate.

The cousin Leo le Seler who she was determined should not see them was acting strangely, she thought, for one so eager to prosecute, and posed some questions about his resolution to have his cousin condemned for something of which he must know she was innocent. The gold had certainly been planted in her clothes-chest, but why had he delayed in having her arrested? Why give her the chance to evade him if he was so committed to his plan?

Because, she assumed, they were blood relatives, and such vindictiveness would bring down Mark of Scepeton's wrath upon his head and because, in spite of his threats, he did not relish the prospect of a trial against the family. Which was probably why he had so far not mentioned these problems to Oriane's father. Because he could not afford a thorough investigation into his affairs? Because, as one sent down from Oxford for bad behaviour, he would not be believed? Or was there more to hide? Because he preferred Oriane to run away from the business and leave it all to him, regardless of his stepfather's will? Well, that much he had achieved, but he had not heard the last of it, and from that point, the schemes in Faythe Fitzhardinge's head were given full rein.

Purposely giving Oriane no time for her thoughts to clear, and consequently for alternative plans to materialise, Lady Fitzhardinge settled her lame duck in a beautiful room overlooking the meadow that sloped down to the river on the same sunny side of the manor as the gardens. Then she left a message for her son to visit her in the solar immediately on his return from the tiltyard. Immediately, that is, after a wash.

Euan Fitzhardinge was not available for quite some time after that interview with his parents, one of whom was in no position to muster any opposition to the other's suggestions as he might well have done in former times, just for the excitement. Euan himself had not opposed them either, except to remark that her plan held no guarantee of success, however neat. If she was expecting instant agreement between both parties, he said, then she was being totally unrealistic for she should know that Mistress Oriane of York couldn't stand the sight of him.

'Nor would I, dear, if you'd been as rude to me as you were to her. But that doesn't mean I'd not be open to persuasion. Anyway, you're a soldier. What d'ye think tactics are for?'

'Mother…tactics and war are not the same as—'

'Yes, they are, dear. Now, go and try. Just to please me. It's time we had some grandsons around the place and I'll not have that pack of mothers and daughters bickering at your father's heels any more. He's getting tired of it.'

'An excellent reason for marriage,' Euan said, somewhat tersely.

'As good as any other.'

The pretence of heartlessness was, of course, only for expediency. Faythe Fitzhardinge was calculating, but not inhuman, and her son Euan was by no means the puppet he appeared to be on this occasion. If the idea had not suited him in the first place, nothing on earth would have induced him to comply with his mother's wishes.

Believing that fate had now called a temporary ceasefire on her beleaguered life, Oriane was unprepared for the sight of the man who opened the door at her call to enter. She stared, speechless.

'I live here. Remember? Fitzhardinge?'

Jolted into a response, she remembered to breathe. 'Er…yes. I'm sorry I'm here in your…it was not my idea, you see. I would never have…'

He closed the door. 'I may come in? I need to speak to you.'

She nodded once, aware that Maddie was moving away to the deep window-seat where she took up some mending. A few clothes lay in neat piles on the chest but Oriane still wore her woollen cloak, the clasp of which she played with, restlessly. Her heavy plaits encircled her head like a coronet, catching the light from the two large windows behind her, giving her the advantage of the light upon his face.

'Will you be seated, mistress?'

She made a slight movement. 'No, I thank you.'

'I have come to offer you a way out of your troubles.'

Still she did not offer him the chance to sit. It was obvious that Lady Faythe had explained her presence at the manor; she would have felt obliged to do that. He would have objected. He was here to tell her so. 'If you are offering me an escort to my father's home, then I thank you. I have little baggage…'

'No, mistress. That is not what I am offering you. Would you *please* sit? This may take some time.'

She backed into a stool and sat, upright and wooden, waiting until he brought another and sat with his back to the light. Determined not to let him take the lead or anticipate her mind, she tried again. 'It need not take any of your time at all, Sir Euan, to tell me that your lady mother was unwise to bring me here, that I should be better….'

'*Will* you allow me to tell you what I am offering you or are you going to run through every possibility while I sit here and say no to each?'

'Then…? Oh, please continue.'

'Thank you. My mother has told me of your cousin's accusations and of your anxiety not to burden your father with the problem at this important time for him. I am willing to reimburse Master le Seler the sum he believes you…mistakenly…owe him and to give you the safety of my own and my family's protection here at Monk Bywater.'

Her eyes hunted for a meaning, jerking from one object to another and finally coming to rest on his face which, as before, she could not fathom. She took a sharp breath, then rose with all the dignity she could summon. 'Sir Euan,' she said, 'I am sure you intend that I should be grateful for this proposition, but I cannot believe that Lady Fitzhardinge is aware that you are making it. Nor would my father believe that a knight would suggest such a thing. Your reputation…'

He stood, his head proudly erect on the strong neck. 'What reputation of mine is relevant in this context, mistress? Do I have a reputation for marriage? If so, it is wholly undeserved.'

She blinked. 'Marriage? For…for marriage?' she whispered.

He flung back his head with an exasperated sigh, then glared at her, reminding her again of the angry soldier she had first met. 'God's truth, woman. What did you think I was offering? Ah…' He flung out a hand. 'No, let me guess…with my reputation…'

'Well, what *was* I supposed to believe? That with all your conquests you can't find enough variety? Do you not pay them well enough these days, Sir Euan?'

She saw the colour of his eyes at last. They were dark, greeny-brown like smoky quartz, and very angry.

He strode to the door and jerked it open, snapping at Maddie on the way. 'Leave us, mistress.'

'No, Maddie!'

Loyal, but full of sense, the maid lay down her sewing, curtsied to them both, and left the room.

Sir Euan came back to Oriane and stood before her more closely than she would have liked. 'Understand me, Mistress Oriane of York. I have never paid a woman for her services in my bed, and if you believe that this is what I am proposing to you then we have nothing more to say to each other. Except that, if I were your father, I would have beaten you into silence rather oftener than he apparently did.'

'But you are not.'

'As you say, I am not.' His brows were pulled forward like two black crags. 'And if you can rid yourself of your prejudice for as long as it takes me to speak, I'll tell you of the bargain I am seeking and then, if you can listen without interrupting like a hysterical hen, I'll tell you what you'll get in return.' He caught her arm as she began to turn away. 'For pity's sake, mistress, I've never known anyone like you for obduracy. Stand still, will you, and hear me. I'm giving you a choice, dammit!'

He knew by her eyes that she would shake his hand off and so loosed his fingers just before it came, robbing her of the pleasure of its resistance. Still, he stood too close with his long arms dangling loose, ready to stop her if she moved away.

But he could not make her face him. 'Say what you have to say, sir. Our views on what constitutes a choice obviously differ. Go ahead.'

'My offer, mistress, is marriage. To me. I need a wife and I need sons...'

'In that order?'

'And the reputation you seem so keen to air need not concern you. I would also wish to take advantage of the connections your father and his intended bride have to offer.'

Her head came round to the front at that unexpected addition. 'What?' she asked.

'These things work both ways. I can see that the lady sets great store by such alliances and the truth is that none of us can afford to overlook them. She has contacts through her late husband with certain men who command the king's armies and I want the same contacts. Marriage to you would provide them. If, of course, you prefer not to accept my offer, your father's marriage to her would probably not materialise either, would it? Because she would cry off at the sound of a family scandal.'

She knew this was true: her father's marriage depended on her own acceptance, ultimately, for though he would no doubt pay for her trial and do his best for her, it would ruin his chances with the widow. Certainly he would not pay Leo off, as this man was offering to do. But what a price, and who was paying most? And had he meant it about settling her so-called account? She would not ask for details.

Her silence led him on, just as if she had answered.

'As I said, I am willing to buy your cousin's silence so that your name will not be dragged through the courts.'

'So that you will gain your precious connections.'

'Just so.'

'And what happens when my cousin demands more, later on?'

He shook his head. 'I could have him quietly killed now, if I'd a mind to it. If he rears his head once more after he's been paid, I will, and I intend to make sure he knows it. As well as that, you will bear the Fitzhardinge name.'

'And the Fitzhardinge sons!'

'Yes, and sons, mistress. Or daughters. Or whatever monsters you believe I might sire. I've grown weary of searching for a suitable wife and the haggling that goes with it. You'll do well enough. You have no grasping parents. You have a courage that borders on the foolhardy, but that's a fault I'd not mind in my sons. You have enough intelligence to please a goldsmith, and honesty, and you're comely enough; that'll do for daughters. You're young. You can breed, presumably?'

Oriane swallowed. 'Do you know, sir, I've never yet had a chance to find that out. Should I go and make some investigations on that subject, then I can come back and tell you whether I'm a good breeder or not?' She flung away from him before he could stop her, livid with anger, then turned to face him from the window-seat where Maddie had been sitting. 'I cannot believe I'm having this conversation,' she said. 'Is this really what your mother wished you to say to me?'

'To offer you my hand, yes. She wishes it. Though I dare say she would have wanted me to phrase it more elegantly, perhaps. But I am a soldier, mistress, not a mincing courtier, and I deal direct.'

'You are attempting to *buy* me like a common whore, sir!'

'I know little of common whores, only uncommon ones who expect no payment. You are an exception, I agree. A financial bargain as well as a physical one. But look at it in another way, if you can. Instead of an uncomfortable trial, this arrangement would give us time to investigate the allegations your cousin has made. I don't give money away quite so easily, you see, and you could hardly do that from the sheriff's cell, could you?' He moved towards her and she backed away until the window-seat pressed against her legs and she sat heavily on to the cushion.

'I'd rather do it from hell!' she said.

'Yes. Well, that's all very noble, and I don't suppose that being married to a Fitzhardinge carries the same hollow ring of martyrdom. But if you think you can clear your name from hell, then go ahead and try. Your father won't thank you for it though, will he?'

'And my brothers. You'd send them home, wouldn't you?'

'No, I wouldn't. They have potential. But they'd have a rough time living it down, wouldn't they? And it wouldn't help their advancement much.' Slowly, he was closing in on her so that she could not move away now without pushing against him. He placed his hands on the cushion at each side of her lap, his head close to hers. 'Think on it. Marriage to me must have some of the advantages hell can't offer.'

'Only you would believe it.'

His wide mouth played with a smile, discarded it, and pulled itself together. 'Give me your answer tomorrow.'

'I don't need to, sir. You can have it now. I am not a breeding sow and I cannot guarantee the terms you have set out for me. And even if I were, there are other boars I would as soon bear a litter to.'

'Hah!' The sound and the smile came together almost upon her skin, easing her back into the deep recess. Her pushing hands on his wide shoulders made not a whit of difference and, as her head reached the sill, he knelt on the cushion and gathered her up with one arm, pulling her hands into one merciless grasp behind her back. Cradled into his shoulder, she was held, immobile and stony-faced. 'You will,' he said, 'because you won't be able to resist the temptation to fight me, to thwart me at every end and turn. And you'd not be able to do that from a cell, would you? You'll marry me, lass.'

She knew that she was about to taste his lips for they spoke against her mouth so that his breath mingled with hers. She heaved against him but there was nowhere to go and his mouth cut off the cry she might have made, and the shock of him held the breath in her lungs until, gradually, when he did not release her, it dissipated against his cheek.

Desperately, and with an effort of concentration that took every scrap of will, she forbade herself to respond, to relax or to make the slightest concession to his assault, even though this was nothing like the abuse of Leo's friends. On the contrary, it was sensual and very practised, and was deliberately testing her to see how long she could remain unmoved.

At the first signal of a cry that began in her breast, a cry of impending weakness, he released her, anticipating its arrival. It was not her full submission he wanted but an acknowledgement that she had, at last, met her match and that, like it or not, he would win. Carefully he backed away, pulling her upright.

She was breathless with anger. 'You are as…as bad as those blackguards who came…the other day…all of a kind…God knows what…what goes on in your heads.' She sprang away from the window-seat, pointing at it. 'And *that* is supposed to endear you to me, is it?'

'No, mistress. It's not.' He stood apart with hands on hips, watching her with some amusement. 'I can live without your endearments as long as you bear me the grandsons my parents desire. That was to discover if you have the makings of a good breeder.' He smiled, wickedly.

Blind fury, outrage and a boiling resentment welled up inside Oriane like a head of steam in a kettle and, in an outburst of uncontrollable violence, she grabbed at a beautifully ornamented scabbard and its dagger that lay on a small table, withdrew the blade and reversed it in her hand without taking her eyes from his. Expertly, she held the blade, balancing the handle towards him.

'Put it down,' he chided as if to a child. 'You'll hurt yourself.'

White-faced, she twisted and threw it at the panelling that lined the wall, more particularly towards a grinning carved head that topped an intersection by the window, barely swaying her skirts with the effort and so fast that it hit its target before he could turn to watch. The blade sank deep between the eyes of the wooden head and vibrated, as delicate as a quill.

In Oriane's eyes was fury and jubilation, mixed.

In Fitzhardinge's there was admiration and some

shock. He walked across the panelling and removed the knife, sheathing it in the scabbard as he reached the door. He turned and looked at her, his glance sweeping from crown to toes and back again. 'I'll get sons on you, woman, if it's the last thing I do.'

'It will be,' she snarled, turning away.

Chapter Five

Maddie returned almost immediately to find her mistress pale and shaken, leaning against the wall and staring out of the open window across to the buttery and dairy, the pantry and kitchen gardens on the far side of the house. On the cushion was Maddie's sewing, now crumpled and very creased.

'What…?' Maddie swallowed the rest of the query wishing that she had been a fly on the wall. Going for the next best thing, she poured wine into a small glass beaker and took it to Oriane, hoping that it would both calm her and make her more articulate at the same time.

Oriane accepted it with neither a look nor a word; her introspection had moved beyond explanation and, if she had thought to be confused before, was even more so now with that man's kiss still on her mouth. She could still taste him. Could she be so sure she'd not responded by even the smallest degree? Closed her eyes? Softened against him? Opened her lips? Would he have noticed? 'We can't stay here, Maddie,' she whispered.

Maddie heard her, but decided to contest it. She was small and pretty, dark and quietly sunny, six years older than Oriane and had been maid to Mark of Scepeton's wife when she died five years ago. She had come to York with her new thirteen-year-old mistress and cared for her with the devotion of combined servant, sister and mother, rarely questioning what Oriane did because there was rarely any need to. She knew why she did things, and had never yet made a mistake that she couldn't put right soon enough.

Similarly, she swallowed the obvious question, as she had earlier, and set about a discreet recitation of the benefits of staying put, at least for a while. She began with the room itself, being the easiest and most obvious. 'It's a bonny view is that, mistress,' she said, using the extra two words at the end of the sentence, as all Lancastrians did. 'And just have a see out o' this one.' She moved to the adjacent wall where a larger three-sided window opened on to a view of a glistening width of river lined with willows that waved green fringes in the wind. The same river that flowed through York.

From somewhere out of sight came the sound of men's shouts and laughter, the neigh of a horse, the crash of shields. 'Your brothers'll be out there, somewhere,' Maddie said.

Oriane made no movement to show that she had heard.

Maddie turned into the room, undaunted by the silence. 'And look at the tapestries; even your uncle's were not as big as these. It'll be cosy enough in here in winter, love, with a fine fire over there, too.' The fireplace was of stone, like the walls, funnel-shaped and sculpted with the Fitzhardinge arms. Now it was empty of all except half a tree sawn into logs, and great dog-irons with heads on the terminals.

Heads looked down from the wooden rail between the windows, grinning cheerfully, one with a hole in his forehead. Maddie kept trying. 'And that great bed. I wonder who uses this room? It's big enough for four, that is.'

The bed was truly beautiful, canopied with oak and curtained with soft green that matched the green silk quilted coverlet and the extravagant pile of pillows. A grey and white squirrel-fur blanket was folded across the lower half where one could sit in the absence of chairs; two oak stools, a small table and two iron-bound chests were the only other furniture.

The sun streamed across a wooden painted floor, highlighting a path of chequers that matched the colours on the heavily embroidered cushions of the window-seats, green, rose-pink and gold. The beams above their heads had been painted in the same colours, filling the room, and on any other day Oriane would have been compelled to compare it with her own drab little chamber at Silver Street.

Maddie lifted the lid of the smallest chest. 'Bed-linen,' she said, and replaced it. The other one was empty, lined with parchment. 'Shall I be putting your things away, love?'

Oriane turned at last. 'No need. We're not staying.'

Maddie sat on the chest. 'Just for a while, eh? Until you get your thoughts ironed out? We can't go back to Silver Street, not while Master Leo's out to make things difficult for you.'

'That seems to be their main purpose in life.'

'What? Who?'

'Men. To make things difficult. Uncle Matthew. My father. Now Leo.'

'Sir Euan?'

'Him! What have I done to...?' She uplifted her hands.

'Now don't go feeling sorry for yourself.'

'I'm not, Maddie. But what am I supposed to do now, I wonder?'

'Why not wait until it sorts itself out?'

'Because I have to decide now, before Leo starts proceedings.'

'The boys would like it if we stayed a bit.'

Oriane stared out towards where the sounds had come from. 'Yes,' she agreed, 'I know they would.'

'And Lady Fitzhardinge. She likes you and you like her.'

'Yes, but I wish I'd known she had this in mind.'

'What in mind?'

'This. Marriage. Paying Leo for his silence.'

Maddie was silent, pitying the poor lass. It was not easy, for the man seemed easily rattled and Oriane was at her most tender. 'Is it Sir Euan's reputation that puts you off, then?'

'Everything puts me off!' Oriane turned back to the window-seat and picked up the squashed fabric. 'Everything.'

Maddie, who missed very little, saw how Oriane's fingers brushed lightly over the dent in the cushion and how they lingered as if to feed on its latent warmth and how, almost stealthily, the crumpled fabric was brought to her face for its scent to be inhaled against the lips.

Everything? Maddie wondered.

* * *

Except for the great hall, Lord and Lady Fitzhardinge's solar was the largest of the private chambers to be used both as family and sleeping quarters. The carved bed would have crowded any of the rooms at Silver Street, but here it left plenty of space and was now awash with greenish light from the opaque windows, casting bright undulations over the linen sheets where Lord Fitzhardinge lay asleep.

With sidelong looks at the bed, the two women tiptoed across to the window-seat and sat facing each other, the hostess reaching for her guest's hand as a gesture of understanding. 'I know, dear. You don't have to explain,' she said. 'If he was not my own son, I probably wouldn't like him, either. Perhaps my hopes of a marriage between you was not so well-timed, but I did believe it would help you out of a difficulty. Do you not think so? There are far more business alliances than love-matches, you know, but that's no reason why there should not be friendship.' She looked across at the white-capped figure on the bed. 'He and I were at daggers-drawn for the best part of a year until we learned to live with each other. Now I don't know how I shall bear life without him.'

'I'm sure it's not entirely your son's fault, my lady,' Oriane said. 'And I know no one whose offer would have been received at this moment, coming so soon after…'

'Yes, yes, of course. I understand.' She touched Oriane's arm again.

'But I need some time to think on my own. I have it in mind to go to the nuns at Clementhorpe. They knew my uncle and they'll give me hospitality until I can work out what's best to do.'

'You won't reconsider Euan's offer to settle with your cousin?'

'I think not, my lady. It would place me under an impossible obligation to him and that would be a grave disadvantage to bring to a marriage. He and I are totally at odds. He doesn't like me any more than I like him. He is used to more experienced women, not people like me. I am not of his world.'

'Oh, dear,' Lady Faythe said, with genuine regret. 'That's what happens when they spend so much of their time living on the edge of danger, roughing it, taking whatever is offered without a thought of a more permanent existence with a wife and family. Euan has always loved that life, and he's still angry that the army physician insisted he give his wound time to heal. He would have preferred to be indispensable. Wouldn't all men?'

Perhaps, Oriane thought, that was one of Leo's problems. But did that give them the right to take out their frustrations on whoever was to hand? She had never had any illusions about the benefits of marriage for family connections, for the consolidation of property or the healing of rifts after a feud, but surely he could have found someone more willing than herself with the same advantages.

Lady Fitzhardinge read her thoughts. 'But it was for your benefit, too, remember. He's never shown any interest in marriage until now.'

'My lady, I don't think for one moment that your son changed his mind for my sake alone. He's far more interested in the connections my father and his intended bride can offer him than he is in me. If I don't marry him, my father's marriage will probably be called off at the prospect of a family scandal, and without those connections, Sir Euan believes he will then lose his chance of moving into a higher position in the king's army quite as soon as he'd like.'

Lady Fitzhardinge frowned. 'Is that what he told you?'

'Yes, my lady.'

She would not contradict a guest, but this took some understanding. There had never been a time she could remember when a Fitzhardinge needed any help in advancement from a wool-merchant, but perhaps times were changing. Whatever they were, Euan must have his reasons, one of which appeared to be that he had discovered an advantage which she had not. All the same, it was typically insensitive of him to have told the girl at this stage.

Had things been different, Oriane might have enjoyed refusing this arrogant and overbearing man, just to teach him a lesson, but the circumstances were of a far more serious nature, and it was not that aspect of her refusal that mattered. It was the fear that, no matter what his reasons for offering marriage, he would make her more unhappy then she could bear.

A night here under this roof would be construed by the Fitzhardinges as coming close to acceptance. With so many people around, she would have no time to think of alternatives. 'My lady, before more time is lost, I beg you to accept my thanks for your help in all things since this horrid business began, but my last request is that you allow me to take my cousin's horse and go with my maid to Clementhorpe. To stay where your son is would be misconstrued, I fear, as it may have been already.'

'Ah, this is so sad. All my best-laid plans…ah, well! I shall send a message to your cousin to tell him that he must not be hasty in this matter, that you need more time. Meanwhile, we'll think what else can be done. I'll have the horse saddled for you. Come.' She led the way to the door. 'Euan is in no doubt of your mind, I suppose?'

'He can be in no doubt whatever, my lady.'

'Then we can look forward to more bad temper. He hates being gainsaid.'

Oriane and Maddie would have walked to the Benedictine nunnery of Clementhorpe if time, not baggage, had been on their hands, for it was no great distance along the York road then away from the river, across the common, and towards the tiny compound of white- and pink-blossomed orchards and walled gardens. Stone-flagged rooftops covered with buttons of moss fell like sleepy eyelids over lancet windows, and smoke rose in an almost vertical wisp from the kitchen buildings next to the refectory.

They felt the aura of peace and safety as they approached the gate; Oriane's uncle had done work for the prioress in the past few years and a welcome was assured. At her call, the porter let them through with a silent smile and signalled the groom to take the horses, and at that point their escort took his leave and headed back to Monk Bywater.

A group of nuns appeared at the carved stone entrance, black-robed and white-wimpled around islands of pink faces. Rosaries and crucifixes were the only relief on their stark habits, unlike those who came forward down the steps at a trot, men in leather jerkins with leather baldrics across their chests instead of crosses; daggers, swords and pouches at their belts instead of rosaries. They pulled up, sharply, staring at Oriane and her maid, then were almost knocked aside by a third man who thrust past them, one arm in a sling.

'There! That's them! I told you, didn't I? Yonder's my horse, too. See?' It was Leo, bright-eyed with fever and, with him, the sheriff's men.

Appraising the situation at a glance, Oriane spoke to the prioress, whose expression gave nothing away. 'Allow me to explain, Reverend Mother. We have come to ask for your hospitality for a few days, at most, while my cousin and I...'

Leo interrupted. 'Your cousin has given you enough time to put matters right. It is now time for you to explain yourself to the court, mistress. I am fortunate in having loyal servants who told me where you'd gone, or I should not have known where to start looking.' He came to stand before her, belligerently.

'They told you I was coming here? To Clementhorpe?'

'Of course. And now we're to have a reckoning, Mistress Oriane, after Master Gerard added up all the amounts you've pilfered.'

'Wait one moment, Master le Seler, if you please!' The prioress came forward with some authority. 'We will not play court, judge and jury at the entrance to this priory, I think, no matter how right you believe yourself to be.' Her gentle contours and wrinkles of laughter were offset by a diamond-cut hardness of eye that would have halted a marauding Viking. 'If you wish to discuss this matter between you then you are welcome to use the refectory while it is still free. Follow me, mistress, if you please.'

They were shown into a large, bare, stone-pillared chamber set with long oak tables and benches, a lectern, and little else. And although they stood in some semblance of courtesy, the prioress listening without comment except to offer Oriane and her maid beakers of weak ale, the argument covered only the same ground as it had earlier that morning at Silver Street. Leo was convinced, he said, that Oriane was responsible for all the thefts and discrepancies, and made his distrust of her obvious by posting the two sheriff's men near the entrances. The fact that Oriane had borrowed Leo's horse did not help her cause, despite the servants' ploy to send him on what they believed would be a wild-goose chase.

Nothing that Oriane could say in her own defence appeared to make any impression on her cousin nor, when Dame Joan the prioress asked for more time for Oriane, did he see this as a positive step. 'She has no defence, Reverend Mother. She promised to do her best to compensate me but so far I've seen no sign of this.' His fair hair was dark with sweat and stuck in points to his forehead.

'With your father's funeral to arrange, Leo, it's hardly surprising, is it? I gathered the impression it was my blood you were after more than compensation.'

'On the contrary, cousin,' Leo said, pretending a reasonableness far removed from his manner, 'if you could repay me for the losses I've suffered, I'd have no more to say about it. But you can't, can you?'

'How much?' A voice from the doorway echoed into the chamber.

With one arm, the sheriff's man was held aside as a party of men flowed towards them and arranged themselves behind Oriane and Maddie.

Only a few short hours ago, the chance to repay Leo had been there for the taking and she had swept it aside as being too expensive for her. Suddenly, the same chance had reappeared, and this time, so close to losing her private battle with Leo, Oriane allowed the new protagonist to take her part for a while.

Maddie caught at her mistress's hand and squeezed it.

Sir Euan bowed politely to the prioress. 'I beg your pardon, Reverend Mother. I mean no discourtesy, but I believe this matter can be resolved instantly without further disrupting your peace.'

'Is that why you've brought all these men with you, Sir Euan? So as not to disrupt our peace?'

'They include the lady's two brothers,' he replied. 'I came here to...'

Paul. Patrick. Oriane heard no more of what Sir Euan was saying until the twins had stepped forward and taken her two hands in the most formal and restrained greeting she had ever received from them. That this was something to do with their new training she could understand, but when her right hand was retained for a fraction longer than need be and a sharp whisper, 'Put it on. Quick!' was breathed upon her cheek with a precise kiss, she took note of the hard uncomfortable thing on her finger, pushing it further on as the twins drew back into line.

It was then that she caught Leo's incredulous echo of the word she had not heard uttered. 'Betrothed? When? When was this, cousin? Show me...come on, show me. Have you a ring?'

'Show him, mistress,' Sir Euan said, 'if you please.'

This was no time or place for reticence: if she wanted to save her skin, then a charade was the only way to do it, for without this man's support she would stand no chance against her cousin. She held her hand out.

'Why did you say nothing of this?' Leo said, staring at the ring that sat heavily upon her finger. A great onyx. Far too large.

'I did not feel it was relevant, cousin. As I was telling you when Sir Euan entered, I thought you were more interested in locking me away than in being repaid, otherwise you would surely have given me time to make some enquiries. I didn't know that Sir Euan would be willing to help me in that enterprise because I have not told him of this matter. It was something about which I hoped you would eventually discuss with me in a reasonable manner, as relatives do, instead of which you descend upon me with the sheriff's men in tow when I come here to seek a few day's hospitality, having lost my benefactor.'

'And how did Sir Euan come to hear of this unhappy state of affairs,' the prioress asked, 'if you did not tell him of it?'

'Perhaps Sir Euan himself can answer that,' Oriane said.

Sir Euan did. 'I don't employ men to stand around

and look decorative,' he said. 'I expect them to use their eyes and ears. Master le Seler has not been too discreet about his business affairs since he returned to York, Reverend Mother.' He glanced at Leo and watched the pink deepen from neck to cheeks. 'He doesn't mind who knows of his campaign against a defenceless woman beneath his own roof. His own cousin. The one who kept his stepfather's business going for five years. I dare say the whole of York knows about it by now, especially with the sheriff's men trotting behind him through the streets all the way to a convent for a siege of a fortnight's duration, perhaps. Did you bring your new plate armour too, lad? Eh?'

Leo le Seler, wishing he'd stayed at home in Silver Street, backed into the shadows where his red face would glow less brightly. 'Perhaps we could continue this conversation in private, Sir Euan,' he said, wiping his brow with his sleeve.

It was clever, Oriane thought, how Fitzhardinge had spun the limelight away from his own doings towards Leo's, answering the question indirectly, and by implication. It was also clever how he had managed to manipulate the potential disaster to his own advantage by obliging her to acknowledge a betrothal which did not exist in fact, but which he would probably now insist upon. By being saved from one quicksand, she had walked into another, her one consolation being that she might now be allowed, without further explanation, to stay here for the few days' respite she had originally intended. If money was indeed to be exchanged, Sir Euan would be entitled to her cooperation, but a few days' grace was surely not too much to ask. And why *had* he come?

Quite disbelieving the accusations against Oriane, Dame Joan had the betrothed couple escorted to the guest-house across the garth where rooms were set aside for travelling ladies and those seeking rest or spiritual refreshment. Smiling, the guest-mistress told Oriane that she was welcome to use the convent's facilities for as long as she wished.

'Two days,' Sir Euan said, closing the door. 'Then I shall come and escort you to Monk Bywater. Monday evening.' He leaned against the door with his hair brushing the underside of the heavy oak beams, watching from beneath lowered brows how Oriane went instantly to throw open the horn-paned window. 'Did you hear me?'

Still unresigned, she turned to face him, hoping that there could be found some way round this. 'Look…' she began, holding a hand to him as if to support some newly formulated alternative.

'Oh, no! I'm *not* looking. What I am about to do is to go and talk of money to that little rat-faced whelp and get him off your back, if you'll pardon the expression. And before I do that I want your word that the ring you wear says what it's meant to say. That you've agreed, once and for all, to marry me. Where is it? You've taken it off already?'

Oriane held out her palm with the ring on it. 'Well, of course I've taken it off. It's yours, not mine. It was for bluff, wasn't it? Well, I thank you; indeed I do most heartily, but this is not the way to go on. I know I owe you…'

'You certainly do, woman. If I pay your cousin to let you off the hook, you owe me the price I demand, with no more hemming and hawing, if you please.

Now, put that ring back on and let me hear your acceptance. Hurry. I have to go.'

She pleaded, silently, with her hands.

Fitzhardinge folded his arms and waited, unmoved.

'A business arrangement,' she whispered. 'Just a business arrangement?'

His eyelids dropped and slowly opened again. 'I need sons,' he said. 'One can hardly get sons on a business arrangement.'

'Haven't you got sons already, somewhere?'

'Dozens, I expect. I need new ones.'

She looked away at the low narrow bed and the creaseless homespun blanket and held a hand beneath her heart. He was cold. He made it sound like needing a new pair of shoes. He disliked her. He wanted sons and those important entries into higher command, whichever came first. 'We dislike each other. Doesn't that matter to you?'

'No. I can get sons on a woman whether we like each other or not.'

'And *me*? Don't my feelings enter into it?'

He lowered his head, dropping his arms and splaying his fingers over his low-belted hips. 'Feelings?' He indicated the door with his head. 'There were plenty of those in the air when the sheriff's men blocked the doors. When cousin Leo put on his persecuted act. When I came in and you played along with that little game. Your feelings entered into it then, I remember. You knew then what message you were sending me, didn't you, Oriane of York?' He advanced into the room, but she turned her back on him. 'It was a bargain. You knew it then just as you know it now. Let's hear no more of feelings. Give me the ring.'

She held it over her shoulder, refusing to turn.

He took her wrist and held it up, opening her fingers and easing the ring once more into place. Then, keeping hold of her, he spoke into her ear. 'Now, your agreement.'

She nodded.

'No. Say it!'

'I will marry you, Euan Fitzhardinge.'

With one swing of her wrist, he turned her. 'Now, again. To my face.'

'I will…' She got no further, for the words were taken in by his mouth which, for a man with no feelings to concern him, was as thoroughly efficient as one might have expected of a soldier with his reputation.

'You will,' he said, lifting his head to look at her. 'Did you hear yourself? You said it.'

'Yes, I heard it,' she whispered. It had sounded to her like a voice from another world. She had a question, but would not ask it of him.

He answered it, nevertheless. 'I came here to get you back. Why else would I have come? To rape the nuns?'

Oriane pushed against his shoulders, hating his coarseness.

'Monday evening. Be prepared. And leave the rest to me. You are out of danger.' Terse, soldier's words. Ungentle. More like battle commands. He had gone before she could think of a suitably wounding reply, before she could recall whether she had kept her eyes open, as she had intended to do.

For all that, the freedom in which she was supposed to be rejoicing was hard to recognise, and for some time after that very unbalanced encounter, Oriane sat on the woollen blanket asking herself, over and over, what had happened to the sane, right-way-up world of a week ago. She was no weakling given to self-pity or swooning, though these two afflictions had been menacingly close of late. Nor was she feeling sorry for herself now. Even so, she lay on the bed in a ball, twisting the heavy ring on her finger and closing her eyes as she knew she had done over there, by the window.

Beyond that, her thoughts were not rosy. They were going to have to talk, soon, and rationally. He would have to ask her father's permission. That, and the agreement of a dowry, jointures, settlements, could take weeks. So would the banns. Between Rogationtide and Trinity Sunday marriages were forbidden. That would take them into June. Then there would be Corpus Christi on the tenth, a great festival in York. There would be no marriages over that period, either.

He would naturally want to consummate their betrothal, as was usually the way, if only to reinforce his pointedly uncaring remark about her breeding qualities. No betrothal was regarded as indissoluble until then, and he of all people would take no risks for fear she should find a way of calling it off. He would lose no time; of that she was sure.

It was that aspect, more than any other, which troubled her most, for like any young woman, she had held in her heart an ideal of how it should be to bond with a man, in joy, with love and carefulness. She had seen men and women coupling vigorously in corners, in fields, had once come across a writhing tangle of three (well, more than two, anyway) bodies in a barn just before she left home to live in York. She had been puzzled, ready to run and call for help thinking that the one lass must be unwilling. Then she heard her speak, and giggle, and then had crept away, utterly confused but filled with a lightness of spirit that told her of a playful element she had never suspected. Her mother had never once hinted of playfulness, nor even joy, and had died in childbirth.

Since then, Oriane had held at the back of her mind a determination to do her own choosing. He would be well connected, of course, but most of all he would have charm, patience and the ability to entertain her, graciously and considerately. He would be strong, but artistic, a poet, musician, scholar, chivalrous knight and wealthy merchant all rolled into one. She would find him and allow him to find her, and they would make love with the tenderness her mother had never implied and with the laughter she herself had witnessed.

Try as she might to make them fit, none of the required attributes would do for the Fitzhardinge except the strength and wealth; a poor total by anyone's reckoning. Unless, that is, she had missed out an element that no one had told her of.

She slid a hand between her thighs, tightening with fear. He would not laugh with her, or be gentle and considerate. He required sons and had said quite clearly that he cared not whether they liked each other; he could do it without even that. He was a soldier, and coarse, and had used women for his pleasure since adolescence and, finding little pleasure with her, would no doubt continue to do so after their marriage. He had held her in a grip more of restraint than desire, as he would have held an escapee. His kisses had been to display possession, not love. He would take, and give nothing. He would neither know nor care if he hurt her, nor would she tell him. She did not want him there.

After that, it seemed as though all her waking moments were devoted to the problem of how to delay, and whereas her sleep at Silver Street had been broken by fears of another kind, now she could scarcely bring herself to believe that the newest problem was every bit as inevitable. In the still May nights, when the sound of bells was hers either to obey or ignore, she lay with her imaginings, devising complicated and unworkable methods of making herself unavailable.

The sisters and other guests left her in peace to enjoy walking with Maddie in the orchard and meadows, tending the little garden beyond her chamber, reading devotions in the guests' parlour or listening to the nuns' choir-practice. At matins and evensong she went to the church which was also used as the parish church for the people of Clementhorpe, and it was during the Monday evensong that the stifled clatter of feet announced yet another late arrival.

Oriane continued her devotion without looking up. A group of people came to stand at her back. A sidelong glance at the floor identified the large dusty riding-boots of Fitzhardinge. To the other side of her, her brothers' boots.

Patrick leaned, keeping his head bowed. 'Prayers for a safe arrival,' he whispered. 'Father sends his love.'

'Father?' Oriane looked up, letting her rosary slip. 'Where have you been?'

'Scepeton,' Paul said, then fell silent as he felt the glare of his master's eyes. The lads nudged each other as they saw their sister's hand being removed from the rosary, taken to Fitzhardinge's lips, and returned with never a glance from either of them.

Chapter Six

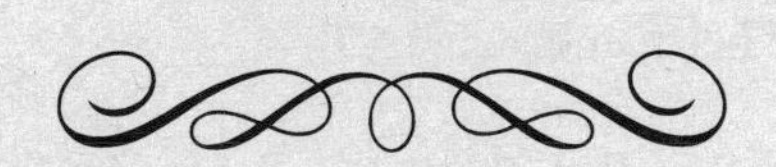

'He comes, my lady,' the tiring-woman said.

'Yes, I see him. You can go, Alice.' Lady Faythe Fitzhardinge put aside the embroidery she had been holding in one hand for the past half-hour and leaned further into the window-recess to catch sight of the riders before they swung away towards the gates. The light was fading, but he had said he would do it and she believed him. He had the girl, too. So, that was settled.

She smiled, her attention now directed towards the man in the bed who studied her with that same intensity that Euan had adopted, making it difficult to tell what they were thinking. Except that now, after thirty years, she was getting rather better at it.

'You'll like her,' she said, sitting on the woollen coverlet.

The voice from the bed was surprisingly deep and rich from one so enfeebled. 'I like her already from what you've told me. He's never gone to these lengths before, has he?'

'To consult the father? No, I'd certainly know of it

if he had. He was determined that Mark of Scepeton should know what's going on in his own family, whether the girl willed it or no. I agreed with him. Your old friend would not thank us for keeping it to ourselves, and as long as the damned cousin keeps quiet, there's no reason why Mistress Cherry should be upset by it.'

'Is that her name? Cherry?'

'Yes.'

The face cracked, the flat chest shook, and a cough turned into a breathless wheeze.

'Here, loveday. Drink this.'

Obediently, he sipped. 'D'ye remember how we fought, eh?' he whispered, lying back on the pillows. 'He'll be the same, I fear. Too damn proud to let a woman see how he feels about her. I hope she stays the course, like you did.'

'She'll stay. She's in love with him.'

'She fled, though, didn't she? Is that a good sign?'

She patted her husband's hand, allowing herself to be caught and held by a grip still stronger then hers. Her laughter was silent. 'Yes, loveday. That's a good sign. He won't let her get far.'

'So what was it you were telling me about Mark of Scepeton's connections? I'd have sworn he's not the type to bother with that kind of thing. A wool-merchant.'

'It's her, apparently. His intended bride.'

'So who can *she* know that Euan needs, for heaven's sake?'

'Nobody, dearest. It's some cock-and-bull story that Euan's told her as a reason why he needs the marriage.

Plain love, attraction, whatever, is too simple for Euan. He couldn't have told her that, could he?'

'No, I suppose not. Not Euan.' He smiled.

'You should have had a word with him, you know.'

'Too late. They'll have to work it out for themselves.'

'They're in for a rough time, then.'

'They're young.'

'They're here.'

Having been through similar tribulations herself, Lady Faythe knew not to expect smiles from the two who entered, though her son's eyes held a distinctly triumphant glitter. She had seen it before after a success. She noted with some relief that he did not have the girl by the wrist but that his great frame was so close behind her that any thought she might have had about an alternative to this would have to wait. She was almost herded into the solar, poor lass, her lovely face serene except for eyes that flashed like the blade of his Toledo steel sword.

The plaits of her hair, almost colourless in this light, were interwoven with green ribbons and wrapped around her head like thick rope, revealing a cap of hair that swept from a widow's peak above her forehead, softened by tendrils that escaped disorderly on to her skin. With the last of the light on one shoulder, she curtsied like a green willow-frond, gracefully unfolding and sweeping forward to receive a kiss to both cheeks.

'We are glad to have you with us again, my dear. Have you supped?'

'I fear not, my lady. Sir Euan wished me to leave immediately.'

'Euan!' Lady Faythe frowned at her son, greeting him with an embrace at the same time. 'You didn't allow Mistress Oriane to have her supper? What are you thinking of?'

'I'm thinking, mother, that the men who have ridden with me all day to get here don't deserve to be kept hanging around while Mistress Oriane of York has her supper. She can have it now, with me.'

The young woman's stony expression needed no confirmation, but the one from the bed reached Lady Fitzhardinge with an implied amusement. Well used to her son's ways, she brushed aside the incivility. 'I shall have your supper sent to your room, my dear. But first, I want Oriane to meet Lord Fitzhardinge. He and your father were friends, you know, a long time ago.'

Oriane knew that, from beyond the ceiling-to-floor bed-curtains, a handsome face had been watching, and if she had feared that Sir Euan's rudeness was inherited from his father, she was now reassured.

'Forgive me, mistress, for being asleep when you visited me twice before. If they had told me then of your loveliness, I would have defied all the sleeping-draughts in Christendom to stay awake.' He held out a gnarled hand and she went, like a daughter, to sit by his side.

The supper of which she had not been allowed to partake at Clementhorpe and which she had missed by some two hours at Monk Bywater Manor was delayed yet again, at Oriane's request, because having been offered the refreshing comforts of a bath, nothing else seemed quite so immediate. Added to that was the delectable thought that, since Sir Euan intended to share her meal, he would now have to wait some more until she had bathed.

Which went to show how little she knew of her future husband's grasp of tactics. Always anticipate what the opposition will do next.

The room, which Lady Fitzhardinge confirmed was to be shared with no one but Maddie, soon bustled with servants bearing a large wooden tub made from one half of a wine barrel padded around the top edge with leather and with a small stool inside. Pages arrived with buckets of water, maids brought towels and pots of soft soap called lye, and Maddie constructed a tent around the tub by extending a white linen sheet from the bed-rail and holding its edge down with two stools. And so, as the hot water arrived, bucket by bucket, Oriane sat in the barrel and watched the new glow from heavy six-pound candles spread into circles of light through the white sheet and the steam, the silent movement of shadowy figures, the suck of the sheet as the door opened and closed.

Savouring the plunge of water as it poured over her back, her closed eyes gave an impression of calmness she did not feel. Nor did hunger pangs help her anxiety, for although the nuns' hospitality was generous, the food was very plain and not well cooked, and she had been famished well before evensong.

The sudden change of light and the swirl of cooler air through the steam jerked her upright. The sheet that had given her some privacy from the servants was hauled from its anchor and looped up over the bed-rail with a lack of ceremony that announced the presence of one person as nothing else could.

'Have you brought the whole damned household in

here to gawp?' Oriane yelped at him. 'Put the curtain back and get out!' She placed her hands on opposite shoulders and glared at the black silhouette against the light, unable to see his face clearly for the drips that ran into her eyes.

'Time you'd finished,' he said. 'Come on, I'll help you out.' He held out a hand.

'I *haven't* finished. Replace the curtain, and let me get on with it in peace.'

He went to sit behind her on the bed. 'I'll wait,' he said.

'I may be some time.'

He sprawled back onto one elbow. 'I can stand the view.'

Her impulse was to throw the sponge or a handful of water at him, but that would have wet her bed, made him laugh (probably), and exposed herself, achieving nothing except his satisfaction. The view of her back she did not intend to enlarge by getting out. 'Maddie!' she called to the empty room. Her command did not conceal the plaintive tone in her voice.

'It's all right, woman, I'm not going to ravish you. I've come for a bath, that's all. I've ridden hard for two days, and I've thought of little else since noon. Now, if you get out, I can get in, d'ye think?'

'Of course.' Her voice was now scathing. 'You'd ride like the wind for your new connections. That's the first thing you'd do, I'm sure.'

'The second. The first was to shut your obnoxious cousin up.'

'Pass me the towel.'

'Please?'

'Pass me the towel. Do you want a cold bath?'

Languidly, he rolled off the bed and came to stand before her; then, piece by piece, he began to remove his clothes, first the soft leather boots, then the belt, then the tunic and the points that tied his shirt and hose together.

This was calculated effrontery. 'And just what do you think your mother would say to this display of bad manners?' she snapped, averting her eyes.

He pulled off his shirt then bent to strip off the clinging dark hose, every move as unselfconscious as if he'd stood before his comrades. Stark naked, smelling of horse and male muskiness and sticky with sweat, he placed a hand on each side of the tub and leaned towards her as he had done before, blocking out the light. 'If you think, mistress, to pluck at my conscience-strings with threats of my lady mother's displeasure, you are wasting your time. She is more aware of my shortcomings than most. She knows that a bath is my pleasure at the end of the day, and to have a woman sponge one down is something she provides for any guest who desires it. Take your hands away from your shoulders.'

'No, damn you! Leave me!' she choked.

Without anger, he took her wrists and prised them away, holding them at the edges of the tub. Her breasts rested upon the foamy surface of the water, with streamers of lather from the soapwort strewn across their smoothly rounded tops like tatters of lace. His study of them, even in the gloom, was calculated to chasten her. 'Now, mistress,' he whispered, 'ask for the towel politely and then get out of here or suffer me to get in with you. Choose.'

'Let me go and I will get my own towel,' she said, looking away from him.

He dropped his head, laughing. *'Brava,'* he whispered.

Feeling her hands released, she turned in the tub as quickly as an eel and looked over the side to find that the stool that she had stepped on to enter the water had been used by Maddie to anchor the sheet and now lay out of reach, tipped on to the straw mat. Already strung to the breaking-point, she could not suppress the tears of humiliation that scalded her eyelids, and her hands covered her face in anticipation of the further shame she would have to endure as a result of her misfired independence. She had turned her back to him not only to hide herself but to avoid seeing what his body was clearly telling her, and whether she understood the phenomenon or not, it was something she had hoped not to encounter so soon, with hunger of a different sort on her mind.

'Oriane.'

'No. *No!*' she said into her hands.

'It's all right...I'm covered. And I have the towel for you, and the stool is by the tub. Stand up. Come on...stand.'

With her back to the light, she eased herself out of the water, accepting the support of his hands to step out over the high rim, then the towel that he wrapped around her. His tone had changed; his game abandoned. He had seen all he came to see.

As if nothing had happened, he dropped his towel and stepped into the tub, sitting with his back to her and allowing her to dry herself in private, which was all she had wanted.

Maddie returned well before Oriane's nerve did, followed by a steady trickle of kitchen lads bearing trays of food.

'Where in heaven's name have you been, Maddie?' Oriane croaked. The watery eyes and the quick jerk of the thumb towards the tub explained the reason for the uncharacteristically petulant query, one that required no answer except sign language to take a look at the food.

Oriane put a hand to her face to cool her cheek, accepting Maddie's ministrations in silence. She had seen naked men before, briefly and at a distance as they jumped into the river after a day's work; her brothers often. Even her father. But this man was unlike any she had seen before, powerfully broad and deep-chested, his arms overloaded with muscles that swept upwards towards the deep-rooted neck like the base of a tree. Her swift glance at his lower half, quickly turned aside, had shown her an outline of hard narrow buttocks and straight legs, knotted and sinewy, with an angry jagged wound across the top of one thigh. She hoped it was painful. Very.

She made a token protest when he dismissed Maddie and the pages who had helped him to dress, certain that the privacy he intended was for appearances' sake.

'Then bring her back, by all means, if you want her to know every detail of what your father and I agreed together. I don't make a habit of discussing my private affairs under the servants' noses, but if…'

'About me…us?'

'Of course.'

'When you'd concluded your connection-seeking, I suppose.'

'If that's what you wish to think.' He picked up a piece of roast hare from the dish and took a bite, waving the bone towards the table. 'Perhaps you should sit down and fortify yourself against the news, if you can eat and listen at the same time.'

'I don't expect I shall be given chance to do otherwise,' she muttered, sitting.

The cook had sent up the most delectable morsels for what he believed would be an intimate meal, everything daintily presented to appeal to his young master and lady. Tiny joints of roast hare, mushroom patties as small as a groat, honeyed pancakes and crisp-fried saffron-coloured girdle-breads. There were pork meatballs in a spicy sauce and petite slices of Leche Lumbard stiffened with dates and almonds, crystallised fruits winking with sugar.

Sir Euan poured wine into silver goblets and handed one to Oriane. 'Better drink to our agreement,' he said, looking at her over the rim. 'We shall have the betrothal ceremony in a week's time.'

She set the goblet down, clumsily. 'A ceremony? Is that necessary?'

'Yes. Let's begin. I can't wait any longer.'

She was sure he referred to his supper, but her appetite had already begun to dwindle. 'I thought we'd already agreed,' she said, studying the gimped edge of a patty. 'I'm wearing your ring. What more do I have to do?'

'Stop worrying,' he said with his mouth full. He lay down his knife. 'The betrothal is as important as the wedding, you know that, and it gives everyone a chance to meet you beforehand. I had to see your father to find out when he'd arranged his wedding, and there are so few days at this time of the year that don't collide with holy days. You know that, too. Your father's already set his for the fourteenth day of June, just after Corpus Christi, so I've set ours for the twentieth.'

Oriane snorted and threw her napkin down, tight-lipped with annoyance. 'It didn't occur to either of you that I might like to be consulted, did it?' She pushed her stool back, scowling. 'That's only a few weeks away.'

'Consulted? No, it didn't, mistress. If you're thinking that it might not be convenient, well, that's no matter. I shall have bedded you well before then.'

'To see if I can breed?'

'No, there'll hardly be time to find that out. To stop you from wriggling out of the contract.'

'And how could I do that, pray, at this late stage? And here, of all places? After your settlement with my cousin? There'll be no need for any bedding, Sir Euan, I thank you. I do not intend to go back on my word.' Her voice quivered with indignation.

'You did not give me your word. That's what the ceremony is for. *Vows.*' He leaned back and, holding up his goblet, drank a toast to her angry face. 'And, having made them, I intend to make sure you keep them. There will be a bedding, mistress, whatever your inclinations.'

Defiantly, Oriane left the table and went to stand by the bed. 'Having well and truly put me off my food, sir, perhaps you would care to take a five-minute break and indulge yourself here and now? After ruining both my bath and my supper, you might as well ruin the rest of the month for me. It would be a fitting conclusion to this episode in my life.'

He placed the goblet on the table and rose, moving towards her like a cat, with stealth, purposely making her believe that he was considering her cynical proposal. Within his reach, she flung up a hand to ward him off.

'No!' Her mouth only framed the word and the eyes that had held a challenge only a moment ago were now darkly fearful.

Taking her wrist in mid-air, he pulled. 'Come along, Oriane. I do not accept that kind of challenge. We will leave the when and where of it to another day. Or night.' He placed her on the deserted stool. 'Now, we will eat our supper in peace before I tell you the rest of my news. Go on, eat.'

Accepting his truce, she continued her meal, not tasting much of it or appreciating the unaccustomed Rhenish wine. While it lasted, she told him of her uncle's will and of her suspicions, and he told her of his settlement with Leo who had now been reimbursed for all he had lost.

'Lost!' Oriane growled. 'The whole of my future determined by his damned lies. And you are taking advantage of the situation.'

'That's enough,' Sir Euan told her. 'You don't resume hostilities when you've only just agreed a truce. That's not allowed, I'm afraid.'

'It is in my kind of battle.'

'I'll try to remember that.' He smiled. 'It's just as well to know that one side has different rules. And anyway, my taking advantage, as you put it, also gave you your freedom. You might try to remember that.'

'Free—?' She caught his eyes, a slight upward movement of his shoulders as he straightened. The retort died.

'Do you want to hear about your dowry?'

She nodded, lowering her eyes. 'Yes. My father's obviously given his blessing?'

'Of course. A marriage between the offspring of old friends is always a good thing. He sends you his love and hopes we'll be there at his wedding feast.'

She looked away, purposely not responding. 'And his settlement on us?'

'Not as much as you were within your right to expect.'

Sharply, her head came up. 'Why not?'

He took a breath to answer, but she was ahead of him.

'Don't tell me he feels obliged to provide for Jane, too? Surely not. Doesn't her ambitious mother have a dowry for her? She's taking my share? What about my mother's lands? She can't touch that, can she? That's mine…he held it in trust for me.'

'Steady, lass. Steady! Have you finished eating? Right, come over here and sit on the bed and I'll tell you. Bring your wine. Perhaps I should have saved that bit of news.' He produced a roll of parchment from somewhere and passed it to her, watching the frown deepen as she read.

'Three horses, five oxen, six cows and calves, six steers and heifers, forty ewes with lambs, six rams and six pigs, five quarters of wheat… What in God's name is a place like *this* going to do with five quarters of wheat and three wretched horses?' She shook the list at him, but he made no reply. 'Five quarters of rye and ten of oats, two of salt, a cape, two mantles, three robes, nine blankets...' Her voice tailed off. 'Uncut cloth, towels and...fifty shillings...oh!' She flung the parchment aside and jumped up, walking into the darkest corner and hiding her face deep in her hands. 'Fifty shillings! Holy Virgin, is that all I'm worth? Fifty miserly shillings?'

'Oriane...'

She lifted her head, her words shaking with distress. 'Have you any idea, any idea at all, how humiliating this is? Have you? To be taken in the first place for the convenience of two men, a business-deal, and then to be foisted off by one's own father with *that*, nine blankets...two quarters of salt? You could breed your sons on the six heifers, couldn't you? Close your eyes and you'd not know the difference.' Her own filled with tears.

'I think I might,' he murmured.

'Tell me the rest,' she whispered. 'Is there more? Has he managed to deprive me of my mother's holdings, too?'

'Yes,' he said. 'Half of them he'll continue to hold until...'

'Until that cow-eyed wench snares some prancing courtier with good connections. Yes, I see. My property will do very well for that, won't it? Holy Mother...' She looked wildly about the room, not observing the hand that covered two long table-knives with napkins. 'Now I know what I'm really worth. He sold me cheaply, didn't he?'

'Oriane...'

'He's not within his rights to do this,' she snapped, cutting him off again.

'He knows the law as well as anyone.'

'But you didn't dispute it, naturally.'

'Oriane, I didn't dispute it because...'

'Because you—'

'*Will* you shut up, woman, and let me get a word in edgeways?' he bellowed. 'I can help to make it better for you, if you'll give me the chance.'

'I don't want you to make it better. I want my property. All of it. He's only listed half the goods I'm entitled to. Nothing from my uncle, after five years...nothing.' Her voice broke into loud gasping sobs and she turned into the wall, holding on to the edge of the soft woollen tapestry with one tight fist and beating at the chest of a harmless falconer with the other.

Again, she was led by the wrist back to his side, given one of the napkins to wipe her nose and eyes, and more red wine to refresh her. It made her choke instead.

'Now, can you listen to me for a moment or two?'

She nodded.

'I realise you've lost some of your marriage-portion from your mother, but my failure to accept your father's terms would not have made any difference, Oriane. It was all he was able to offer; all I wanted him to offer. He's to be married himself now, remember.'

'That's not the point,' she said. 'It was to have been mine.'

'Yes, but I shall try to compensate you for the loss

so that, if you should be widowed, you stand to own a considerable amount of property in your own right.'

'A jointure?' she said.

'No, not a jointure. It's from me, not my parents. A dower. I'll take you to see some of it tomorrow, if you wish—those that are near enough.'

'Those?'

'There are twenty-four properties in all.'

She sniffed, dabbing at her cheeks. 'Now I know you are jesting.'

'I am not jesting, Oriane. They will be my wedding-gift to you.'

'And mine to you will be the clothes I brought from Silver Street, three old nags of my father's, five oxen,' she said, swaying.

'And sons,' he said, thinking she might not hear.

'Ah, yes. The sons, of course. And no interfering parents. If you start now, the sons might be in place for the twentieth day of June...just. Or you could—' she swallowed the words in a yawn of utter exhaustion and fell against his shoulder '—you could wait for the five heifers to arrive...and the sows...'

Shifting sideways, Sir Euan picked her up and lay her in the middle of the bed where she curled herself into a ball, her eyes already closed by spiked lashes that glistened with tears. He sat, watching her slow breathing beneath the glorious curve of her breasts and remembering how, earlier, they had rested on the shelf of water. Then he left and closed the door quietly so as not to wake her, calling on the way down for Maddie to go to her.

Towards dawn, when the effects of the wine began to wear off, Oriane watched the new light fill the room and listened to the sounds of an awakening manor that reminded her of home at Scepeton, the insistent wood-pigeons and cockerels, the complaining cows, the hounds' excited yelps of recognition.

Her memories of the previous evening were, as usual, of anger and some unnamed fear that she was losing control of her life. In half-sleep, she tried to recapture and identify the disturbing thoughts and knew that they were to do with Fitzhardinge. He had looked at her, spoken to her as no one had done before of intimate things that were so far ahead of her experience that she had never planned for them, nor had ever wanted to; things that concerned the end-product, not the preamble. She resented that. He assumed a matter-of-factness that she was not ready for. He had set a date; but first, a betrothal ceremony. In a week. She crossed her arms over her breasts, but the memory came back of how he had uncrossed them. So she opened them again and felt the memory of his hands over hers while she had looked away so as not to see him.

The Rogationtide festivities which had begun while Oriane was at Clementhorpe gave each day an impetus that caught her in its tide and swept her towards the betrothal ceremony for which she was unready in every sense.

Village work did not stop, but each day found extra hours for riotous games, horse-racing, dancing and practical jests, mummers and musicians and the inevitable feasting and drinking that lasted well into the warm dry nights. Then, in the soft darkness, men and women might exchange clothes and visit each others' houses with consequences they preferred not to anticipate and, in the harsh daylight, a girl was tied to a cart at the centre of the village and publicly whipped for fornication. The deed had happened three weeks earlier and seemed vaguely irrelevant now, but it deterred no one, not even her, and was watched in the same festive mood as the bear-baiting and cockfighting.

The gates of the manor stayed open all week for the villagers to watch the archery displays, the sword-play and the jousting in the tiltyard where a tiered stand had been erected. The ladies of the household, wives and lovers, their maids and companions sat with Oriane of York, complacently telling her who was who inside the anonymous helms over the heads of plate-armoured men. Sir Tomas Vittorini and Sir Geffrey d'Azure had both begged favours from her on different days, and she had obliged by tying her scarves around their arms and bestowing laughing kisses when they won.

D'Azure was tall and fair and, like his two friends Fitzhardinge and Vittorini, was adored by the women. Together, they made an impressive trio, two of them dark, bearded and boldly handsome, one fair and comely, and there were occasions when Oriane had difficulty telling their voices apart but for the elaborate crests that topped the visored helms of each.

Fitzhardinge's gallantry was more restrained than that of his friends. The more exaggerated their attentions to Oriane, the fewer his compliments, and while his gallantry was not lacking in all the outward courtesies, he did and said no more than was absolutely necessary, and even that was executed with a formality that made people look from one unsmiling face to the other and back again. In low voices well out of earshot, the women wondered how she could be so unmoved by his rampant maleness, and the men wondered what it would take to melt the bastard's cold heart if this one couldn't do it. Or had she?

Tomas and Geffrey pushed their chivalry to the limits, hoping to find out how far Fitzhardinge would allow them to go, but he refused to respond, apparently so sure of his prize that no more effort on his part was needed. He had taken her, with an impressive party of friends and manor-officials, to see seven of the properties in and around York, two rural estates and manors, two corn mills and three shops, the rents from which would yield annually as much as her father could expect from all of his together. He had brushed aside her thanks and reminded her with his eyes how she was expected to repay him and she had remembered something about heifers and sows and a heavy Rhenish wine, wondering if the same dosage would obliterate to the same degree the details of his unavoidable intention. So far, it had not been necessary to find out.

Sir Tomas had found his friend's coolness impossible to understand. It had served well enough with other women who had found it exciting, a challenge, never a bar to their enthusiasm, and then Euan had taken whatever was offered without ever overreaching, let alone taking anyone who was unwilling. What had happened in Mistress Oriane's case was difficult to conjecture when Fitzhardinge had left them in no doubt as to his seriousness in making her his. Yet the dispassionate acceptance of his victory might have been no more than just another three broken lances in the lists, a round of applause, a bow, another horse and suit of armour as payment. No more or less than his due. The man was indeed heartless.

Tomas flirted with her outrageously, in sight and out of sight of his friend. Geffrey aided and abetted him, joining in whenever he could if only to make the lass part with one of those ravishing smiles. Recklessly, and enjoying himself too much for caution, Tomas put it to Euan that he was on course to lose his bride-to-be if he didn't pay her more attention.

'I pay her as much attention as she desires, my friend,' Euan said, lifting his chin to have his buckles undone. 'If it pleases you to make good my omissions, go to it. But I think you will be disappointed. The lady is mine and she knows it. That's all there is to it.'

Tomas looked down his beautifully curved beak, lifting one angled brow. 'Omissions?' The word lingered, delving into the darkly concealed eyes of his friend and employer. He pursed his lips in thought, then relaxed. 'You give me leave to try, eh?'

Euan waited until the squire had gathered the armour together and left the sun-washed canvas pavilion before he made his reply. Then it was clear and deliberate, albeit as soft as a whisper. 'Do not mistake me, Tomas. We are talking of omissions, not of initiations. The lady is untried by my choosing and will remain so until I decide otherwise. Keep her happy, by all means, but no more than that. Is that clear?'

'Happy during the daylight hours. They're longer at this time of the year, remember? You think you'll restore the balance, do you, when you choose to get round to it? We Italians do not let the grass grow so long beneath our feet, Euan.'

'You Italians are too impulsive; I've told you that before. You should study the English methods more carefully.'

'My God, Euan, you push the lady's patience too far.'

Fitzhardinge picked up his shirt and threw it at the returning squire. 'You must not flatter me, Tomas. It's not the lady's patience that's being tested.' He held out his arms for the shirt sleeves, and Tomas was left to place the emphasis on whichever two words he pleased.

Chapter Seven

On the face of it, so to speak, the smiles Oriane directed towards Sir Geffrey and Sir Tomas implied an acceptance, even a happiness with her new situation. They were not the only ones to seek her smiles: Lady Faythe spent the whole of one morning with her dressmaker and Oriane, ordering a complete remake of her wardrobe and telling the astonished seamstress that she'd have to send for more help from the village if she couldn't have them ready by the end of the week. Silk from Lucca, velvets from Venice, cloth of baudekin from Cyprus, Italian half-silks brocaded with gold, taffeta and sendal, fine linens and fur-edged mantles for the cooler summer evenings, soft leather shoes and stockings of…

'No…no, my lady, I beg you. No stockings in this heat.'

'Veils, then. No, wait! Veils are on the way out, now. Let's look at the linen of Laon, lawn they call it nowadays. You must have new undergowns, Oriane, my dear. And, Alice, bring my jewellery casket.'

It would have been churlish not to smile.

Alone in her room, or with only Maddie as witness, smiles gave way to set jaws and clenched fists and the eternal questions that centred round the happenings which had plunged her into the midst of this parody of life. Making small-talk and flirting with the men was all very well for a day, perhaps, but the one for whom her eyes searched in contravention to her strongest commands did not seek her company. After the ride to York, he left her to her own devices while he attended to matters of manorial importance, those which his father would normally have controlled. By day, he was to be found with his estate steward, his bailiff and reeve, his constable and master-at-arms and his knights. At mealtimes, he coaxed no conversation from her, nor offered any. Each evening before bed, he came to bathe in her room only because it had been his before hers and because it was the easiest of the private rooms to be reached with hot water from the kitchen. At these times, Oriane invariably found something to do that kept her from seeing his nakedness and never once did she accept his unfailing invitation to use the water before him.

Instead, she wondered maliciously how many others he had made the same offer to, how many he had shared a bath with. And the bed, for that matter. That cheeky-faced lass she'd seen him talking to with his hand on the wall behind her, or the woman with the straw hat at the jousting who had asked her if she'd dressed his wound yet, then turned to giggle with her neighbour.

The day before the one set for the betrothal ceremony, Lady Faythe told her that she was expected to join them in the afternoon's falconry. This would normally have posed no problem, for Oriane was a good horsewoman and experienced with her father's hawks, but she had already refused Sir Euan's earlier lukewarm invitation, which had been issued, it seemed to her, as though he preferred her not to accept. Lady Faythe issued expectancies rather than invitations. No one ever refused.

On seeing her immediately surrounded by his knightly friends, Sir Euan's assumption was that they had invited her and that she had accepted, after all. His response was typically brusque. 'Oh, you've come, I see. Well, what are you going to fly, a merlin or a hobby?'

She would rather he had shown some pleasure, and surprised herself at the hurt his manner caused her. 'A sparrowhawk, if you please,' she said. 'Unless you have some reason to believe I cannot manage one?'

Remembering the dagger, he replied, 'On the contrary, which is why I was surprised when you declined my invitation.'

With Lady Faythe's approval and willing assistance from the men, Oriane flew her hawk impeccably through the lower wooded slopes where it darted fast and low to take blackbird and thrush and even a partridge. Sir Euan, carrying his new lanner falcon, watched without comment. Later on, as they moved upwards into open country, she hooded her sparrowhawk and passed it to the cadge-man who transported the frame of birds on his shoulders.

Sir Tomas, observing Oriane's slow removal of the heavy gauntlet from her hand, the tightened dimple on one cheek, the lowered eyes, moved to her side until his stirrup almost touched her toe. 'You should be well pleased with that performance, mistress,' he said.

Her head lifted. 'Yes.' Her reply was an effort. Her smile even more so.

The rest of the party were now moving on, giving the peregrines and the new lanner falcon all their attention.

'What is it, mistress? Your smile and words say one thing, your eyes another.'

She withdrew them from the scene beyond but it was too late to hide the direction of her search. Caught out and utterly without words to explain, her eyes flew to Sir Tomas's as if for refuge and stayed there, bathing comfortably in the deep brown Italian-velvet darkness.

If it could have been defined at all, the notion took shape in her mind at that moment, though more as an experience already in progress than a cold-blooded plan of action. Comfort was what she needed, wanted, craved. Sir Tomas's eyes offered it.

In the complicated ritual of requests and offers and fearful refusals that mean a hundred different things in different lights, Oriane's intention dissipated as quickly as it had materialised, like a soap-bubble. She could neither answer his question nor hold his warm inviting eyes.

'You are fearful. Is all this going a little to fa—?'

'Yes...yes, Sir Tomas!' She leapt at the chance of an explanation. Here was the opening, offered, already understood. 'Yes, it *is* going too fast. Oh dear, this sounds foolish.' It did, to her, used to managing a shop, a household, servants, her life. Childish and foolish.

'No, mistress. Not so. Much has happened to you, I believe, over the last two weeks; everything of importance. Life-changes. We usually give ourselves time to recover from one before we take on the next, but sometimes…'

She nodded. 'Yes, sometimes we have to take…'

'No, sometimes the *anticipation* of the next change is worse than the event.'

His understanding was so accurate that Oriane stared, leaping again into the soft brown-ness. This time, she did not anticipate him.

'You have nothing to fear from him. I remember telling you once before that Sir Euan is still angry, and you found little sympathy with that. Now, you can see for yourself, and until he learns to deal with it, you will be caught in the crossfire, mistress. It will need all your resources to endure it without becoming disenchanted. But you need not fear him.'

'I was never enchanted, Sir Tomas. He had no need of me, in the first place.'

'Not from where you stand, perhaps, but he never does anything without good reason, Mistress Oriane. I would trust him with my life. I often have.'

'But I *am* fearful,' she whispered, 'despite what you say. Look at him.' She led his glance towards the powerful figure on the black horse, his arms raised to receive the falcon. 'He'll have no care for my newness. He's a soldier. He shows more tenderness to his new bird than to me.'

'That's what you fear most? Tomorrow?'

She swung her head away in a low arc, not daring to ask openly for his understanding of that. What man could?

'Could it be that your own fear is worse than what it fears? If you were to go to him willingly, perhaps…?'

She stopped him with an impatient gesture. 'Willingly? I thought you knew, Sir Tomas, that I am not willing. I object to his method of finding a wife and I am not the kind of woman to grovel in doting adoration when the hero rides in on his pure white horse to release me from the dragon's lair. I thank him very much, but I can hate my saviour *and* the dragon with equal fervour.'

'I see you know your Saint George in some detail.' He smiled.

'Yes, I'm sure he was a delightful man, but every woman has her own ideal and hates the thought of letting it go. You may be right about my own fear making matters worse, but that's not going to go away, things being as they are, is it? Even you must see that.' She looked again at the distant figure of Sir Euan, holding down his rearing horse as someone's temperamental falcon swooped across its nose. The allusion would have been difficult to miss.

'*Even* me?'

Instantly, she was sorry. She put a hand out to touch his arm but it was caught in his long brown fingers and taken to meet his lips. Following it, her eyes were lured back into his and enveloped, held and soothed.

'You really hate him, mistress? Dislike, surely. Not hate.'

But his words did not register enough to warrant a reply, for his grasp of the difficulties that beset her was more than she could have hoped, more than she could have expected from anyone or have spoken so frankly. Added to that, she was already bathing in his physical comfort, the gentle touch, the dark and tender voice, the compassionate expression with firmness and strength in the mouth. He would be strong, supportive. Dare she suggest it? Her breath tightened. 'Tomas,' she whispered. 'Help me. Please?' She gulped, searching for the shock she half-expected to register, and the longer he was silent, the more she believed he would consider her most unusual and intimate plea.

He did not flinch from it, nor did he answer directly, though she knew that he understood her meaning. 'Are you quite sure that that is the kind of help you need?' he said.

'It is the only kind of help that I need. To be shown how it should be. So that I'm not so…so new to it…not so pained by it.'

'A woman need not be pained, mistress.'

'I will. I know it. With him, I will be hurt. And then what will my chances be of ever knowing anything different? What I fear will become fact on every occasion, won't it?' She looked away, her face burning at the shameless talk to a man she had known only a few days. She backed her palfrey further into the shade of the lone tree on the windy hill-top and pulled the gauze scarf around her cheeks. Perhaps she should not have spoken her thoughts, after all. Beyond them, horses and riders and servants grouped and regrouped. 'We should join them,' she said, gathering the reins.

'Wait, mistress.' Sir Tomas leaned forward and took her reins to check the move. Her silk-covered legs lay close together on the same side of the horse in the newest mode and her hands lay within easy reach of his. Letting go of the rein, he touched them with one finger, like the caress of a moth. 'Wait. I know that was not easy for you to say, or to wait for my reply. I wanted to give you the chance to withdraw it and then I decided that I didn't want you to. I am trying to study the English methods of prudence, you see, but I find it difficult.'

'Thank you, Sir Tomas, but I do not wish to withdraw it, either.'

'And I am honoured to have been chosen. But have you thought that Sir Euan will be able to tell, when he eventually comes to you, that you are…have already…er, not as he expected?'

'Not a virgin? No, this was not something I had planned. I gave it no thought.'

'It is possible for a man of Sir Euan's experience to be able to tell, you see. I can think of no way round that problem.'

'But he's never asked. He assumed, I suppose, but I doubt he'd know or care. He's only intent on getting sons, no more, no less, and he's already said that my feelings don't enter into it. He certainly won't change his mind on that before tomorrow.'

'He said that?'

'He told me he can get sons on a woman whether he likes her or not.'

Sir Tomas sighed into the breeze so that she would not hear, narrowing his eyes against the light and letting his studied gaze rest upon his friend. English restraint at its very noblest, he thought. 'I see,' he said. 'He has made you unhappy, and in my country that is a mortal sin. I will do what I can to put that right, and we must both exercise a typically English caution in the matter.'

'I would never admit to anyone that I had gone to such lengths as this, Sir Tomas, let alone boast of it. My virginity is something I have always held dear, but if I am forced to relinquish it, I have a mind to control whom I relinquish it to and in what manner. After that, I shall be able to bear whatever follows with a stout heart, having known just one night of pleasure.'

She was not prepared for his warning. 'That, mistress, is the theory. The practice is somewhat different, you may find.'

'How so?'

He pulled her horse's head up from the grass and handed the reins to her. 'You are used to business transactions, but the business of love has side-effects rather like a drug. Not as easy to give up as to begin.'

The satisfaction of having at last made a decision that concerned her immediate future carried Oriane through the rest of the afternoon without ever once being soured by the concept that she could be motivated by revenge. Nor did she go along with Sir Tomas's chivalrous warning that her emotions might become entangled beyond her governance.

She did not fancy herself in love with him nor that he was in love with her, but if Sir Euan could to it with anyone, then so (presumably) could Tomas. At any rate, he had not seemed concerned about that possibility, and she needed him only for one night to help her over the first stumbling-block. It *was* a business transaction, whatever he chose to believe, and if he feared that she might beg for more of the same, then he would discover soon enough that she did not propose to spend night after night swapping lover and betrothed or being habitually unfaithful. Once would do perfectly well. A night of his comfort was all she required.

The time until then passed more slowly than any she had ever experienced. There had been the meal taken *al fresco* up on top of the hill when Sir Euan had pointedly seated her on a cushion between himself and Lady Faythe, which Oriane saw more as a gesture of rebuke than of possession. He made some show, after that, of being more attentive and even praised her, in an offhand fashion, for her skill with the unpredictable sparrowhawk.

'You did well,' he said, 'for a woman. I'm beginning to wonder if there's anything you cannot do well.'

'It will take you a lifetime to find that out, sir, if you continue to take so little notice of me.' With a new confidence, she was able to smile as she spoke.

He looked sharply at her and placed a sugared fruit on her knee. 'Here, lady. Sink your neat little talons into that. There are ways of discovering what a woman does well without tying her to a man's side all day long, and one does not continue the chase once the deer has been brought down.'

A huff of amusement escaped at his mixture of metaphors. 'With birds, women and deer, sir, you are going to be too fully occupied to do your duty with the heifers and sows. Perhaps you had better limit your activities.' She turned to speak to Lady Faythe and Sir Geffrey before he could think of anything to cap that.

Her comments must have had some effect because

he kept her by him for the rest of the afternoon, and when she would have given Sir Geffrey the attention he requested, Sir Euan took a place by her side that put paid to any flirtatious nonsense his friend might have had in mind.

The twins, Patrick and Paul, were more patently in awe of Sir Euan than their sister, telling her in the courtyard that he had not allowed them to accompany him because they had shared a task between them that had been given to only one. 'He's fearsome,' they told Oriane, with relish, adding fuel to her own distorted image. 'One wrong move and he tears you apart.' The timing of their depiction was unfortunate, to say the least.

Oriane had cut short the rest of their ghoulish tidings and had gone to her cool room where the floor had been swept and recovered with a scattering of sweet-smelling herbs. She had ordered the tub and water for her bath at what she knew was an inconvenient time for the kitchen-hands, so that she could bathe without interruption. It was also inconvenient for Sir Euan, for the water was almost cold by the time he came to bathe, though he said nothing of it.

The supper, more elaborate than usual, lasted interminably through several courses, rituals, minstrels and entertainments that strung Oriane's nerves well beyond the limit of her tastebuds. To avoid Sir Tomas Vittorini's eyes became a supreme effort of will, nor could she know, as is the case with deception, whether her avoidance was overt or not. Again, Sir Euan did all that courtesy demanded, both at the meal and afterwards, taking her to the door of her chamber well past the time when she would normally have been abed and bidding her a pleasant night's sleep, reminding her, as if she needed it, that they had a busy day ahead of them on the morrow.

She bade Maddie dress her hair, as usual, in one long plait and, in her weary state, could not decide whether to warn the maid of the expected visitor or not. So she didn't, and Maddie was asleep on her small pallet by the side window long before her mistress. When no sound nearer than the night calls of the owl and the bark of a fox disturbed the air of the chamber, Oriane began to wonder whether Sir Tomas had, after all, understood what she required of him. She wished also that she had not drunk the red wine that Sir Euan so attentively plied her with, for any lessening of either her control or her awareness was not what she had in mind. Quite the opposite.

She had slept, against her will, when she became aware that he stood within the enclosed space around her bed. She had left open the curtained side opposite the window for the cooling air, but now it was closed and he was invisible, and she would have to use every sense except sight to perceive him. Which, for all she knew, might simplify matters.

'Is that you?' she whispered, not minding the absurdity of the question.

She heard the smile in his voice. 'Yes, mistress. It's me.' He sat beside her on the bed and searched for her hand and instantly she knew by the warmth that flowed from him that his upper half, at least, was naked.

'Where's Maddie?' she said, sitting up.

The smile again. 'Bound and gagged,' he said.

'What…?'

'No—' he caressed her wrist '—asleep. Does she expect me?'

She shook her head, then realised he'd not see that. 'No. If she hears anything, she'll know what to think.'

'What, that *he's* here with you?'

'Yes.' It was her turn to smile. 'All cats are grey…'

'In the dark. I thought that damn meal would never end.'

'Sir Euan gave me that Rhenish stuff. I must tell him one day that it's too strong for me.'

'Perhaps he knows.'

'He knows nothing of me, Tomas. Nothing at all.'

'Ssh…' He slid his hand up her arm and down again until, wanting him to continue the gentle caress, she reached out and encountered his bearded chin.

'You've trimmed your beard,' she said.

He took her hand and held it firmly in his grasp. 'Yes. Fitzhardinge did it for me. Didn't you notice at supper?'

'No. I tried not to look at you.'

Silently, his hand stopped its rhythmical sweep and took her upper arms, drawing her gently towards him until she was held within his embrace, her cool breasts against his skin. 'Come, lady, this is what you need, I believe. Now, tell me of these fears.'

Her cheek was against his collarbone, her nose beneath his chin, tactile sensations that added to the faint aroma of soap, and smoke from the hall. 'I told you, Tomas.'

'I know, but if you give me details, I can banish them for you. And what's all this about, eh?' He lifted the heavy plait and brushed her cheek with it then, holding her to him, he began to fumble behind her back and she knew that he was unplaiting it. Finally, he shook it free. 'There,' he said, letting it fall over them both. 'That's what this stuff is for.'

'Won't it get in the way?'

'Probably.' He laughed, softly. 'But I take it you wish to know what will pleasure your husband-to-be as well as yourself, do you?'

'No,' she said, nosing his skin. 'I do not.'

'All right. Then this is for me alone.' He slid a hand into her hair and held a fistful of it on top of her head, pulling her back with it until her face was upturned to his and cradled into his shoulder. His kiss was careful and sensitive and allowed her to breathe, roaming across her mouth in a leisurely amble that gave her time to feel every move and to make her own reciprocal foray across the new territory. He led her on, waiting and enticing, cleverly showing her what to do, where to go, unhurried and sensuous. It was a conversation she could never have imagined, a duet, a wordless song that tipped them both sideways on to the bed in a pile of silky hair. He brought the duet to an end and began a poem in which he slid his mouth downwards, moving over her throat and encircling her face in a garland of kisses.

'Tomas,' she murmured, drowsily, already half-drunk with sensations.

He slowed and stopped, his lips just touching her nose. 'I think,' he whispered, 'that either you learn remarkably quickly or that you know more about this business than you have led me to believe.'

'No,' she said. 'The only person to have kissed me before is Sir Euan himself.'

'Ah. And you didn't enjoy that, I take it?'

Her reply was delayed while she explored his smooth, rock-hard shoulder. 'I…I don't know, Tomas. His kisses were angry. Not like yours.'

'And you fear that his lovemaking will be the same? Angry?'

'Yes, I told you. I don't want to give myself to a harsh lover until I've first known how it should be. Are we ready to…to, you know…?'

She could almost see the laugh that dropped softly on to her. Then his lips on her ear said, 'No, lady. Nowhere near ready. I think we might start this way.' He sat up and pulled her with him, drawing the sheet away and easing her forward till she stood at the side of the bed, close against him.

Having always believed that lovemaking was strictly a lying-down activity, Oriane was puzzled by this but did as he instructed her, laying her hands upon his shoulders and giving up her mouth again to his. She quivered with anticipation as his hands roamed freely into her hair, over her neck and shoulders, and her arms moved of their own accord from their resting-place.

He took them and replaced them. 'Stay there,' he murmured.

She felt him resume his slow progress until his hands hovered above her breasts. She gasped, her fingers opening in ecstacy, her nipples just touching the palms of his hands, her skin encompassed and raked softly by his fingertips. His mouth opened to receive her moan, drawing more into it with practised ease while his fingers drew upon the softly pointed peaks to prepare a way for his lips.

Beneath her hands, she felt his shoulders descend,

but could not move away from the bed behind her legs. A soft warmth enclosed one breast, a sensation that melted her knees and started an ache between her legs that forced her hands away from their designated place into his hair, pulling him harder into her. He moved to the other side, kissing and licking, nudging the underside of the soft curve with his mouth before moving downwards over her softly firm belly.

She struggled to contain the cries being withheld for Maddie's sake. Tomas, knowing what was happening to her, pushed his arm between her opening thighs, placed his large hand beneath her buttocks and lifted her in one backward heave on to the bed.

She thought then, in some hazy place at the back of her mind, that this would be all. She was ready for him. She ached. This must be well past the beginning and towards the conclusion. But she was mistaken. 'Now, Tomas? Now?'

'No, lady. Not yet,' he said, and continued the journey where he had left off with hands and lips, exploring every surface, every crevice, causing Oriane to grab wildly at his hand when the taut strings of her senses threatened to break.

'Please, Tomas…no more. Do it now…please.'

He lay over her, holding her hand away over her head. 'Then I shall have to come back another time and show you.'

'Yes…yes, come back. But now you must do it. If it hurts I shall not know nor care, for the ache consumes me.'

Waiting and unafraid, she lay in a cocoon of expectancy, wanting only the relief that she knew must come from the final act. At his touch, her thighs opened for him and his hand led the way, caressing the path like a night-time reconnaissance into forbidden realms, opening the locked gates with skilful fingers and taking her lurch of pain into his mouth with a kiss that comforted and gentled. A moment or two to recover, his voice low against her ear, his hands once more under her knees, pushing upwards, then she accepted his body completely with a sigh that grew into the rhythmic and ragged panting of love.

If it hurt, it was a dull throbbing exquisite hurt that drew the breath from her lungs and fuelled a slow-burning fire where the ache had been. Tomas's body above her, hard yet not heavy, held her down while his lips roamed her face, telling her things no one had ever spoken of before, describing her intimate parts as if no other woman, before or since, had ever had any to speak of.

She had not known that Tomas had wanted her so desperately, had always thought his flirtations to be meaningless. His ardour surprised and excited her. But, in her mind, a spark of fantasy mingled with his eloquence and, while his body took possession of hers, she could imagine with no great difficulty that this was the man who had first kissed her, the one whom she disliked, looked for, listened for and dreamed of. The one to whom she was nothing but a potential breeder. She could caress his shoulders and massively strong arms, his muscled back and neck, his hair, and she could believe that, here in the darkness, he was her lover. He would never have said the things that Tomas was saying, but she could pretend. And then she could forget again.

Knowing nothing of the timing of these things,

Oriane was content to allow Tomas to dictate the pace. He was skilled; he did not leave her to her own devices or immerse himself in his own delights to the exclusion of hers, and she was grateful for his attentions, his queries about her pleasure. Twice he asked her if he should stop and twice she told him that that was the last thing she wanted. Then, he had asked her if he should go more slowly, like this, and she had almost screamed with the pleasure of it and laughed when he said that he doubted he could keep that up for long, anyway.

Later, much later, he had told her in a low growl to hold on tightly and, while it lasted, she was a wild horse that he rode across fiery plains before exploding into a million white fragments, like a starburst, never to be the same again. She heard him groan into her hair as if in pain and she had tried to comfort him with a hand on his face, but he had removed her hand and held it away, telling her that she was a gem, a priceless jewel, a peerless woman, which she took to be the kind of thing that lovers said to each other after such an all-consuming experience.

Yet, from Tomas, it sounded anything but trite, and dimly into her mind crept the possibility that he actually cared for her more than he had led her to believe. If that was so, he had hidden it well, until now.

As thoughts began to replace senses, Oriane knew that she had been right to ask Tomas for this, for anything less would be worthless and ugly and would probably have broken her heart. The pragmatism of her day-to-day life did not extend to her dreams; they were precious and fragile and had been nurtured since adolescence. They should not be sacrificed for the sake of convenience, neither hers nor Fitzhardinge's.

In her innocence, she had believed that one such experience would be enough to sustain her throughout her married life. That was beforehand.

'What was it you said about the theory and the practice yesterday, Tomas?'

He eased himself away, wincing at some stiffness, and drew the sheet up between them. 'Remind me, lady. What did I refer to?'

'About the practice being different. That it might not be so easy to give up. Like a drug, you said.'

Tenderly, he pulled her close into his arms, her hair across his throat. He laid his hand over hers, on his chest. 'And you told me it was to be for one night only. Do you still feel that way? And might I remind you, here in the darkness, that you agreed I should return and show you more?'

'Yes, I remember. I think.' She smiled and he caught its sound, returning one of his own.

'You're having second thoughts?'

'No, Tomas. I think that, perhaps, once is not enough.'

'You are right, Mistress Oriane of York. Once is nowhere near enough.'

The respite a man needed after making love was something to which Oriane had never devoted one iota of thought. So she was not particulary surprised when Sir Tomas Vittorini, being supremely fit, began his lovemaking again, this time even more slowly than before, which gave Oriane all the time she needed to release her tightly cloistered dream of being loved by the one who disliked her so. Her act must have been an accomplished one, for she managed to deceive both Sir Tomas and herself.

Beyond the curtain drawn back to where Oriane had left it the night before, the faint light of the early dawn verified that it was no dream. His singular male aroma still clung to her, to the crumpled sheet and the dented pillow, to her hair that had veiled his face when, laughing, he had rolled with her during their second joyful coupling. It had been everything she had wanted but could never have dreamed of, for what he brought to it had been learned in a different world from hers.

She had not asked him, nor had he ventured the information, but she knew that such knowledge could hardly be instinctive, only the abundant cordiality that had given her the courage to confide in him in the first place. His experience was apparent and had served her well, and she would not spoil it by prying into its origins.

Hugging the sheet to her, she sat upon the pillows, savouring a faint tremor along the secret path where he had so effectively forced an entry, and wondered distantly whether Fitzhardinge would be able to tell. After last night, she was no longer so sure. They had talked in low sleepy whispers about the need to be discreet, about the certainty that she would now have to allow Fitzhardinge to consummate the betrothal without any exaggerated display of reticence. She and Tomas must not reveal any sign of greater friendship than before, not even by a glance, a whisper. She was Fitzhardinge's woman, Tomas reminded her, and whatever her feelings for the man, she must do nothing to suggest otherwise, for Tomas's sake as well as her own. In any case, he was not the ogre she believed him to be, Tomas assured her, as she may well discover, if she gave him time.

He had not asked her to elaborate on the reasons for her dislike, for he must have known them as well as anyone else who had been at that first humiliating meeting, nor could she have explained her own uncompromising attitude, for it was unidentifiable, even to herself. She had fallen asleep in mid-ponder; when she awoke, Tomas had gone.

That morning, the butterfly emerged from the chrysalis in other more obvious ways, for the new gowns arrived on the arms of Lady Faythe and her tiring-women, the seamstress herself, Maddie, and assorted other ladies who came ostensibly to see the transformation. Both Oriane and her maid were of the unspoken opinion that they had come to take a closer look at the body Euan Fitzhardinge would at last claim for his own and to discover for themselves what she had that they didn't. Maddie, who had not slept through the whispered activities behind the curtains any more than she had missed its effects on the tumbled bed and its occupant in the morning, kept her own counsel about the night's events until her mistress should choose to remark on them to her.

There were kirtles of silks and softest linen; long-sleeved cote-hardies with buttons everywhere—the latest fashion; sleeveless surcoats to match and contrast, banded with inkle-loom braids, with fur and with embroidery; mantles of velvet, cashmere, camel-hair and wool; scarves of gossamer; jewelled belts and soft coloured-leather shoes with bells on the toes; and hair-cauls of fine gold mesh studded with pearls. All this,

Oriane mused, grinding her teeth, was what her father should have been providing. Or even her uncle, had not her malicious cousin had other ideas. If anything lessened her pleasure in the overwhelming array of textiles, that thought did, for she knew herself to be already in their debt.

Collectively, they decided on a pale pink, brocaded silk cote-hardie that hugged her body from the waist upward like a second skin, buttoning coyly up to her chin and down each sleeve from elbow to wrist. Over that, and because the day was already hot, a lighter silk full-skirted surcoat of deep amber gold, banded with gold-and-pink silk roses around its deep cutaway side-openings. The train at the back swept across the floor and swirled around her feet like a confection of spun-sugar, leading all eyes upwards over the womanly curves towards the white-gold cascade that fell in heavy ripples over neck and shoulders and back. Last, she removed the heavy ring from her finger which would be returned to her betrothed before the ceremony; she felt light-headed without it.

Chapter Eight

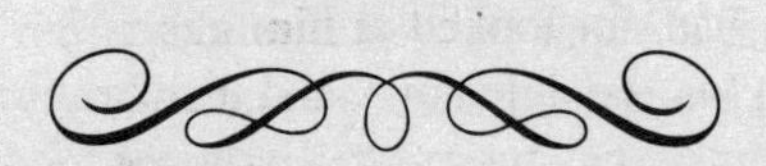

Formal though the ceremony was, it was not the crowded or noisy affair that Oriane had dreaded, but intimate, and decidedly unbalanced without any representative from her own family except her brothers, and even they were under Fitzhardinge's rule. In the solar, where Lord Fitzhardinge could observe from his white-curtained bed, the quietly spoken vows and the chaste kiss were exchanged. The new ring, which fitted her finger perfectly, was infinitely more to her taste than the first which had been thrust at her in such bizarre circumstances: two clasped hands beneath a ruby heart, a beautiful piece of workmanship which she was able to appreciate as well as anyone there.

She stood, twisting the gold band into a comfortable groove at the base of her finger, knowing that its strangeness would have to be learnt all over again in a few weeks, this time in its final resting-place on the left.

'You are subdued, lady,' Fitzhardinge said, his voice intentionally low so as not to be overheard.

She had not realised it but, looking back, saw that

her manner had indeed been almost downcast, submissive. At least, that was how he would have seen it. To her, it tokened a preoccupation with her new state that had taken precedence in her mind over everything else, even the ceremony. Tomas had looked at her intently, and they had smiled as he kissed her hand but no more than that and, apart from noticing his trimmed beard, she had not looked at him again.

Instantly on the defensive, and unable to make light of the remark, she stung. 'And you, sir? You are satisfied now, I hope?'

'More than you could ever imagine, lady. I shall leave you in peace now, until after our wedding.' He bowed slightly. 'Except for the daily courtesies and duties which we must observe for my parents' sakes, you are safe from me.'

'You mean, you take my word alone?'

'For your peace of mind, Oriane of York, I will take your word as it stands. There, perhaps that will bring a smile to your face.' He took her newly ringed hand to his lips and kissed it.

For her peace of mind? He must have wondered, Oriane thought later, why his pronouncement failed to raise a smile but produced an expression of consternation. Had she but known his mind before this, there would have been no urgency to request Tomas's help, but with weeks to go before the wedding and a monthly flow somewhere in between, it was now Fitzhardinge's involvement she needed if she was not to risk being pregnant by Tomas before then. How typical of the man to change his mind after his previous insistence. Now she would have to take matters into her own hands yet again.

At her request, the shameful list itemizing the dowry from her father was not read out, nor were the Fitzhardinge settlements, and the proceedings thereafter moved out of doors to a feast in the newly shorn meadow at the back of the manor-house. Tables had been set up beneath coloured awnings between the walled garden and the river, and here the household and guests were served with a spectacular array of food that, for all it was a fast-day, was no less inventive for that. Coffered pies of eels and herring, spiced sauces, oysters, mussels, lobsters and crabs, crayfish and carp from the stewpond, wild mushrooms, saffron eggs and Yorkshire curd tarts.

Throughout the feast, Oriane put on a brave show of being happy and at ease and managed to forget, periodically, the new problem that now beset her. But the secret delight she took from being at his side and from his gallantry was not something she allowed herself to admit, not for a moment. Such thoughts had been allowed to escape last night, but they were not for the daylight.

She accepted Fitzhardinge's attentions, fully believing that they were for show only, that his dislike of her was genuinely due to his frustration at having to fulfill this domestic role instead of being in France in the thick of some skirmish. Then, marriage would be the last thing on his mind, and it was both her fortune and her misfortune that their paths had crossed when they did. How was she going to persuade him to change his mind about accepting her vow alone, without the consummation, in the light of her former protestation?

After the feast came the rough games, hilariously

riotous contests enacted by the young men and squires who enjoyed the chance of putting to the test their newly learned skills. Jousting in the river was one of them when, instead of tilting at the quintain on horseback, they stood in boats and were rowed, with lances at the ready. At the top of the pole in the water, the shield that hung on the swinging bar was balanced on its opposite side by a heavy sand-filled bag which would swing round and hit the head of whoever scored a hit on the shield, if he did not duck fast enough. Even then, the jolt was enough to unbalance him, and there were few lads who did not have to swim back to the riverbank, spitting and laughing.

There was pick-a-back wrestling where contestants wrestled from atop a partner's shoulders, there was nine-pin bowling at nine pegs called wallops. Oriane won the day at this, even from the men's distance. There was a game of water-handball with a pig's bladder and a great deal of cheating and ducking of opponents with bystanders eventually joining in. Later on there were morris dancers and dancing-in-a-ring to the wail of bagpipes, drums and a harp. And as if their master's son's betrothal had been no more than another element in the Rogationtide festivities, the day drew to a close unnoticed except by the young, who started eating again. The children's parchment windmills-on-sticks were waved homewards and the dancing continued to the foot-tapping and hand-clapping of those too old to join in. The sky filled with streamers of pink, orange, red, fringed with green and the deep indigo of night, and a disorientated moth bumped into Oriane's head.

Fitzhardinge took her wrist and walked with her

through the grass back to the courtyard, calling last instructions to his squires on the way. To Oriane, he was not inclined to speak, only to look, to pass her through each doorway with a hand on her elbow, through to the stairway, the gallery and the upper rooms.

'The solar, or your room, lady? Which is it to be?'

In that moment, the solution to the dilemma was born. 'I owe thanks to your lady mother for this special day,' she said. 'I must bid her a good night before I retire.'

During the thanks to his mother, and sensing Oriane's distraction, Fitzhardinge took her wrist again and drew her towards the door of the solar with a less-than-subtle excuse that they must leave his father to sleep.

'Euan...!' Lady Faythe's whisper and hesitant hand on his arm almost stopped him, but not quite.

'Yes, Mother.' He patted her hand and eased Oriane ahead of him, closing the door firmly against the unwanted advice.

At the door to her room Oriane paused, almost certain that he had intended to leave her there. 'Will you be bathing in here this evening?' she asked.

'Not tonight,' he said. 'I have business to attend to.'

'Oh...I see. I wondered...'

'Wondered what? Speak freely, lady, we are alone now. There is no need for you to strive for cordiality any longer with none to hear us. You have done well, but the effort must have tired you.'

That wounded her, and it must have showed. She *had* tried, and had claimed a certain measure of success. Had it all been for nothing? 'I'm sorry.' She turned away with her hand on the latch, but he placed his fingers over hers.

'What was it you wondered? Whether thanks were due to me, also?'

'Yes. As a matter of fact, I had already decided that they were, but if you are in no mood to accept them...'

He slipped his hand under hers and released the catch, pushing the door open and following her inside. He leaned against it like a young oak against its parent, a blend of browns and deeply dagged plum colours accentuated by gold and amethysts, topaz and beryl. His hose were parti-coloured and patterned with gold-embroidered diamonds. The long tippets hanging from his elbows reached the floor like a peacock's tail-feathers. 'Now,' he said, watching her walk to the centre of the room, 'what did you have in mind, exactly?'

She turned, her heart already aching with the irony of it, with not knowing how to break down their barricades of ill will. 'I wished to thank you, that's all.' She spread her hands, looking anywhere except at him. The room was darkening and there was little to see except patches of lambent light. 'You have been at pains to make this day happy for me and I am sorry if my efforts to enjoy it appeared obvious. It was not so very difficult for me to enjoy myself, I assure you.'

He pushed himself away from the shadowy door and stood before her with hands splayed over his low jewelled belt, his head back in the attitude of cynicism she had seen on former occasions. 'And you have it in mind to *thank* me? Was that it, or is there something specific that warrants this privacy?' His look swept the room, noting the sheets turned down ready for sleep, and Maddie's absence. The reedy pipes and the low thud of the drum came in on a warm breeze through the open window, underscoring the tension between them.

Oriane's courage almost failed her. She must try to unbend more, but in the glare of this man's hostility, how could she? 'You said earlier, Sir Euan, that you intended to leave me in peace.'

'Yes?'

'Well, I am willing to...er...' A pent-up breath hurtled from her lungs like a groan of despair and she turned away again, unable to continue.

There was a long pause before he spoke. 'I see. I am to be rewarded. Is that it?'

Among the shadowy figures on the tapestried wall, a kindly-faced man caught Oriane's eye, encouraging her. 'I can see how it is sure to seem like that...'

'It does.'

'...but...but I am in your debt, do you not see that? For ever in your *debt*. The dowry. Your help. Your settlement of property on me. Hospitality. This day. I have given nothing and I have nothing to give, Sir Euan.' There were angry tears in her eyes as she rounded on him. 'This is all I have to repay you. Have you ever been in a position where you cannot pay your debts? Have you? Until I bear you sons, Sir Euan, I shall be nothing but an embarrassment to you. You have made that quite clear, despite your care of me today, yet my only currency is this—' she tapped her chest '—and the sooner I can begin paying this way, the easier I shall feel. I'm sorry.' She turned back to the encouraging figure. 'This is not what I intended to say, I meant simply to say that I am grateful to you, that's all. And whatever you want of me you can take.'

'Take?'

'All right, not *take*! Have. Have it...whatever!'

'It's of no more value to you, then?'

'Yes!' she snarled, glaring at him through her tears. 'Of *course* it's of value to me. That's why I'm saying this to you. Is it better or worse than the six sows, the two mantles, the sheep with lambs? It's all I've got, isn't it?'

Her wrists were taken away from her face and held in his strong grasp. 'Tomorrow, Oriane of York, we shall go to Silver Street and find your uncle's will.'

'Tomorrow's the Sabbath.'

'I don't care if it's Christmas Day. We shall go and find it.'

'But what of Leo?'

'He's away. He went yesterday.'

She looked at him through her tears. 'How do you know that?'

'Because, lady, I have made it my business to find out.'

'You want to find it for my sake?'

'For both our sakes. What's yours will be mine and that's what this conversation is all about, isn't it? Possessions. Dues. Gifts. Rewards. Call 'em what you like. Your wanting to give me something you haven't got. Yet.'

'Yes,' she croaked.

'Well, then, since you do have something you wish me to accept in advance, I will please you by accepting it.'

'In anger?'

'No, not in anger. In whatever frame of mind you offer it, I will accept it the same.'

With caution? Trepidation? Wild jubilation? The fear that had hounded her before last night's experience had now receded, and the prospect of dwelling in her fantasy for real stood before her, even though he would not be with her as Tomas had been, caring and devoted, pandering to her selfishness. It was a risk she was surprisingly willing to take, not only because she needed his involvement for her own safety but because, whatever reasons she had given him, her heart bade her balance this man's cold indifference against Tomas's ardour and choose which she preferred.

In whatever frame of mind you offer it.

Unfortunately, the experience of one night, however passionate, was hardly enough to give her the confidence she required to offer herself in any frame of mind except the one held towards a man who had already assured her that her feelings, her endearments, her inclinations were nothing to him. He could do it with her whether he liked her or not, and clearly he did not.

In the circumstances, he could want nothing from her budding repertoire of delights except the part that produced sons. And so, never having been unclothed by a man nor known the desire it could produce, Oriane did what she assumed he would prefer her to do and went behind her bed-curtains to undress.

Without Maddie's assistance, it took a little longer, but most of the buttons were for show and she wore only two garments. Laying her head carefully upon the pillows, she left her hair as it was, twisted beneath her head, the sheet pulled tightly up to her chin.

'I'm ready,' she said, clenching her fists.

He drew the curtain aside and stood outlined against the fading light of the window, naked and immense, his face in darkness. Taking the sheet from her hands, he drew it slowly down to her feet, then sat as Tomas had done as if to talk, to put her at her ease. But instead of that, he removed the hands that had automatically flown to her breast, studying in the dimness what lay before him, ramrod straight, like a tomb-effigy.

'This is your thanks to me, Oriane of York? Your gift?'

Her teeth chattered on the word, sending it out like a breath. 'Yes.'

'A gift indeed,' he said. 'Not bestowed lightly, I imagine.'

'No indeed, sir. Not bestowed lightly.'

'Then since the light does not help me, I must discover my gift by another method.' His hand had begun a slow exploration as he spoke, moving purposefully over her neck and shoulders and downwards in gentle sweeps as though he was examining a valuable horse, covering her breast with one great hand. Tomas had caressed her with his mouth; this man sought information, moving over stomach and thighs to the place where Tomas had unleashed such joy.

She grabbed at his hand as it slid deep into the crevice of her legs, half in fear at what he might discover but also in a response to the excitement of his nearness, his nakedness, the touch of his fingers on her skin. She felt the onyx ring beneath her palm, the one she had worn until this morning.

His hand rested under hers. 'What is it, lady? The gift is withdrawn?'

'No.'

'Then you have nothing to fear. I shall not take more than you are willing to give. May I proceed?'

She removed her restraining hand and held his shoulder while he explored further, not knowing whether this was for his benefit or hers. Then he positioned himself above her and took her without more ado, with neither kiss nor caress nor soft words, nor enquiries after her comfort.

Yet in another way, this was the counterpart to what Tomas had offered her, the mate, the complement, removing the need for fantasy. It was reality and, while it lasted, was distressing only inasmuch as she could never tell him what it meant to be possessed by one such as he, even he who could have done it with anyone. She gave nothing to it because she was convinced he did not want that. He gave nothing more for the same reason. When it was over in a few moments, he was the one who could walk away and leave without a word, drawing the curtains together behind him, only the click of the door latch, the whine of pipes and the monotonous thud of drums to drown out the beat of her heart.

It was quiet and dark when Maddie returned, full of whispered apologies. But Oriane was half-asleep and in no mind to remonstrate that her maid had taken a yard when given an inch, and she allowed her to redress her hair, almost asleep again before it was finished.

Nor did she protest when Tomas's warm arms closed about her and drew her close to him, still soft with sleep. She had not expected him on this of all nights, but was glad that his curiosity had brought him to her, and his wish to be of comfort.

'He came?' he whispered.

'Yes.'

'Was it bad? Did he hurt you?'

'No, he didn't hurt me. I don't think he enjoyed it any more than I did. It was a duty, that's all.'

Tomas kissed her, but she responded only half-heartedly and begged him just to hold her, no more, and when he asked if Fitzhardinge had observed that the gates were already unlocked (he spoke in metaphors to make her smile) she obliged and said that his perceptions were probably blunted by over-use, for he had noticed nothing unusual. Nestling closely, her hand slid down his well-muscled buttock and thigh, but was caught and brought to his chest and held, while she fell into her imaginings once again before sleep.

His hand smoothing her breast wakened her far enough to feel his hardness against her back. Then, with long deliberate sweeps down her body as Fitzhardinge had done, Tomas turned her to him and parted her legs, entering her without a word and unwittingly participating in a delusion so close to reality that, in her part-waking state, he became the one she wanted and no other.

This time, in silence, she gave unreservedly with an intensity she knew he would misunderstand, and he demanded with a desperation she could never have matched, for he was strong and vigorous. Taking hold of her plait, he held her head immobile and drank in her kisses like a man parched with thirst, consuming her, utterly.

Dawn had streaked the sky with duck-egg green by the time he left her, satiated and too exhausted to speak. He kissed her hand as he had many times before and left her to sleep. Except that she didn't, but lay with tears streaming into her hair and listening to the peacocks wail to each other from the garden wall.

Maddie, the fist to notice the reddened nose, immediately reached for her tally-stick on which notches were marked in sets of four. Counting from the narrow red cord tied around the lower set, she sniffed loudly and held the stick up before her mistress. 'There,' she said. 'That's what it's all about, see? You're due.'

Oriane nodded, relieved that her tears were so easily accounted for. It would save her having to make something up.

Observant Tomas, too discreet to mention the swollen eyelids and lips, took her hand and led her to her mare, a dapple-grey palfrey that Sir Euan had singled out for her use. Instead of commenting, he let Oriane see his appreciative scrutiny of the apricot velvet surcoat over the cream linen kirtle, the wide neckline of which scooped low across her bosom. The figure-hugging linen gown revealed every curve, and Tomas noted them all, including the hair that hung loose over her shoulders. A golden circlet sat straight across her brow, keeping the hair in place that would, after the wedding, be bound up for good.

'As you like it, Tomas,' Oriane murmured.

'Golden rain,' he replied, taking her hand. 'You are more content now, mistress? Your fears are allayed?'

She inclined her head, aware of his underlying meaning. 'It's all right. Women's tears. No reason,' she said. If only Sir Euan had shown the same concern.

Sir Tomas rode by her side, saying little except to point out what he knew would give her pleasure, the giant hogweed by the river's edge, the creamy plumes of meadowsweet, the bright blue cranesbill; Oriane was thankful for his company. In the circumstances, she fancied it would not have been difficult to fall in love with him, for he had all the qualities a woman desired except wealth, though his lovemaking could have made up for that. His disloyalty was not what one expected from a knight, of course, nor were all knights as pure in thought and deed as they were made out to be. But his role as her instructor would be terminated as soon as her monthly courses appeared, she knew he understood that, and besides, who was ever going to know what had passed between them?

Her gratification on that score was balanced by the knowledge that her intended 'gift' to Sir Euan had gone sadly astray, although she had dressed up its real purpose in the finer clothes of goodwill. She had not expected to enjoy it but had thought that he might, and that he might also have shown some small token of tenderness. Or even the passion he had displayed earlier. As it was, he had apparently enjoyed it no more than she had, and his physical presence was now all she had to remind her of that event. Which he would doubtless be in no hurry to repeat.

And for all Tomas's skill, she knew her scheme to have been less than successful, for now she needed them both for different reasons, far more than she would ever be able to admit to them. So much for her intentions.

Sunday morning in York was alive to a different kind of music from the weekly cries of traders and journeymen, of merchants on the wharves, apprentices and beggars with dogs yapping at their heels. Sunday crowds, clean-dressed and sober, elbowed their way through the pilgrims towards the nearest peal of bells, clutching at their best gowns and steering children away from the slops that ran along the gutters and tutting with disapproval at the inert bodies of drunks in doorways. Intent on their hazardous obstacle-course but merrily returning salutations, they drew to one side with envious stares as the Fitzhardinge cavalcade headed along Jubbergate to Silver Street.

Oriane searched the crowds for familiar faces to re-assure herself that she was still remembered here. Twice, she was greeted, and she was able to turn and smile, warmed by the contact.

Sir Euan had told her that Leo le Seler was away from home and that, but for their betrothal yesterday, their visit would have been made earlier, a revelation that placed his seemingly impulsive offer of last evening in context. Despite all attempts to find out how he knew of her cousin's activities, she could discover nothing except that he was being watched. Oriane pressed Sir Euan on this. 'You believe he's up to something?' she said.

'Well, don't you? His father out of the way. You next, by hook or by crook. I'd call that being up to something, certainly.'

'He could not have been responsible for his step-father's death, Sir Euan. He was as upset by it as any son would be and, anyway, he himself was wounded. That's why he's behaving so strangely, I'm sure. He was feverishly ill when we saw him at Clementhorpe, you remember.'

'Aye, wound fever's common enough. But he'd only to get help from St Mary's or from that fool at St Leonard's. He could have asked *you* for help instead of accusing you of theft. The idiot deserves all he's got coming to him.'

That kind of talk was not to Oriane's liking, but she knew it was useless to reply. The man was hard. Even his two newest squires said so, totally unable to understand her sudden betrothal, unless it was their father's doing. Still, she could not resist a jibe as they clattered into the courtyard behind the goldsmith's shop. 'So, I suppose you must know where my cousin has gone and when he's due to return, Sir Euan?' She pulled aside the soft blanket that covered her legs as she sat astride the saddle.

Sir Euan reached up to help her dismount, ignoring the bait. 'Come on,' he said. At his silent command, several of their escort left on foot to return to the front of the shop, and Oriane took this as the answer to her question.

It was not difficult to gain access, for although most of the servants were at church, the two kitchen lads and the groom were in the yard and, in the hall, a maid was lifting the cat off the table. She smiled happily as Oriane entered. 'Oh, Mistress Oriane, it's been that strange without you.' She tipped her head towards the door that led towards the workshop and the front of the house. 'Master Leo's away, but Master Gerard's in there.'

Sir Euan took Oriane by the elbow. 'Then we shall not disturb him,' he said, softly. 'Come, lady. To the solar first, I think.' Without needing to ask the way, he escorted her upstairs. The plan was a general one for town shops; a solar above the shop at the front, smaller rooms off that. Below, the great single-storey hall with kitchen at the back; above, lofts for the apprentices.

The solar was empty except for Uncle Matthew's bed and the table where the reliquary still stood as they had last seen it after the funeral; as Oriane had seen it through the crack in the doorway. She hesitated, experiencing a recurrence of that eerie scene and the guilt of her silent witness.

Sir Euan held out his palm. 'Your key, if you please.'

Obediently, she delved into her pouch while protesting, 'But I told you, it doesn't fit.'

'I don't disbelieve you, but I want to see for myself.' He placed the little gold thing in the lock at the base of the casket. 'I want to know why it doesn't turn. Obviously, it was made for this casket but not for this lock. Now, where...?' He removed the key and bent to search for another keyhole as Oriane did.

'I'm not even sure that it *was* my uncle's will Leo was reading when I saw him,' Oriane said. 'They could have been other papers to do with the reliquary. Instructions. That kind of thing.'

'Well, that may be, but why would your uncle give you a key without telling you what it unlocked?'

'He would have told me if he'd lived longer, though I cannot help feeling that whatever he's concealed in here is intended for the monks at St Mary's. They know about it, of course, and I dare say they're expecting to receive it, eventually. Abbot William and he were good friends, you know.'

'Then I believe we should take it to them, lady, without delay.'

'What, now?'

'Why not? Your cousin can hardly object, can he?'

'Not object to theft?'

'You would merely be carrying out your uncle's wishes. The abbot can't come here personally to collect it without an invitation.'

'But what about the papers inside? If the will…'

'If the will is still in there, young le Seler has broken the law by not making it public. If it's not in there, he can have no possible objection to the casket going to the abbey where your uncle intended it. Either way, it's much the best thing to do. We shall never find out unless we remove it from here, shall we?'

'But without Leo's key, how do we—?'

'We force the lock. Easy. I have a man who—'

'Force it? The abbot would never allow that.'

'If he thought there was something in it he should know about, he certainly would, my girl.'

His stance, his strong chin, his very sureness was like a rock, a life-raft. Until now, she had forgotten the sweetness of such protection. Now, at his word, she would have agreed to anything and felt secure.

Perversely, she prolonged the argument. 'Gerard's here,' she said.

'He's at the front, we're at the back.' Anticipating her acceptance, he undid his cloak at the neck and handed it to her. 'Spread that on the bed. I'm going to carry it over. Ready?'

The casket was solid gold and crusted with gems,

but to a man used to fighting inside plate armour it presented no problem when, wrapped securely in his cloak, it was carried quietly downstairs and through the hall to the horses waiting outside.

Two of the squires swung round the courtyard gate, each trying to be first with the news. 'Sir! He's on his way into town. He'll be at the Bootham Bar shortly, sir.'

'Damn! So soon. That means we shan't be able to look elsewhere.' Sir Euan helped Oriane up into the saddle, leapt into his own and took the precious bundle up in front of him. 'Come, quickly. We don't want another confrontation, do we? Tomas, take Mistress Oriane along Petergate to the postern gate of the abbey. You'll probably meet friend Leo coming through the bar. I'll get into the abbey by the river wall and through the guest house. I'll see you there. Hurry!' Sending two men with Sir Tomas and Oriane and taking two with him, he watched them go then turned and trotted along Silver Street and across the empty Thursday Market.

Oriane could not resist a furtive whisper. 'You don't think he suspects, do you?'

Tomas did not smile at her foolishness but kept his eyes peeled for signs of Leo le Seler. 'Of course not,' he said. 'He trusts me.' Which was supposed to put Oriane's mind at rest, but did not.

Their impromptu visit to the abbey, though not exactly futile, did not further their discovery of Matthew le Seler's will that day, for while the prior and Father Petrus were both delighted to receive the reliquary into their safekeeping at last, their abbot, Father William, was taking a short retreat at the priory of Finchale near

Chester-le-Street. This being the case, neither Sir Euan nor Oriane saw any reason to acquaint them with the facts about the will or the keys, for without the abbot's permission, no one would be allowed to see the reliquary until its formal presentation. Not even Leo, the monks informed them. It looked as if there was no option but to wait until the prior's return and to see what action cousin Leo would take when he discovered that his precious hiding-place had itself gone into hiding.

Sir Euan found the disappointment easier to bear than Oriane who was hard-pressed to pretend that another week was of no consequence when it meant the difference between being an impoverished bride-to-be and a wealthy one. It was humiliating enough to have to accept this man's aid, but the idea of being able to buy herself out of the situation was still on her mind, and the few intervening weeks were now at a premium. Seven more days before she could discover what she was worth stretched before her like the prospect of seven years.

That evening after supper, suspecting a complacency on Tomas's part after his intense loving of last night, she allowed Sir Geffrey d'Azure to be her companion in Lady Faythe's well-kept garden and to sit with her on the turf-bench to read in French the story of Tristan and Iseult. Not understanding a word did not detract from her appreciation of the language or his deep voice, only the sight of Sir Tomas entertaining one of Lady Faythe's ladies did that, his concentration shared only by his lute. He need not, Oriane thought, have looked quite so happily engrossed.

Nor did Sir Euan give her cause for relief when he eventually came to sit by her side. When Oriane asked him what he'd been doing until then, he mixed his sarcasm with what she feared might be the truth. 'Why, upholding my reputation, lady. What else? Isn't that what you wished me to say?'

Maddie had been long asleep when the door opened and a figure stepped silently inside, hesitating at the light of the full moon that filled the chamber, bringing with it the smell of summer meadows and newly cut grass. Oriane, however, was sitting on her pillow with her knees drawn up beneath her chin, staring at the moon, then at the shadowy recess by the door. She made neither movement nor greeting.

The figure whispered. 'Close the curtains, lady, if you please.'

'I prefer to keep them open.'

'You did not expect me?'

'No, Tomas. Why should I? I thought you'd be elsewhere.'

'Ah. You're angry.'

'Not in the least, but we must talk some time, I suppose.'

'Then draw the curtains, in case...' Even from the shadows, his reference to Maddie's sleeping form could be recognised.

With a lack of grace, she reached out and pulled the curtain along the rail, cutting out the silvery light from one side, then resumed the less than welcoming position.

Almost before she had pulled the sheet up around her knees, Tomas had reached the part-enclosed bed and slid the other curtain across the bottom end so that all Oriane could see of him was a dim shape. He seated himself on the bed. 'Could you not sleep, lady? You were thinking about the will?'

From her fleeting image, she had the impression that he was wearing a long loose robe and now, as he moved up to face her, she heard the faint rustle of silk from his shoulders. 'About everything,' she said. 'About that, and about my monthly courses being late.'

'Late? How late?'

'A few days, that's all. But I'm usually on time. I shall take an infusion tomorrow; Maddie and I know quite a few simples that'll help.'

He leaned towards her. 'You want it to come, then? You do not wish to bear a child? There's no fear now, you know, that he will think...'

She made an impatient move, looking away from where he sat into the deepest shadows. 'Oh, Tomas, how men's minds work! Of course I don't want to be pregnant when there's a chance that I might bear a child that looks like you. I didn't think it could happen so soon.'

'Ah, yes. Of course.'

His reply was so subdued that she knew he had misunderstood. 'Oh, Tomas! I didn't mean *that*. You are the handsomest of men and if I was not...if things were different, I would be honoured to have sons that looked like you. But...'

She heard his huff of relieved laughter. 'Yes, I know. But are these herb infusions not dangerous?'

'Well...'

'Well, what? Are they?'

She sighed and fell silent. Then, 'What would it matter, Tomas?' She was glad when he made no protestation or demanded a retraction from her.

He took her hands from her knees and held her wrists. 'It might solve your problems,' he told her with gentleness, 'but it is not what Sir Euan wants.'

'Oh, no,' she agreed. 'I know what he wants. Sons. I want dignity, and love, Tomas. And respect. Happiness. Ordinary things like a household to run and a garden to create, and a still-room, and to learn how to speak your language, and Geffrey's, and to play the lute, and chess. I want a loving husband who will laugh with me as you do, whom I can turn to for advice and support.'

'Sir Euan has not helped?'

'Yes, oh, yes, of course he has, and I'm grateful for that.'

There was another silence. 'You think you may learn to love him, in time?'

'He'd not notice, or care. Once I can find out if my uncle has left me anything, I may be in a position to suggest paying Sir Euan back for my debt, and enough to release me from our contract.'

He spoke quickly, and with an uncompromising finality. 'Too late for that.'

'Yes, I suppose it may be, but if both parties agree...' She felt his thumbs move backwards and forwards across her wrists and absorbed, through the contact of skin, some of the disquiet her suggestion had caused him.

'No...no, lady. Don't ever think it. He'd not agree, I know it. Far better to find a way through the difficulties than to retreat. You have me to help you, for as long as you need me.'

'Tomas, you have been more than kind to me, but I'm hardly being fair on you. I was reminded this evening why I cannot lay claim to your time any longer.'

'This evening?'

She could feel his frown. 'The Lady Sophie obviously looks for your company and you enjoy hers. I cannot keep you from others. Once my flow begins we must meet no more.' She dropped her head upon her knees, then felt the bed move as he stood to renew his place by her side, drawing her into his arms, knees and all, sliding a hand inside the sheet and on to her buttocks.

'Ssh! We'll settle the problem of Lady Sophie when the time comes, shall we? She's no more to me than any of the others. Until then, you may have to get used to the idea of either bearing a son like me or a daughter as lovely as yourself. I'd say the chances were even.'

'A daughter?'

'Yes,' he laughed, 'a daughter. They're like sons, I believe, only prettier and gentler, and…' His hand caressed the soft inside of her thigh.

Oriane allowed herself to be swung round on to the bed and submerged by his body. The gown had gone. His skin was smooth and hard beneath her exploring fingers, his back a knotty terrain of muscles on each side of a valley that led to a deep cleft. Her hands travelled the great expanse.

'And you must not do anything to make your courses begin. I'm sure you and Maddie know what you're doing, but if anything happened to you, Sir

Euan would never forgive himself. He cares about you more than you know, lady.'

'Oh, Tomas, that's nons—'

'It's not nonsense. I know him better than anyone, and I know that you are the only woman he's ever asked to share his life.' Lying above her, he unplaited her hair and spread it out in the darkness. 'Or made such an effort to clear her name.' He eased the sheet away from between them.

'Isn't that more to do with finding out who soiled the Fitzhardinge name while he was away?'

'No, lady, it's not. Now, can we stop talking about this third party and devote some time to more interesting matters? This may be our last meeting for a week.'

'For always, Tomas. Our last for always.'

'I think not.' His mouth covered her retort, holding the word at bay so skilfully that it dissolved before she could recall it. Attempting, Oriane suspected, to convince her that this could never be her last time with him, Tomas urged her surrender to his caressing hands and lips with a slowness that stretched the hours into light-years of shimmering pleasure.

Yet he would never know how, after he left, she cried herself to sleep as the dawn broke, inconsolable again even in Maddie's tender arms.

'Ssh…what is it, love?' Maddie mopped her brow with the sheet. 'Ye did this last time he came. Did he hurt ye?'

'No, Maddie. Not that. Just the wrong man, that's all. Nothing anyone can put right now.'

The wrong man! Holy Mother of God! The kindly maid took her mistress into her arms and rocked her, thinking her own thoughts and wondering how this muddle had ever begun, in the first place. 'I'll go down and get you a posset, shall I, love?'

'Yes, please, Maddie.'

But by the time the milky drink was brought, her mistress was damply asleep, regardless of the cockerel's lusty crow and the peacocks' cries. Maddie sipped the hot posset herself, then set about tidying the crumpled bed around Oriane, for it looked like a battlefield.

Chapter Nine

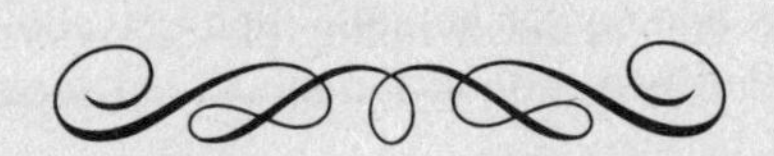

Maddie's passion for tidiness meant that she discovered the good news before her mistress, and the bright red stain for which they had both hoped made its appearance without the aid of lovage, mugwort, white dead-nettle or parsley. And such was the evidence over a wide area of both over- and under-sheets that Maddie was quite sure it had started during the pleasures of the night and must also be known to the one who had caused the tears. Knowing men's horror of such things, Maddie had every reason to expect that the bathtub would already have been in use that morning, but she got it for her mistress, nevertheless.

Outwardly calm, refreshed and vastly relieved, Oriane was dressed in a loose blue kirtle that tied beneath her breasts. She was having her hair braided for coolness when Fitzhardinge entered, knocking after the door was opened. Oriane reacted with some asperity. 'It is as well to knock at some stage, though I always do it beforehand,' she said.

He circled her, smiling. 'Unlike myself, you were well trained.' He went to sit on the newly made bed and leaned his arms across his knees, watching the blue ribbons and the fair hair intertwine beneath Maddie's deft fingers. 'Tomorrow at first light,' he said, 'we set out for Ketils Ing. I should be obliged if you would pack all you need for the next couple of weeks.'

Oriane turned to face him, too quickly for Maddie who had to grab at the swinging plait. 'Where? A journey? Now? But that's ridiculous. You know I need to see Abbot William as soon as he returns.'

'Yes, but that won't be for a week. And anyway, there's no particular hurry, is there? The thing'll be quite safe until we get to it.'

'There *is* a hurry. You know there is. Of all times to make a journey, this must be the most inconvenient. And what is it at Ketils Ing that won't wait? Can't you go alone?'

'One of my manors, and no, I shall not go alone. You will accompany me. It's only a couple of miles away from your father and I thought you might like the chance to entertain him and his lady. Wouldn't you? Your brothers will be going.'

'You have a manor there? I never heard of a manor-house at Ketils Ing.'

'You wouldn't. You've been in York for the last five years, haven't you? It's a new one, just completed on the site of the old moat-house, but there's still the inside to be put right, gardens to plant, stores, still-room, dairy, pantry, all that. We shall take the stewards with us and you'll need to be there to say how you want it. Unless you prefer to leave it to me, of course.' He stood, suggesting indifference.

'No…er, gardens, did you say?'

'Several. We'll have to recruit some men to put them straight. Perhaps I should take Diggon and his lads.'

'And a still-room, and dairy?'

'A buttery and pantry—' he stared out of the window '—chapel, solar, more rooms than you'll know what to do with. They'll all need hangings and furnishings; I can't take everything from here. Beds, bedding—' he waved a hand across the room '—all this can go. You can have eight of the mules and panniers, but all the rest are being used for other stuff, cooking things, food and stores, some new furniture I've had made, but not enough.'

'My bed? Where do I sleep tonight?'

'On the floor, like the rest of us. It won't be the first time?'

'No.'

'We'll stay overnight at St Aelfled's Priory. The prioress expects us.'

'Dame Constance. I know her. I used to…' She stopped, aware that she was sounding too enthusiastic. She pulled the smile back into line.

'Yes. You used to stay there as a child. The nuns taught you to read.' He strode towards the door and was through it before her astonishment showed.

Pulled by some second thought, he returned and, as Maddie moved away, approached Oriane to study her with some keenness. His eyes, she noticed, were like river-water in the bright morning-light, brown, flecked with green. Last time she had seen them opened wide enough for inspection they had been more like deep sea-water. Without flinching, she allowed him to take her chin in his hand and rest it on his fingers.

'You have been weeping, lady. Are you unwell?'

Taken aback by his sudden concern, she had no time to dissemble. 'I am well, sir, I thank you. Women's tears, that's all.' It was what she had said to Tomas and he had appeared to understand.

'Women's tears? You cannot believe yourself to be pregnant already, surely?'

The blunt question caught her off-balance. 'No, sir. I assure you that I am not pregnant. I imagine neither of us should be too surprised at that.'

'No, indeed.' At his cool agreement, the words that she had meant to sting him rebounded on her instead. 'We shall take the journey in easy stages,' he said, letting her chin go, 'and you will travel in my mother's litter, not on horseback.'

'I would rather…'

'You would rather do whatever is opposite to my wishes. Yes, I realise that, but my mother is preparing it for you with great enthusiasm and I presume you would not wish to hurt her feelings?'

'No, indeed, sir. I would not.'

He inclined his head, acknowledging her compliance. 'I will send the marshall and the second steward to you, if that is convenient. You will want to tell them of your needs. Take whatever ladies will be useful to you and let me know so that I can have horses prepared. I shall not be too far away, if you should need me.' He turned to go.

'Thank you, Sir Euan. Before you go, may I know what you have discovered about my cousin? He returned to Silver Street yesterday but you did not say where he had been. Did you find out?'

'Yes. He'd been to the forest to see his outlaw

friends, lady.' He stood with one hand on the latch, expressionless.

'Friends? Outlaws? Oh, surely not. You think...?'

'It's too soon to think anything for certain. All I know is that there's some connection between them, and that cannot be a good thing. I shall find out what form it takes, eventually. Leave it to me.'

Organising came naturally to Oriane, but a departure on this scale and at such short notice required more experience than hers. The marshall, responsible for the domestic staff, and the under-steward, whose role was to order supplies for the household, were helpful and discreet, accepting her suggestions, answering questions and recognising that, once she understood the ropes, she would be fully capable of managing the event. To be Sir Euan's wife, she would have to do this three or four times a year from one manor to the next. She went with them to examine supplies, make lists, check the hangings and bed-linen, the plate and cutlery, the size of the waggons, choose the servants.

Lady Faythe, thankful to see Oriane animated at last, reminded her of things, lent her women, made recommendations, but never imposed. And, too busy to ponder for long on this sudden decision, Oriane gave some thought instead to the problem of how they were all going to be fed on arrival.

'Men sent on ahead this morning, mistress,' she was told. 'They'll have the ovens baking and the vat brewing well afore we get there.' Rooms would be aired and swept clean, doors would be hung, windows polished—yes, real glass, they told her—fires lit, rushes laid, candles fixed, water heated, food prepared.

For Lady Faythe's sake, as well as her own, Oriane inspected the carved wooden litter which was to be her own mode of transport, and though she had reservations about the comfort of a long shallow box carried on shafts between two strong horses, the feather mattress and embroidered cushions, velvet padding and curtained sides gave credence to Lady Faythe's guarantee that she'd be able to fall asleep in it.

'If she doesn't fall out first.' Patrick's *sotto voce* comment was heard by Sir Euan who swiped mildly at the lad's ears, intentionally missing them.

'If your sister falls out, lad, you and your brother will both be sent back here. You two will be riding the horses that carry her, so you'd better learn how to manoeuvre it. Go on, both of you. Get up in the saddles and do an hour's practice before supper.'

'But, sir,' Paul whispered, 'it's supper time now.'

'An hour, I said. No less.' Sir Euan took Oriane's elbow, sharing a smile with her that must surely have been their first.

With ten oxen to pull the heaviest waggons, twenty-four sumpter horses, mules, hackneys, palfreys and Oriane's litter, the furthest they could manage in one day was twenty-five miles, and although the sky was again cloudless, the tumbling streams sprang, every so often, from deep limestone caverns to cool ankles and to slake thirsts. From her shaded position, Oriane found the journey more comfortable than the twins had led her to believe as long as the track was reasonably level, and she was relieved not to have to suffer chapped thighs for two days of this heat and at this particular time.

At each stop by a river, the young pages and squires stripped off and dived in to cool themselves while the toll was paid to cross the bridge.

'Wheel loose!' was yelled on their first morning. Then, amidst groans and grumbles at the delay, the cavalcade was halted while the smith fixed a spoke or reset a pinion.

The second time this happened was in the middle of a shallow river-crossing where every man and boy was required to help hold up the loaded cart while the broken wheel was repaired. Watching from the bank, the women stood giggling near Oriane's litter as the men discarded tunics, surcoats, shirts and hose, dropping them on the grassy pebbles to wade in, wearing only their braes.

The women's examination of half-naked torsos was every bit as thorough as the men's would have been, given the opportunity, and the giggles faded as backs bent and strained beneath the great cart and the knights displayed, unwittingly and without exception, the terrible scars they had acquired during their years of fighting. Familiar to their squires, they were new to most of the women who viewed them with a mixture of pity and wonder.

Surreptitiously, Oriane had sneaked many a glance at the great wound on Sir Euan's thigh which, although healing, was still red and pink, reaching diagonally almost to his knee. What she had never seen was Tomas's back, for her hands had painted a perfect mental image of hard knotted muscles beneath smooth skin, deep valleys and clefts flawed by no scars. The picture in her mind, however, was incompatible with reality, for here were two strong white scars of proud tissue that stood out in relief from the bronzed skin, long tracks across his shoulder-blade that disappeared beneath his left arm, made by a sword-cut beneath his shield. No exploratory hand, not even a casual caress in half-sleep, could have missed a disfiguration like that.

Unable to drag her eyes away from the contradiction, or to sidetrack into its causes, she stared at each of the men in turn, willing the light or the water's reflections to play her some trick. Oblivious to the women's scrutiny, the men bent, turned, stood and fell over, revealing marks that would have identified them to a blind woman, though Sir Euan and Sir Tomas's stature and colouring were similar enough to delay a positive recognition for some time. Especially if one's hands had never been allowed to reach a raw thigh-wound. Or if they had been held away from a handsomely curved nose or…no, away from where it *should* have been.

She shook her head. This was preposterous. There must be a mistake. But mistake or not, a phrase recurred within her memory to drown out all other hypotheses, a phrase that Tomas had used only yesterday. *He trusts me.* And she had foolishly expected him to betray the carefully nurtured trust of many years for a whim of her own, she who had known both men for only a few days. Illogically, she kept up her examination of the wet glistening bodies, trying by some leap of imagination to place Sir Tomas's head on Sir Euan's neck, for the latter was the only one with a totally unmarked back, or wide enough shoulders, or long enough legs covered thickly in dark hair that she had stroked with the soft soles of her feet.

In many respects, the two men were similar; in detail they were not. And she, being new to the game, had been fooled. Confounded by her own stupidity, affronted by their ingenuity, she turned to Maddie. 'Help me get out of this thing, if you please. The heat is stifling me.'

Striding through a field of cowslips away from the noisy river scene, she was still unable fully to accept the man's audacity, her mind alternately racing ahead and coming to abrupt halts (with her feet) when the awful evidence returned and was then challenged with being impossible. He could not, *would* not do such a thing. Why not? She had helped him to it. It had been her plan to deceive, so why be indignant when he had done the same? But surely he could not expect her to be fooled for long? Well, between them they had managed quite well so far; Tomas's back had apparently been easier for them to forget than her innocence.

Once more on the road, she subjected them to detailed scrutiny, comparing ear-lobes, mouths, gestures, voices, hands and every reachable surface. Fingers. The onyx ring. Tomas's hands were ringless. Once, she had felt Sir Euan's hand beneath hers, but her memory of his last visit yielded no firm conclusion. For now, she would have to play along with it, allow them to assume her continued ignorance and, if it was difficult, she had only herself to blame. She would be more observant, try them out and reach a conclusion when more evidence was before her. Then she would decide what to do. She changed her position to the opposite end of the litter as the track became steeper, too outraged and bewildered to feign sleep.

Nor did sleep come to her any easier in the quiet

little cell that she shared with Maddie at the lonely priory of St Aelfled's, for everything she knew about the one to whom she was betrothed had now to be viewed in a different light. Every look, every clasp of his fingers over hers, every word was now loaded with a knowledge of her that she had been sure he did not have. Believing he was Tomas, she had boasted of it to him. How he must have laughed to himself. *There will be a bedding, mistress, whatever your inclinations.* Sure that the gift she had presented to him with such fearful indifference had been her own answer to that warning; she had taken matters into her own hands without knowing that they were, in every sense, entirely in his.

'Maddie! Are you asleep?'

Maddie turned on to her back. 'No, love. What is it?'

'These last few nights...you know...?'

'When he came to you, is that what you mean?'

'Mmm. Were you asleep? Did you see him?'

'I was awake most of the time. I saw him. Why?'

'Did you...did you see him clearly?'

The gist of the questioning was not hard to follow, even at this time of the night. Maddie leaned up on one elbow. 'You're asking me who it *was*? You're not sure? God in heaven, love, is that what you meant when you said it was the wrong man? Who d'ye think it was?'

'Well...Sir Tomas Vittorini.'

Maddie flopped back with a sigh. 'Holy saints! Why would...?' She leaned up again, staring at the blackness where she knew Oriane to be. 'Love, it was Sir *Euan*. Did you not know?'

The reply was whispered, incredulous, dreading the truth she had already guessed. 'No, not then. It was dark, Maddie. Always so dark. Are you sure it was? How d'ye know?'

'Course I'm sure. I saw him. And besides that, I know exactly where Sir Tomas was these last three nights.'

'With Lady Sophie?'

'Yes. She made damn sure we all knew. Wouldn't anybody? I thought Sir Euan came when it was dark because that's the way you preferred it. But why on earth should you have thought it was Sir Tomas? Is that why you wept, because you wanted it to be...? Oh, *love*!' She lifted an arm towards her mistress and found her face, wet with tears. 'Oh, what a mix-up. It was today, when you saw them naked? They're not so alike, then, are they?'

'Their voices, Maddie. He made his sound the same. And then at supper tonight, I realised that it's only Sir Euan who calls me "lady". The others all call me "mistress", as I am until I'm married. And he trimmed Sir Tomas's beard to make it more like his, so they're both in this together, laughing at me. I should have known!' Angrily, she beat her fist into the pillow. 'I'll never be able to look them in the face again.'

'Hush, love. That makes no sense, does it? Don't weep so. He'd not have come to you for three nights if he'd not wanted you so desperately, would he?' Maddie had heard, as well as seen. There had been moments when her presence had been overlooked and the cries of love had escaped their curtained boundaries. 'Whatever you believed, whatever you expected from Sir Tomas, it was Sir Euan who came.'

'He tricked me, Maddie!' Oriane thumped the pillow again.

'Was it not your intention to trick him, then, with Sir Tomas?'

'No, not trick. Deceive, yes, but that's not the same.'

It was a fine point, but Maddie saw it clearly enough, even without knowing the details. 'Well, he knows he'll not be able to come to you at nights for a while, so why not get your own back and keep him away for good? If neither of them knows when your courses have finished, he'll have to stay away, won't he?' Maddie was beginning to warm to the art of scheming.

'I've already told Sir Tom—Euan not to come any more, but he wouldn't accept it. Now I understand why he could afford to take that risk and why he asked if I thought I might be pregnant. I've a mind to keep up the pretence though, Maddie.' Not even to her maid could she confess that the drug had already taken its hold, as Sir Tomas warned her it would.

'That's it. Neither of us was watching when they came out of the river so they're not to know that we've noticed anything. Let them keep on believing you're deceived, and keep on pretending that Sir Euan is Sir Tomas. Play them at their own game, love.'

But what was the game, and what were the rules? What was Sir Euan's purpose in taking his friend's part not once, as she had requested, but repeatedly? Was it to trick her into the fear of bearing Tomas's child? To make her carry the guilt for as long as he chose? Was he revelling, masochistically, in her deceit, just to prove his own cynicism?

That theory, of course, reflected his daytime manner which, if he had truly wanted to hurt her, he could also have imposed upon her in the guise of Sir Tomas. But he had not. Far from it. And even the dispassionate coupling after the betrothal was not a failure to be held entirely at his door for he had offered her no less than she had offered him, the use of a body, not until later when, as Tomas, he had returned to comfort her and remind her of how it could have been.

He'd had no need to do that, for he could not have known of her longing to lay beneath him despite the absence of word or caress. After all that, he had taken to heart the needs that she had listed, unwittingly, to his other self. Surely this impromptu journey was evidence of something like regard.

What had he called her? A priceless gem. A peerless woman. Just for an instant, she had believed that her lover cared for her. On the last occasion, he had said, 'He cares about you more than you know, lady. I know him better than anyone.'

She woke at the sound of the bell for Prime with his words set to music. Maddie was already up and half-packed, humming 'Oranges and Lemons' in the same key.

Ketil, a Danish farmer of the ninth century looking for new land away from the sea's greedy reach, had laid claim to several thousand acres on the hills of the English north country. He had called his land after himself to avoid confusion: Ketilwell, Ketilthorpe, Ketils Ing, an ing being a water-meadow by the river;

valuable land. In later centuries, Ketil's lands were handed down to his descendants, then taken forcibly by the first Norman king and parcelled out to the knights who had fought for him at Hastings in 1066. That was how the Fitzhardinges came to own them and how Ketil's descendants came to be working as serfs, owned, like the land itself.

The first Fitzhardinges, preferring the more civilised south, never discovered the true value of their acquisition, the lead and the silver that went with it, the hard millstone grit or the limestone, the seams of coal, the peat moors and the good stocks of fish in the rivers and tarns, the timber and hunting in the forests, the rich meadows in the valleys and the short juicy hill-grass for the sheep. Later Fitzhardinges woke up to the beauty of the land, but by that time the wild Scots from across the border had, too. Reclusive monks came from France to build great abbeys and to farm sheep on a massive scale that required granges to house the away-from-home shepherd-monks, the lay-brothers and bailiffs.

Pestilence came, carried by pilgrims and itinerant workers from the towns; Ketils Ing and the surrounding villages were no proof against that. The fortified manor-house became roofless and open to the rooks; the workforce declined. The local Cistercian abbey, on the lookout for more property, offered to buy it, but Lord Fitzhardinge had gone up to look at it last year and decided that, if it was good enough for the wily monks to repair, it was good enough for his son, whenever he should choose to settle down.

His timing had been faultless, for the builders were still on site when Sir Euan and his party arrived towards mid-afternoon on the second day of their journey, tired and dusty and eyeing the shining moat that surrounded the manor's high walls.

Tugging her thoughts away from matters of the heart towards organising the household, Oriane saw that there would be much to keep her occupied, for the buildings were set around a central courtyard and were larger than the manor-house at Monk Bywater. Within the crenellated walls, the white stone rose in a medley of arches, windows and new additions that contrasted sharply with the older lichen- and moss-covered nucleus. Masons still shouted orders to men high up on wooden scaffolding, and apprentices in grimy aprons hurriedly swept aside chippings of stone and gobbets of mortar, clearing the courtyard of buckets and stone-saws, chisels and mallets.

Sir Euan was less than pleased to arrive surrounded by workmen's mess but, ankle deep in wood-shavings and blowing away clouds of sawdust, Oriane drew her betrothed away from the chaos and led him through the chambers, the passageways, the steps from solar, to chapel, to office. Assessing their size, location and convenience, they designated each place to its rightful occupant, exclaiming at the views, the large windows, the real fireplaces, the newly plastered walls ready for painting, the Flemish tiled floors, the wainscotting of sweet-scented fir from Norway. Sir Euan had exaggerated in only one respect; Oriane *did* know what to do with so many rooms.

Sir Euan seemed relieved by her enthusiastic involvement and wondered if the prospect of organising on a grand scale would eventually replace her former antagonism to his plans for her future, though when Sir Tomas ventured to remark to his friend on her new naturalism, the reply was as cynical as ever.

'Well then, perhaps we'd better leave her up here, Tomas. At least we've discovered what makes her amenable.'

Tomas fingered the new panelling. 'I thought you'd already done that, Euan. Am I mistaken?'

'Hah! In the dark? When she thinks I'm you? Hardly a success, I'd say.'

'Then tell her. What have you to lose?'

'My bollocks, man. I'd rather take on a dozen lances, Tomas, I thank you.'

'Afraid?' Tomas blocked the blow with his forearm and followed his friend from the room, chuckling.

Before bed, Oriane found time to sit with her brothers outside the mews where the precious falcons had been quietly settled, some still muttering their objections. 'Well,' she said, leaning against the cool wall, 'I suppose the first thing tomorrow will be to ride over and see father. He'll be surprised.'

'And his lady,' Paul added.

'Ah, the lady. Mistress Cherry and her daughter.' Oriane was intentionally flippant. 'Yes, she'll be able to boast of her connections again, won't she? And Fitzhardinge will be able to boast of his. How convenient for them both.'

'Eh?' said Patrick. 'I'm sure she will, but Sir Euan won't be boasting to her, Orrie. He doesn't boast to anyone.'

'Well, why d'ye think he's marrying me, love? For my money? It's for connections, I tell you. She knows people of rank, her late husband's cronies, who can advance your beloved taskmaster in the king's army. That's what he's after. Didn't you know?'

In the loaded silence, Patrick and Paul stared at her and at each other, weighing up who should be first to protest. Patrick, the dominant one of the two, was first. 'Orrie, what are you talking about? Sir Euan needing advancement? If he advances any more, love, he'll be sitting on King Edward's lap. He's a *commander*. He needs no connections. He's there. And I'm damned sure there's no one Mistress Cherry knows who'll be of the slightest interest to the Fitzhardinges. You've got it wrong, love.'

She was unable to argue. This was a part of him that they knew better than she did, for she had never bothered to enquire.

Paul added his affirmation. 'He's high in the king's favour already, Orrie, that's why he's so riled at having to take time to heal his wound. Because while he's not there they'll fill his position with somebody else and he's worked hard to get where he is. He's the best, and he hates having to back off. What did you think he was, eh? A cavalryman with a bunch of trained mercenaries?'

She had not thought of anything except that he was a soldier, insensitive, a brute. Until yesterday she had not seen him in anything but a distorted light and now a new picture was beginning to emerge. So, he had lied about needing her family. Then what did he need?

Patrick, dangling his long bruised hands between his knees, was being charitable. 'As for Father's new lady,' he said, 'she's all talk, but it's only insecurity. She name-drops, but so do lots of people of her age, just to impress. We've learnt to take no notice and Father just laughs. It'll soon wear off once she's married.'

'And Jane?'

Patrick's head dropped lower in laughter.

'And who told Sir Euan that I'd spent some years at St Aelfled's?'

'He did,' they both replied, nodding at each other. They stood to attention, bowing politely, leaving her alone as Sir Euan appeared round the corner of the kennels and came to sit on the wooden bench by her side, swatting at a cloud of midges that danced by the last light.

'I didn't mean to break up a family conference,' he said. 'You will wish to visit your father soon, perhaps?'

'I was going to suggest it, but if you have other plans…'

'No. You will want to be around tomorrow to attend to matters here. The day after that, if you're rested by then.'

She watched his strong brown hands and the dusting of dark hairs on the backs, unable to dissociate them now from the sensations he had aroused by their skilful explorations. Of course. With his reputation, a certain proficiency was to be expected. What she had just learned, however, weakened her case against him even further, and whereas she might not have suffered his presence so close a few days ago, she now took the opportunity to relate the sight of him to the man who had begun the teaching. Tempted to challenge him, there and then, on the anomalies of his behaviour, she cast around for a way into the topic. Her silence, a mite too long, was misread as discontent.

Sir Euan glanced at her, his eyes travelling down her profile to her lap where one thumb swung to and fro across her skin. 'You are missing York already?' he said.

'I was happy in York, sir, until recently.' She had meant, until Leo's arrival, but realised its ambiguity too late. 'But I've always regarded the dales as my home.' She took a deep breath. Sir Euan, could we not...could you...?'

'No,' he said. 'I couldn't.'

She turned to stare at him in disbelief. 'You don't...'

'Yes, I do. And the answer is no. The agreement includes a marriage, lady. Don't ask me to reconsider and don't remonstrate with your father about the dowry; he's made his offer and I've accepted it. That's all there is to it. We'll attend to the will when we return to York.'

'But that's not...'

'Yes, it is. Perfectly fair and proper. There's plenty to do here without bothering about—'

'Can you not hear me out!' she snapped, jumping to her feet. 'At least you can listen to me, can't you?'

He was on his feet as soon as she had moved, close enough to reach out one long arm and scoop her towards him, bending her slender back. 'I can listen, Oriane, when the information is something I need. I do not need your objections. They grow monotonous.'

By whatever means, she was in his arms. Angry or not, what did it matter? He would not come to her bed tonight, nor would he give her an inch of ground in daylight, but here was a twilight zone where the image and its reflection could fuse, briefly.

Despite her frustration at being misunderstood, her body craved for the hard enclosure of his arms and would not respond to her distant command to resist him. Ineffectually, and with none of the resolution she had shown when he came to her aid at Silver Street, she beat at his shoulder with one hand while clinging to his sleeve with the other. As her eyes closed, the lips that she had believed were Tomas's came to claim her, as they had done during those three nights.

Leaving no room for her to renew her interruptions, this was a kiss closed to reason, sweeping her along like the hillside torrents and bearing in its depths the soft resistance of her mewing cries. Swept into his power, she blended all that she knew of him and savoured it in one intoxicating brew. Like a leaf, she lay back on his arms and allowed herself to be carried, swirling, tasting the familiar mouth, feeling the exciting contrast of beard and skin, listening to the swish of his hand across her ear and the pulse of waves beneath it.

His hand moved downwards, slipping beneath the surcoat over the fine cotton of her kirtle and onto her breast. The warmth of his fingers was a warning that one of them must call a halt, for this could go no further.

'No,' she cried, twisting away. 'You must not.' Her head reeled; words came out harshly and unchosen.

His hand stayed over her breast but his head and shoulders straightened, and Oriane knew by his deep breathing that his anger with her was by no means spent. 'Ah, no. I must not, must I? Not having been invited. I must await your next gift, of course.'

His bitter words took away what was left of her breath and, when she might have reminded him that her monthly flux was a bar to further intimacies or assured him that he was mistaken about the nature of her so-called gift, a shake of her head was all she could manage. The fleeting reality had become a dream again.

He took her silence as agreement, and his desire to wound her in retaliation was barely controlled. Bending his darkly thatched head, he held aside the panel of the surcoat and took into his mouth the breast he was holding, wetting the cotton with his tongue and spreading a circle of heat that reached as far as her knees.

A cry rose into her throat, doubling her over till her face almost touched the thick softness of his hair. The longing to bury herself into it was almost irresistible. Then, standing rigidly, she forced herself not to respond.

Coldly, politely, he readjusted her clothing and released her. 'Come, lady—' he held out a hand '—you will need to bathe after that mauling. We'll go and see what they've done with the bathtub, shall we?' He led her past the unmade garden where the struggling plants went as unnoticed as the flush that burned her throat and cheeks.

'Barbarian!' She hissed pure venom into the bubbles that hid the offending blush. 'Lout! Peasant! Ill-bred, uncivilised know-all!' Contradictions were of no account. 'If only he'd let me get a word in edgeways instead of flying off the handle, he might begin to understand. Clod-pole!'

'Yes, love,' Maddie agreed. 'But you know what men are like. They all think they know what we're going to say even afore we've thunk it. Then they have the gall to say we're impossible to understand.'

'It's as if he's *expecting* me to disapprove of everything all the time,' Oriane complained, squirming deeper. 'He's not even prepared to give me a chance.'

'Well, love, you can hardly blame him for getting the idea that you dislike him.'

'Uncompromising brute! He can think what he damn well likes. In a place of this size I should be able to avoid him easily enough. Heaven knows there's plenty to keep me occupied, Maddie.'

Completely overlooking, for the time being, her change of heart from reluctant betrothed to future lady of the manor, Oriane found it easy enough to evade the man who was as adept at crossing swords with her as she was with him. At meal times, their manner towards each other was cool and polite while in private her grumbles tended to dwell on what he had forbidden her to do than the opposite, which was by far the greater. The one day that she had set aside for putting the place in order stretched into two, which suggested to Sir Euan that she was not as eager to see her father as she had been at Silver Street. He did not dissuade her.

There were plenty of extra hands from the village willing to set the garden to rights, and though the reeve had told Oriane it would count as boon-work, and therefore not paid for in money, she made sure that the food and drink was plentiful enough to tempt them back each day. At Monk Bywater, neither the garden nor the house were hers to rule; here, she was free to organise each plot for simples and pot-herbs, set the beehives and appoint a bee-ward, find a sheltered place for fruit-bushes and another for dyeing-plants, for the women up here had expressed envy of her colourful clothes. The still-room was refurbished with shelves and drying-racks, bottles and dishes, pestles and mortars and chopping-boards. Lists were made and dispatched to the Scepeton apothecary, others made ready for their return to York, the scribe who shadowed Oriane becoming known as 'The Quill' from the sheaf of goose-feather pens he stuck through his bushy grey hair and behind his ears.

Following orders to the letter, Lady Faythe's servants from Monk Bywater, who did not want to be there, did the least they could get away with. So, with a penetrating keenness, she held meetings with the house-steward, pantler and butler to hire more kitchen servants, dairymaids and laundresses, a man to see to the rats that invaded the storerooms, men to clear out the filthy stew-pond and to stock it with new fish.

She ordered the carpenter to construct a pigeon-cote, then to make trellises for the garden, then a rose-arbour, then panels for the turf-seats and, ignoring his shocked expression, gave the village poacher the job of warrener (which he already held, unofficially) to set up a colony of rabbits for the manor tables. With plump pigeons, fish and rabbits, fruit and vegetables from the gardens, delicacies from the still-room, venison and game from the forest and field, the household would cost less to feed than it did at Monk Bywater where the proximity to York had contributed to the decline of such things.

Indoors, the pace was every bit as breathless, and the domestic servants who had been used to Lady Faythe's ways were soon replaced by smiling lasses from Ketils Ing and Scepeton who were glad of the work. If the place was reasonably clean before, it now began to gleam and smell of beeswax, lavender, southernwood, lemon balm and rosemary.

With her hair tied up in a white kerchief, Oriane stood in the centre of the women's chamber supervising the measuring of the walls for new tapestries. One of the merchants in York dealt in such goods from Brussels and Arras; she knew him well, for he had wanted to court her, once. The scribe, scratching busily on his parchment, looked up to catch her last words, the noise from the courtyard below making him frown. The yap of hounds, the hollow clop of hooves and the shouts of greetings were not what Oriane had expected to hear before tomorrow, at Scepeton. Now, gowned in her oldest linen smock with a tear in one sleeve and a stained second-best apron around her middle, she was given no choice but to go down and receive her father, her father's impeccably dressed lady, and the lady's impossibly uncommunicative daughter. The resentments which she had put behind her over the last two days recurred with alarming haste.

Chapter Ten

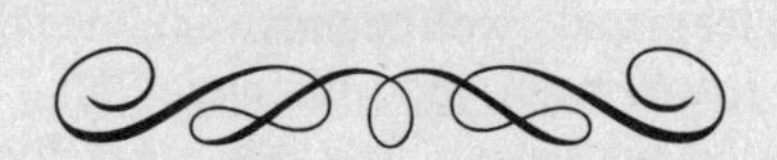

If the uncharitable thought crossed her mind, on the stone staircase leading down to the courtyard, that her father and his lady must have guessed how she would be occupied, two days into a new manor, there was no trace of it on her face as she blinked and smiled at the brightly colourful group below. And if they had thought for one moment (which they did) that she might have preferred more notice of their visit, her welcoming smile and open arms dispelled their fears.

By a whisker, her father reached her first, swinging her off the ground with his embrace before pulling himself together with mock exaggeration to perform his part of the formal greeting, laughing at their pantomime. From the corner of her eye, Oriane saw Mistress Cherry draw back, new to this father-and-daughter game, intrigued, amused, suddenly hesitant to perform her own strictly correct new-mother new-daughter version.

Feeling a certain empathy with the woman's uncharacteristic lack of confidence, Oriane turned to her and made the same laughing greeting in reverse, drawing her into the game that concluded with a friendly hug and thereby taking upon herself the pattern of the new relationship. For Jane, whom she knew to be too embarrassed to act out the same charade, she reserved a more restrained clasp of hands, a kiss to both cheeks and a smile which the lass returned with relief in her eyes before they swivelled apprehensively towards Mark of Scepeton's wolfhounds.

In the cool solar beyond the great hall, Oriane had every reason not to envy Mistress Cherry's fashionably clinging tightness and heavy surcoat of deep red taffeta, or her daughter's high-necked yellow cote-hardie that cruelly accentuated every fold of puppy-fat as much as the contours of her young breasts. Settling the guests like a conjurer with a flock of gaudy parrots, Oriane took charge of her sparkling domain, relieved by the smooth greeting and by the obvious appreciation of the well-appointed room, the servants' efficiency, the variety of nutty biscuits and honey bread-cakes still warm from the kitchen. Nevertheless, at the first opportunity, she slipped out of the room with the intention of changing into a more fitting bliaud with embroidered bands, but too late to evade Fitzhardinge's notice.

Held back in the passageway by one arm, she expected some remark on her appearance from the one whose scrutiny she had been careful not to acknowledge. 'They're in time for dinner,' he said in a low voice. 'Were you going to…?'

'No,' she replied. 'I already have. The hall-steward is prepared for them.'

His eyebrows hitched and lowered again. 'That was well done, lady. You look…'

'Yes, I'm sorry.' She looked down at her plain kirtle with the torn sleeve, a faded blue embellished only at the neckline with locks of hair escaping from the white kerchief. 'I was working, and unprepared.'

'If you will allow me to finish, I was about to say that you look a great deal more comfortable than they do. If they will arrive unannounced, they must take us as they find us. I have no objection to the way you look, lady.' His own appearance verified his sentiment, for he had been in the armoury and forge and was wearing the minimum of clothing short of indecency. With shirt open down the front and sleeves rolled up to the elbows, he made no concessions to female sensibilities.

Oriane was not as comfortable as she appeared and made some show of tucking her hair up, but her hands were removed as Sir Euan attended to the matter in typically down-to-earth fashion, whisking the white linen away and shaking her hair over her shoulders.

'There, that's more appropriate, I think. If that dumpy child can wear her hair loose, let's show 'em how it should look.'

'That dumpy child,' Oriane whispered, looking down the passageway towards the solar, 'has hardly taken her eyes off you since they arrived. Haven't you noticed? You could have married closer into the Cherry family, you know, if you'd been more patient.'

'I still could, if I wanted to,' he said, sliding his hand around her throat and pushing up her stubborn chin with his thumb. 'But I find it more to my taste to quieten you than to get her to talk.' With his body, he pushed her against the cool wall, holding her there with his hand and lips while she did nothing to check him that could have been taken as serious.

The sound of laughter and chatter from the solar ebbing and flowing along the passageway reminded them both of their duties and drew them apart like two wary opponents, each waiting for the other to strike, he not releasing her until he was sure her sharp tongue was sheathed.

'Much more to my taste, lady. I take it your courses have finished?'

The bluntness of his question gave her no time to lie, coming so soon after his subduing kiss. Breathing like a runner, she nodded.

'Then you may find it convenient to offer me another gift soon, Mistress Oriane of York, presented with more packaging, perhaps?'

'Churl!' she snarled, twisting away, riled by his teasing laughter. A small figure stood halfway between them and the door to the solar, its head lowered, watching. 'Jane!'

Oriane saw her flinch and half turn away, too embarrassed to make any reply. The need to remedy Jane's discomfort blotted out the effect of his taunting request, but Sir Euan was quicker than either of them and, thrusting Oriane's kerchief into her hand, he called to the girl, his strong voice halting her before she could disappear entirely.

As if nothing exceptional had happened, he caught her up. 'I have some pups down in the stables that need a good home. Could you manage one, d'ye think? Can you spare a moment to see them now?' He called into the solar to extract Tomas and Geffrey and, between three noisy knights, the blushing lass was escorted away like a yellow butterfly on the west wind.

Now Oriane was thrown into even more confusion, knowing that she was supposed to show her father some contentment with her future and some obligation to him for withholding half of her dowry in favour of a dumpy girl who could scarcely string two words together. The heifers, sheep and quarters of salt still rankled as she led them on a tour of the manor, which might be one way of steering clear of the forbidden subject. In theory.

In fact, almost everything they saw, every renovated room, every plan for developments and the implied wealth that this entailed all pointed directly towards the good bargain her father had made and the good fortune of herself. And, though nothing to that effect was actually spoken, the inference was inescapable.

Her confusion was further compounded by the conflict of emotions which on one side yearned for Fitzhardinge's love and, on the other, the sense of betrayal that surrounded the tactics of him and Sir Tomas. Up here at Ketils Ing, she had the perfect excuse to be uninvolved, but his last remark to her, and Tomas's light touch upon her arm as he passed showed that more decisions must soon be made, the last thing she needed at this point.

Half-expecting to be besieged with advice from the black-haired, plaited, coiled and glittering Mistress Cherry, Oriane was mystified as well as relieved to hear nothing but praise for her efforts of the last two days. Her own south-facing solar overlooked the gardens through a wide ceiling-high oriel window. The large five-sided bay of glass was large enough to seat several people on the seats built into the thickness of the wall, a perfect place in all seasons. To one side of the solar was a small room for Maddie built over the still-room, and a garderobe on the outer wall that fed directly into the moat, twenty or so feet below.

'A maid's room?' Mistress Cherry turned her heavily painted eyes towards Mark of Scepeton. 'And a still? Do show me, Oriane.'

Her future husband warned her, 'Before you get any fancy ideas, my girl, the answer is no, you can't have an oriel built, nor a maid's room, and you'll have to be content with a distillery in the corner of the dairy. So.'

The lady rolled her eyes heavenwards and winked at Oriane. 'Yes, dear,' she said.

'The answer is "no, dear"' he chided her with mock-sternness.

'No, dear,' she replied, obediently. Their smiles said otherwise.

There had never been any of this parent-child talk between Oriane's mother and father, nor had Oriane known of the phenomenon until she had come to York and experienced it amongst the servants. It had enchanted her that a relationship could assume roles other than the usual adult-to-adult, even if only for a sentence or two.

She saw more evidence of it later at the dinner table when Mistress Cherry had tapped Mark of Scepeton's fingers when he had reached too far for a dish of crayfish in egg sauce. He had pulled a child's face and she had laughed, merrily, comforting and scolding at the same time, and Oriane could see how this new ingredient was making her father happier than she had ever seen him. She was glad, then, of her earlier decision not to spoil this with her own problems, which she believed he would not fully understand in view of her pretence at contentment, and if the element of light-heartedness was absent, her father seemed unconcerned by it.

Not so Mistress Katherine Cherry, whose darkly observant eyes had missed nothing of Oriane's demeanour towards her betrothed. They walked together in the large unformed garden, their feet barely skimming the gravel pathways, their introspective glances washing over the newest textures.

'What is it between you and Sir Euan, Oriane? You speak to each other with coolness, yet you must have warmer feelings for him, surely? He's an exceptionally fine-looking man. I wouldn't mind my Jane marrying him.'

There was no denial, but neither was there agreement nor explanation.

Not easily put off, Mistress Cherry led the way to the newly panelled turf bench which had already been filled with earth and topped with a growing layer of chamomile flowers. The pungent scent was released as they sat. 'Your father and I,' she continued, 'are both quite noisy people, aren't we? And I believe your mother was a quiet lady, not given to sharing her thoughts. Am I right? If that's how you are, too, then you must miss her a great deal. I shall never try to take her place, Oriane, but I should like it if we could be friends. I was so afraid of taking on a grown family; I nearly didn't agree.'

'Then that would have been a great pity, mistress, for my father has never looked so happy.'

'Thank you. That means a lot to me. Your mother; would she have approved?'

'Huh!' Oriane's laugh brought no smile. 'Probably not. My mother approved of very little. Looking back, I don't think she and my father were as well suited as you and he. Their relationship was never as loving. At least—' she reconsidered '—not the loving that a child of thirteen would recognise. There was little joy in it, I think.'

'Then I'm sad for that. But tell me no more of their marriage, Oriane. I would not have it seem that I am prying.'

'You asked if I was like her.'

'Yes.'

Oriane plucked a white chamomile flower-head and twirled it in her fingers. 'I don't think I'm like either of them. I loved Leo's mother, my aunt, better than my own. I still think of her as my mother, in a sense.'

'So you lost two mothers and a close uncle within five years. That's quite a loss, Oriane. You must be relieved that your future is more secure now that your cousin's ridiculous demands have been met. Is it too soon for you to show your happiness?'

'My cousin?'

'Leo. Oh, dear.' Mistress Cherry put a hand on Oriane's arm as if to steady herself after a stumble. 'Have I said more than I should? Tch, tch! I was referring to his silly accusations, but I'm sorry if I was supposed to say nothing of it. But surely Sir Euan told you…?'

'Yes, yes, of course, I know that Sir Euan paid him off, but I had hoped that my father would not get to hear of it, Mistress Katherine. It was for his sake, and yours, that I said nothing to him of the business.'

'Not speak of it? To your father? Why ever not, dear? He's the obvious person to deal with it, surely?'

'Not when he's about to contract a marriage, mistress. How would you have felt about marrying into a family in which the daughter is hung for theft? You'd not have gone ahead with it, would you? Think of the disgrace.'

'Ah!' The sigh was immense. 'Oriane, my dear, if you knew.' The burst of laughter seemed to Oriane the least appropriate of responses, but she waited politely for the rest of the sentence. 'If you knew what my own family have been accused of over the years, and hanged for on occasion, you'd know how little weight it carries to encounter more of the same. Undoubtedly these things happen, my dear, usually to the nicest people, but that's how life is. We can't afford to be put off by them, and your father's certainly not. Why should you have thought it? Did you not learn to know him so well?' In another tone, this might have sounded like a complaint, but for all her gaudy appearance, Mistress Cherry's motherly concern was genuine.

'No, not that. I thought I knew him well enough. It was to protect his happiness that I accepted Sir Euan's offer, believing that that would take care of the problem. Never for one moment did I believe he'd *tell* him, after all. It didn't even cross my mind to demand Sir Euan's silence on the matter. It was not something I believed he'd boast of to you.'

Mistress Katherine observed the heightened colour and the sparks of anger, and sympathised. But here were misunderstandings on a large scale. 'No, oh no, dear, you've got it wrong. Sir Euan didn't boast of it, but he did believe your father should know what was going on inside his own family. Can you imagine what your father would think if he discovered years later that you'd been in such a terrible position without him being aware of it? He would never forgive such a lack of trust, would he?'

Oriane stood, kicking at the wooden panelling with her sandalled toe. 'That was not why I remained silent on the matter, mistress. *You* can see that, can't you?' She glanced at the blackened eyes to be sure of the understanding. The nod was reassuring. 'But when we first met, you seemed to be…oh dear, this is going to sound critical of you and I don't mean it to. You seemed to be very impressed by the people you know, people with influence, and I was sure you'd be outraged by any suggestion of scandal. It was nothing to do with lack of trust. Sir Euan's offer was the only way out, at the time. A bargain between us.'

'A bargain?'

'Yes.' She kicked again and turned aside. 'Sons. He needs sons.' She did not see the dimples form in Mistress Katherine's cheeks and by the time she had turned back, they had disappeared.

'Then I am greatly at fault, Oriane. So fearful was I of meeting you and all those at your uncle's funeral, so hard did I try to bolster up my own family background with good connections that I obviously overdid it. I have a record of overdoing things; you must have noticed that by now. You are so very lovely, unlike my poor dear Jane, and that sapped my confidence too, even at my ripe age.' She smiled, giving Oriane a glimpse of the obvious self-consciousness beneath the show. It was as Paul had said. 'And then Sir Euan and his mother were there, and I tried even harder to make a good impression.'

'There was no need, Mistress Katherine. We're a perfectly ordinary lot, and Sir Euan's not easily…' She looked away again into the distant haze where the hills overlapped in blue layers. 'I wish it would rain.'

'Sir Euan is not easily what?'

She came to sit down again, finding the exact form of words difficult. 'He told me, when we made the bargain I spoke of, that he needed connections with our family because of the people you know who can get him the command he desires in the fighting abroad. That's what he said. The boys tell me he's already a commander and as well connected as anyone could be at his age, and now I'm wondering, after all this, how much more he's told me that's untrue.'

Mistress Cherry's shaking head caught at the low sunbeams on the gold braid in her coiled plaits. 'Now that,' she said, solemnly, 'would be laughable if it were not so serious. Especially about my connections with people in the army. My late husband was a master-fuller, so you can see how your father and I met. Nothing to do with the king's army. Of course, I suppose that as long as I kept up the pretence of knowing such people, you would never discover the truth, though Sir Euan must know perfectly well who is known to whom. He's no fool, is he?'

'No, indeed. *He's* not the fool.'

'Now, dear, you must not allow all this to upset you. He must think highly of you to do what he did, do you not think so?'

'I told you, mistress, he wants sons.'

'Yes, dear. He could get sons on half the women of York, I should think, but he chose you, didn't he?'

'Without a dowry to speak of. Perhaps he is a fool, after all.'

'But that's not true, Oriane. Something happened to hold back the property that should have been yours from your mother, and Sir Euan must have told you what...ah, no...of course, he didn't, did he?'

'Told me what he and my father agreed I should bring to the marriage? Yes, mistress, he did. And you can imagine how precious I feel, can you not, to be sent off with *half* of what I expected? Oh yes, my father certainly got off lightly, didn't he?'

'Is that what you believe, Oriane? That your father offered only half what you'd expected? Well then, I'd better be the one to tell you how it happened, since neither of them will.' Mistress Cherry took Oriane's arm and turned her towards the moat wall that glowed pink in the late afternoon sun. 'Come, sit here with me and I'll tell you. You said a moment ago that Sir Euan paid Leo to drop the charges by refunding the lost money. The truth is, my dear, that when he came up to Scepeton while you were staying at Clementhorpe, your father said that the money should be contributed by equal shares from both of them, not only Sir Euan. To have insisted on paying it all himself, which he could have, would have excluded your father from helping which would not have endeared him to his future son-in-law, would it? So your father paid half, which is quite a lot, and because of that, Sir Euan insisted that the dowry should be reduced by at least half to allow your father to recover until the money can be paid back. A temporary measure,

Oriane, that's all. If you learned this in a way that wounded you, then it may have been because he didn't want you to know that he'd told your father, against your wishes.'

'So why didn't he explain this to me, rationally?'

'Would you have believed him? Trusted him?'

Oriane pushed a cushion of moss into the river and watched it bob away on a silvery reflection. She had believed so little of him that was good. 'He told me that some of my mother's dower lands were being held in trust for Jane,' she said, following the moss's progress under the bridge. 'Is that correct, or did he slant that information, too?'

'It's correct, my dear. But you ought to be told why, even though the truth does me no credit. I never intended you to know this, but your father and I had a liaison many years ago when he and my late husband did some business together. Jane is your half-sister. I'm sorry, Oriane.' The coloured lids dropped, then lifted again to look steadily at Oriane. The anxiety showed.

The truth was far better than the lie. 'I can guess the rest, I think. My mother learned of this and requested that half her dower lands should be apportioned to Jane. Sir Euan didn't explain that to me.'

'He wouldn't. No one knows of this except yourself. Not even Jane.'

Having intended to take a man into her own bed while promised to another, Oriane was in no position to make a judgment on the reasons for her father's unfaithfulness, nor this woman's. 'My mother,' she said, '*would* request that. It was like her.

Disapproving, but never vindictive. I wonder if she did it to recompense my father for the joyless marriage.'

'Whatever her reasons, it was exceptionably charitable and very loving, even though it deprives you of what you expected. I hope it makes it a little easier for you to bear. Believe me, Oriane, your dowry does not reflect your father's regard and love for you. He adores you.'

Oriane smiled and covered the older woman's hand with hers. 'You had no more children?' she asked.

'No more. And I had no dowry for Jane, until this, because we were not wealthy and mine was a joyless marriage, too. My late husband lost most of his money in a fire at our home and we had to live in one of the fulling mills until a new house was built, but it was never completed because he couldn't pay the builders and no one would give him credit because he'd always refused the same service to others. He was not generally well-liked, I'm ashamed to say.'

'Live in a fulling mill? The noise must have been appalling.'

'It was,' she laughed. 'But it was only for a year. He died soon after.'

'And my father learned of this and came to the rescue?'

The laugh deepened, shaking the mounds of golden flesh. 'Like a knight on a white charger. Well, bay, anyway. He paid for the house to be completed so that Jane and I could live in it, and we waited a full year before coming together again, out of respect for propriety. He's a saint, Oriane, and if I had not already been in love with him, I certainly should have been after that.'

'You make each other laugh,' Oriane said. 'You are fortunate.'

'And you do not believe yourself to be fortunate, my dear? Is that it? With a place like this, one of how many—seven or eight? And a man who rescues you from a trial you'd stand no chance of winning with such damning evidence against you? A man who obviously thinks...'

'No, mistress, you are mistaken. He does this not from the heart but because I came along conveniently at a time when his parents wished him to find a wife. The marriage negotiations with my father were child's play compared to the haggling he'd have to endure from a noblewoman's parents. His father is ill, you know, and wants to see him settled before he dies. Sir Euan sees this match as a business contract, that's all.'

'Yes, well—' Mistress Cherry brushed the loose moss from her red taffeta and slid off the wall '—I've seen a few business contracts in my time, love, but never one as lopsided as this that you speak of.'

'You think it costs me nothing? I can get used to being mistress of his manors. I shall even get used to bearing his sons, I expect, but I shall never get used to his coldness. He dislikes me, mistress, because in obeying his parents' wishes he is being kept from his chosen profession, fighting. I am in the way of his ambition.' She did not reveal that the only time he gave in to the tenderness was in the dark when she became anonymous and when he himself was unrecognised. She did not add that she yearned for him, even with the coldness.

The farewell was noisy and good-humoured, with the two grown wolfhounds playfully nosing Jane's new pup and the lass herself smiling shyly at the three young squires who had been appointed as her escorts. Already Oriane could see the change in her. It had been an inspired move, and kindly.

Their waves to the departing guests gave no indication of the confrontation that both Oriane and Sir Euan knew would develop as soon as the last of the party disappeared beyond the gatehouse. She strode back towards the house, expecting that he would follow, but his hand slipped beneath her upper arm and drew her back to face him.

'This way,' he said, tipping his head towards the kitchen garden. His eyes, glittering between narrowed lids, were hidden again.

She followed him through the garden to the back of the house where her own pleasance was still being set out. They evaded wheelbarrows, piles of timber and gravel and walked on towards the half-built trellised arbour. Bare arches of willow were already in place to form a shelter, and it was upon one of these staves that he placed a hand, barring her progress beyond him.

He turned to her. 'Now, lady. Try, if you will, to recall my instructions not to remonstrate with your father about the terms of your dowry.' He stood with hunched shoulders to look at her more intently, deliberately standing close. Too close.

Stony-faced and already angry, she told him, 'I did not speak to my father about the dowry. And you might try to recall your promise not to speak to my father about his nephew's allegations against me. *If you will.*'

'I made no such promise. Your memory is at fault.'

'Then we are quits, sir.' She made an effort to dodge round him but he sidestepped and herded her backwards till the willow frame pressed into her.

'Then allow me to rephrase it. You spoke to your father's confidante of the matter, knowing how she will relay your messages.'

'There were no messages,' Oriane snapped. 'And there was no law about speaking to Mistress Cherry on matters that concern us both closely. I cannot form a bond with a stepmother, sir, unless I am allowed to speak freely to her, and the subject of the dowry arose quite naturally out of other things. What I need to know is why *you* took it upon yourself to draw my father into my private affairs at this particular time when you knew full well that that was exactly what I was anxious to avoid. If I'd wanted him to know I would have told him and saved myself the burden of being the Fitzhardinge breeder for the rest of my life.' Her voice, unsteady to begin with, now rose, and the anger that she had striven to contain since her conversation with Mistress Cherry gradually welled up like a head of steam. 'You have taken care to mislead me at every opportunity, about the dowry, the connections.'

'If you were misled about the dowry, wench, it's because you would not let me explain but cut off my every word and then fell asleep in mid-tantrum. I ought to have beaten you awake, I suppose? And since then…'

'Rubbish! If you knew Mistress Cherry's affairs to be no more than a sham, why did you make them an excuse for an alliance? You did know, presumably?'

'Of course, I knew. They were easy enough to see through, God knows.'

'Yet you told me you needed her influence. You lied.'

'Tactics.'

'Lies! Deceit! And you were willing to threaten my father's happiness, his future, by telling him something he had no need to know. That was unforgivable.' She looked for a way out of the embryo arbour but again he moved to prevent her escape.

'Happiness my foot!' he said, scathingly. 'He knew damn well that his bride-to-be has a family history of arson, murder, robbery, the lot. She's as familiar with trouble as she is with fresh air. Her late husband, the fuller, was a notorious rogue; that's why your father stopped dealing with him. One more legal problem would not have deterred either of them, Oriane, otherwise I should not have risked it. There was no risk. He had a right to know; you're his daughter, Leo's his nephew.'

'He relinquished his guardianship of me when he sent me to live with my uncle. And anyway, you should have discussed it with me.'

'Legally, you are still his responsibility, uncle or no uncle. Why else d'ye think I sought his blessing? And I *did* discuss it with you but you were not seeing the facts clearly. You are too intransigent, woman. How could you pretend that you could manage without your father when all your cousin's evidence is rock-solid until we can expose him? No witnesses. Nothing.'

'You manipulated my misfortune to your advantage,' she snarled, facing him. 'Why? To bed me and then rush off back to France. What kind of a bargain is that, then?'

'A bargain you were willing enough to make at Clementhorpe when your clever little cousin brought the sheriff's men to collect you. Remember?' He took her by the shoulders. 'And why the fuss about me rushing off back to France? That's what I am. A soldier. Will you not be glad to see the back of me as soon as you start to breed? Eh?'

The lance, couched firmly and aimed with pinpoint accuracy, pierced her paper-thin armour and reached the tenderest and most vulnerable place in her heart. Gasps of air were sucked in to staunch the pain, tears rushed to blind her and hands grasped at the crumpled and faded fabric of her kirtle. Shaking her head, she dodged him and ran, weaving blindly by some sixth sense round the obstacles and on into the long grass of the orchard where she fell, face down, to water the parched earth with her sobs.

By that same sixth sense she became aware that she was not alone. Without raising her head, she accepted the square of linen which she knew she'd left in her solar. 'Maddie,' she said, dabbing at her cheeks.

'No, mistress, unfortunately I am not half so pretty.'

Dabbing with more purpose, she sat up and saw Tomas's long legs bent to support a relaxed hand. He was leaning against the rough grey bark of a crab-apple tree, watching a spider abseil from the end of one finger onto his pointed shoe. 'I'm all right, Tomas. Really. It's nothing.'

'Ah. Women's tears again. You expect me to believe that?'

'No.'

'I'm relieved. It would have been difficult. So what is it? Things are not working out according to plan? The drug has taken hold already? You are not as in control as you hoped?'

She shook out the dampened square and held it up to the light. The thickened tone of her words, the hiccup of uncontrolled lungs were proof of a passing storm. 'You warned me that this would happen, Tomas. I put the blame on you.'

'Blame me, by all means, mistress, but may I know why?'

'Do you not know?' The silence told her that perhaps he did but, even in her distress, she understood how delicate was the rope by which she balanced from one footing to the next. One wrong move could be critical.

'Yes, I see. Then you are right to blame me. I should have observed your request for a single occasion but I found it as impossible as you, mistress. It takes more strength than I possess to overcome it. I challenge anyone with the same. What will you do?'

Talk was the best antidote to weeping. She folded the kerchief diagonally and placed over her head, tying its points beneath her hair. 'I shall request your help to reverse the situation, Tomas,' she said.

Unperturbed, he smiled. 'That's what we call the cold-water method,' he said. 'We have to use it in camp sometimes, but it's cruelly drastic. I take it we are talking of extreme measures?'

'Yes, Thomas. We are. You must not come to me again. It's too dangerous.'

'For whom?'

The hesitation gave her time to think in both directions. 'For you. Does Sir Euan not suspect anything between us?'

'I'd not be sitting here alone with you in a secluded orchard if Fitzhardinge thought I'd seduced you, I assure you. He would have my guts for harp-strings. You're getting a false picture of him if you believe him to be cold. He's not.'

'No. Three women a night, is it?'

'Where'd you hear that? Your brothers?'

She nodded and wiped her nose with her skirt hem.

'Thought as much. Squires' talk. Dilute it by nine parts to one.'

'That makes it about, what, one-third of a woman per night?'

'It makes it no women at all since his wound in France.'

'Then he must be getting quite desperate. I suppose that, and his wound, and his exile from the battlefield account for his bad temper.'

'The same yardstick, then, probably accounts for my affability.'

She snorted. 'Tomas, you are laughing at me. And you are getting nicely off the subject. I meant what I said a moment ago.'

'Forgive me; I forget what you said a moment ago.'

She took his offered hand and allowed him to pull her to her feet. 'Then make an effort to remember, if you please, Tomas. And how did you know that I was here, anyway?'

'Your maid.'

But when Oriane reached the solar, Maddie was preparing to dress her mistress for supper. 'Where *have* you been, love?' she complained. 'Sir Euan came up from the garden an hour ago.' The square of white linen which she had used in the morning was still on the stool where she had left it.

She was asleep before the pillow was warm. Scalloped and folded, the curtains and covers were as redundant as fires in the oppressive warmth of the chamber which even the faint passage of air from the open window did little to cool.

Her solar here at Ketils Ing was at the opposite end of the upper passageway from the great solar and here was no Maddie to sleep by her window but in the little room that projected into the courtyard. Consequently, there was no one to observe the slow lifting of the latch or the figure that slipped silently across to the bed where Oriane lay nakedly sprawled.

So sure had she been that her message would be passed on and complied with, especially after the argument, that a possible visit from her night-time lover had not even been contemplated, not even for a second. Yet since her discovery on the journey, the thoughts which had at first centred around her dream that Sir Tomas was Sir Euan had now become a reality of such importance that it would take all her wits to keep up the pretence that Sir Euan was Sir Tomas. And being roused in the middle of one's sleep by a warm hand on one's back that slid up to the waist and down to the ankles was not good news for those same wits, however sharp in the daytime.

Her first remembrance was that it was Sir Tomas who had disregarded her instruction that his visits must cease, and in her half-conscious annoyance, swung round with her forearm extended, hitting out and catching him a loud smack with the back of her hand across the shoulder. 'No, Tomas! No! I told you...no!' After that, it dawned on her that something was not right.

The courteous Tomas, who would immediately have taken such a strenuous no for an answer, responded by catching the hand and replacing it firmly on the bed, holding it down while he bent to lift her plait and kiss the back of her neck. 'I heard you, lady,' he said. 'I heard you. Shall we discuss terms?'

She was angry then, for several reasons, one of which was that when she would have threatened to tell Sir Euan, she realised the pointlessness of it. And anyway, they had quarrelled. His sheer effrontery was enough to force a shout into her pillow. 'No! I said no! Get off me, damn you! I don't *want* you!'

Suddenly, she never knew how, she found herself on her back with him over her, preventing more resistance, his fierce whispers clearing her brain.

'Don't keep me away, lady. I burn for you. You needed me first; now I need you. Give yourself to me...I must have you.' His lips diverted her.

Coming from either man, the appeal made equal sense. Coming from the one she wanted, it melted her heart, softening her limbs. No longer needing the dream of his lean weight on her body, she allowed fact and fiction to unite, mentally and physically. She wanted to cry out to him that he was all she desired, that her need was as great as his, but she held it back, too precious a jewel to bestow on a misunderstanding.

Her bodily responses were equal to no such clever ambiguity, bounding from her release with a force barely under control. He was too engrossed in her capitulation to remark on her surprising swing of mood from north to south, nor did he notice how her hands kept within defined limits, her voice on its previous delusive course. Nevertheless, in clinging to him with an explosion of relief, she did not call out the name of her supposed lover as she had before. That, knowing what she did, would have been a cruelty she was incapable of.

The prowess that Sir Tomas had suggested she dilute became easier to believe as the blackest shadows faded into grey and each short sleep moved into lengthier hours of loving. On the soft goose-feather bed he was the passionately attentive lover, patient with her inexperience. Last, on the floor, he was the soldier, taking her soundlessly and with a detached vigour that excited her by its unrefined urgency.

She had winced when her head became jammed against the carved bed-leg and, without speaking or breaking his rhythm, he had roughly swung her away on the sheet with a hand beneath her back. Pettishly, she had bitten him and he had retaliated only by keeping himself out of reach and laughing, softly, 'You'd fight me then, would you, wench? Eh?' And this was so transparently a Fitzhardinge response rather than Sir Tomas's that all the anger and pain that had been so carefully portioned out until now surged into her heels, her back, neck and arms.

Twisting and beating, she could do nothing to stop the pulse of his loins, nor could she escape for long the grip of his fingers over her wrists. The end to the bout came quickly and with something like regret on her part. He released her, carefully wiping her down with the sheet and wrapping her in it, folding her into his arms and then, picking her up like a child, he lay her on the bed. Gathered close against him, she was rocked and comforted, still panting.

'I could not let you win, sweetheart. Don't be angry.' His lips and neat beard caressed her forehead. 'You are a valiant opponent, but I can give you no quarter while I am so disadvantaged. Ssh…you did well. Are you hurt?'

'No, not hurt.'

'What, then?'

She turned her face to receive his kiss. 'Spent,' she said.

The chamber was already taking on the pale new colours of dawn when he rolled smoothly off the uncurtained bed, sure that Oriane slept. Soundlessly, he pulled on his loose floor-length gown and knotted the belt, sliding one hand tenderly down his thigh and letting out a long slow breath through pursed lips. Now, before the light caught him full face, he must leave the motionless figure with the hair coiling around her arms like ropes of gilded silver.

'You will learn to come to my hand, Oriane of York,' he whispered. 'Until you do, I shall not spare you, even though I burn.'

Oriane heard the latch click as distinctly as she had heard his farewell, and though sleep begged to be given a chance, she lay with grey eyes wide open and his words revolving in her head like the premonition of an early winter.

Chapter Eleven

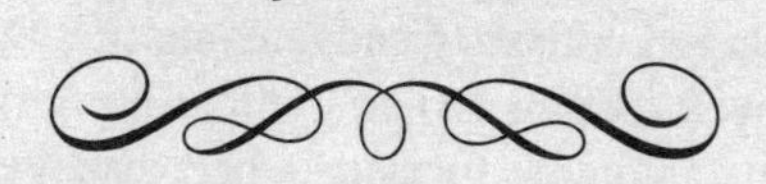

Wielding their hoods like nets, young girls chased after butterflies while their brothers sat with angled birch-rods by the deepest pools, calling excitedly at each brown darting shadow. On the banks of the exhausted river, toddlers seesawed on the logs their fathers had cut and ignored the cavalcade of horses and sumpter-mules that picked its way, only hock-deep, across to the other side. The last ten days at Ketils Ing had provided the party with some freshness from the hills but still none of the longed-for rain, and the prospect of the stifling humidity ahead of them in York did nothing to lighten their step. Only Oriane felt the pace too slow.

Initially to put the manor to rights ready for a more protracted stay later in the summer, their visit had lasted only until their lists of requirements could wait no longer for consultation with the merchants, smiths and craftsmen. Combined with the hunting and hawking, with visits to and from her father that had fostered a growing regard for her future stepmother, the days of arranging and planning had sped quickly; the nights even more so. But paramount in Oriane's thoughts had been the need to consult Abbot William of St Mary's about the reliquary's secret which, by now, her cousin Leo would be frantic to repossess.

The subject had been excluded from her polite and innocuous conversations with Sir Euan, thereby maintaining an outward appearance of amity to all except their most perceptive friends. Even the twins were taken in by it. But in Oriane's mind the problem festered like a wound, for since her discovery of Sir Euan's far greater involvement in her affairs, she could no longer be convinced that the terms of the will mattered to him even a fraction as much as they mattered to her. How could he be expected to understand her obsession? He had called her a priceless gem, but she was a goldsmith's niece and knew the importance of a fair exchange, and she was at one end of an uneven bargain which had become more so since the dissolution of the fabricated connections. Supposing the longed-for sons did not materialise? What had she brought to the marriage then?

Impatiently, she kicked her heels into the palfrey's flanks, urging it out of the water and up onto the bank, having scorned the litter and suggested its relegation to the back of one of the ox-waggons.

'Anxious to be back in York, mistress?' Tomas said, prancing by her side.

'To get to the tapestry-merchant,' she replied. 'He's an old flame of mine.'

'Then I may have to accompany you,' he laughed.

To keep up the pretence, her smile was coquettish; she must continue to deceive Tomas as well as Sir Euan. These last nights of muggy warmth had been a strain on Oriane's natural honesty when she would have preferred to remove all barriers between them, mental as well as physical. But the factors which would have made this possible never came together. It was as if, having travelled so far down this road, they could make no turning for fear of causing more pain. Each night, his lovemaking convinced her of his infatuation, though the words of love never passed his lips. That, she supposed, would have trespassed on Tomas's loyalty too far. Nor did she ever use Tomas's name now, though every other endearment was offered and accepted, both of them skating on the very brink of disclosure.

As long as this was how it must be, she brought to it all the sweetest compliance at her command, ignoring the cold-war days when his apparent dislike of her provoked the inevitable retaliation, when sparks flew and grievances were aired so comprehensively that she could not bring herself to offer him the gift he waited for. It would have been the perfect catalyst, had they known how to reach for it.

Their arrival at Monk Bywater was well timed and saved the dispatch of a messenger to inform them that Lord Fitzhardinge had weakened over the last few days. Fully committed to staying near his father, Sir Euan's concerns would, Oriane assumed, be miles away from Matthew le Seler's will, leaving her no alternative but to make her own plans. She gave no serious thought to the possibility that this might displease Sir Euan. It was, after all, her own affair.

'You did *what*?'

Lady Faythe Fitzhardinge closed the heavy door to

the solar and led the way down the stone steps, flying her white wimple behind her like a flag of peace. 'Don't shout, Euan. You heard what I said; I approved of her going. She's got my shopping list, too.' At the bottom step she turned and noted how his long limbs had loosened with the nursing of the last few weeks, how the skin around his eyes had changed from bruising to a healthy tan. 'You're looking better, at last, my boy,' she said.

Exasperated, he held open the door for her to pass through. 'Mother, you know why she's desperate to get to York, don't you? It's not the tapestry-merchant so much as—'

'The abbot. Yes, dear, I know that. She told me.'

'She told you. There, you see. She knew damn well I wanted to be there and took the first chance to disobey my commands.'

'Not commands, dear. You haven't been commanding her, have you? She's your betrothed, you know, not your sergeant-at-arms, or whatever you call him.' She led him across the hall, doling out suggestions to the servants and placing tubs of beeswax on the trestles for polishing. She knew Euan would follow.

'Mother—' he pursued her into the screens passage where smells of food wafted in from the kitchen beyond '—you were the one to suggest tactics, remember?'

'Those are not commands, Euan dear. Your father tried those on me, and they always had the opposite effect to the one he wanted.'

'Then he should have beaten you,' he muttered.

The bright light from the outer door caused her to screw up her eyes, making it difficult for Euan to see whether this was laughter or pain. 'Only once,' she said, more softly, 'when he couldn't think of anything else to do. It didn't help.'

'It does with men.'

Lady Faythe stopped so suddenly that her son almost trampled her underfoot. She clung to his arm, yanking the hem of her surcoat clear of his blue pointed toes. 'And that, my child, is the root of your problem. Women are not scaled-down versions of men, Euan. They're not even the same breed. You may know what you're doing in bed, no...you need not frown at me for saying so, but if you had thought to listen to her, to understand her, you would not need to talk of commands and disobeyings.'

They stood very still, close together, mother and son.

'I cannot show her any weakness, Mother. She's ever ready to go her own way, even now, and I cannot allow that to happen. Like she has this morning, knowing that I wished to be there.'

'And are you so unsure of her that you must put a ball and chain around her ankle? Do you not recall the wager between the sun and the north wind, Euan?' She saw by the lift of his eyebrows that he did not, so she leaned on his arm and led him at a more sedate pace towards the well where they sat in the shade of its thatch. 'Oriane managed a business most successfully, and, by the sound of things and the length of her shopping list, she's having no problems with the housekeeping, either. You cannot take such a woman and expect her to be as meek as a mouse, you know. She may have been glad enough to accept your offer of help—indeed, I know that she *was*—but giving a person aid does not give you rights over them for evermore. It was your choice. She did not beg you.'

'She's got a bee in her hair about her uncle's will.'

'And so would you, dear boy, if you'd had the same people manage her life as she has. You're sure of your worth, Euan; you've never had to give it a second thought. Oriane is not so fortunate, and now the last remaining things of value to her are being removed, one by one. Have you not seen that?'

'I have, Mother. I gave her property to make up for that, and the new manor to set up. I've accepted all her suggestions. What more can I do?'

The wimpled head tipped, catching the fleeting glimpse of conscience in his eyes and the telltale huff of laughter that followed. 'Do I need to tell you, then?' she said.

'No, Mother. Did someone go with her?' Twisting the onyx ring on his finger, he allowed his mouth to relax.

'Sir Tomas and Sir Geffrey.' She stood, touched his hand and walked off towards the buttery, calling over her shoulder, 'Was that right?'

His fingers opened themselves to sudden concern, submitting to a thumb that brushed gently over the onyx, feeling its smooth prominence.

Tomas. My ring. Your back…my god…your back!

Motionless, he stared down into the dark well then, dipping a hand into the bucket, scooped out a handful of the ice-cold water and splashed it over his face. 'Wake up, you damned fool!' he hissed. 'Wake up, for pity's sake. What are you thinking of?'

The refreshing coolness of the south transept continued into the eastern side of the cloister where the echo of Tomas's feet deadened and sounded again as they approached the vaulted entrance to the chapter house. A hush of black-gowned monks swept past, drawing behind them the welcome smile of the abbot, Father William.

'Come, mistress, Sir Tomas, this way, if you please. Chapter has just finished.' Nodding to the young monk who had led them this far, he ushered Oriane and Sir Tomas round a cluster of pillars and into a long narrow windowless chamber where torches flickered in the draught from doors at each end. 'My private parlour,' he said, his sandalled feet flapping down the steps. 'Whoever built it must have wanted all the abbots to choke to death. We'll leave one door open, shall we?'

The reliquary stood on an oak table surrounded by rolls of parchment, maps, an astrolabe, ink-horns and quills, leatherbound books and a large gilded cross on a square base. Oriane recognised that, too. She seated herself on the stone bench that ran from end to end of one wall and waited for Father William's signal. Begin, he would say.

He did not, but waited for Father Petrus to join them, then said, 'Ah, Petrus. Mistress Oriane has come about the will and we shall need you to stay as witness. You met Sir Tomas at Matthew's funeral, I believe.'

The two men bowed, and Tomas took his seat as Oriane spoke.

'You know why I've come, Father? How is that?'

Father William cleared away a pile of scrolls and brought the heavy reliquary within his range, displaying a strength his loose gown had disguised. 'How do

I know?' He held out his hand to Father Petrus, palm up, and received a key into it. 'That,' he said. 'The key. I expected someone to bring the reliquary to us at some stage, but I must admit to wondering whether the will would still be where your uncle placed it. I take it you did not find his key?'

Oriane was on her feet again, peering at the little duplicate in the abbot's hand. 'Where did you get it?' she said. Then, realising the abruptness of her question, began again. 'Father, is that the same key that Leo had, or another one?'

'Ah,' he said, looking at his infirmarer, 'that answers my question. So young Leo found his stepfather's key. This one, mistress, was given to me by your uncle about six months ago when the locks were in place.' He closed his fingers around the key and smiled again, waiting for her response.

'A duplicate? So you knew where the will was? We looked everywhere, Father. My cousin was sure I was concealing it from him.'

His eyebrows wriggled like grey-haired caterpillars. 'I would have told you, mistress, if I had realised you didn't know. And if your uncle had been prepared for his demise he would no doubt have made sure that you knew its whereabouts, too. But I suppose he left his key where he could get at it when he needed it. He made me the executor of his will, you see. Do sit down. Yet I could do little until the reliquary was brought here. It was Matthew's way of making sure that it fell into the right hands, I suppose, placing it where he knew I would get it, eventually. You realise, of course, that I was bound to seek Master Leo's agreement to read the will? I invited him to tell me when he was free to come, but he sent a message by return to say that he was too ill. He did not want to see Father Petrus, or anyone else, for that matter, though I have wondered since if that message came from his own lips or from those of his servant.'

'Master Gerard?'

He nodded. 'He sent no word to say that he'd found the key or that he was aware of the contents of the will. In which case, we are free to proceed with its reading.'

Seeing Oriane search for a coherent explanation, Tomas told the two monks of Leo's threats, his embezzlement, his attempt to have Oriane arrested and of Fitzhardinge's help. Leo le Seler, he told them, had seen the will and replaced it, pretending to know nothing of it.

'We saw that the ribbon had been untied when we checked to see if it was still there. I suppose it should have occurred to me that that's what had happened.'

'His arm, Father. It was in a sling. He couldn't tie it.'

'And you are now in the care of the Fitzhardinges?' He glanced at Oriane's ring.

'I am betrothed to Sir Euan, Father.'

'Ah, then you will not be too affected by the terms of the will, I take it.' It was a mild bait, but Oriane rose to it.

'Not so, Father. I need to know how the business will continue and how this will have a bearing on my future.'

You have already chosen your future, mistress. The abbot's thoughts were as clear as if he had spoken them out loud, yet he merely hesitated and then conceded the point. 'Well, now, I can be of some help there, because I know to whom the Silver Street property belongs, mistress.'

'Doesn't it...didn't it belong to my uncle?'

'No. He had it on lease from St Mary's Abbey until...'

'Until?'

'Until this,' he nodded towards the reliquary, 'was finished. Then it was his plan to join us here to spend the last of his days. A payment in advance, you might say. We had already accepted him, conditionally. Sadly, we have him only in death.'

Oriane swayed against Tomas who leaned towards her, comforting and solid. 'It's not unusual, mistress,' he said. 'The abbey owns a great number of properties in York. Donated, you know. Come, let's hear the will.' He led her to the table.

The key fitted and turned soundlessly in the lock, pulling forward the shallow drawer which held flat sheets of parchment and the loose blue ribbon.

The caterpillar brows squirmed and met briefly over the sheets which the abbot handed, one by one, to the infirmarer who said, 'Well done, Matthew. Nothing much wrong with the Latin,' and handed them back.

'Latin?' Oriane said. 'I didn't know...'

'Oh, yes. Quite proficient, too. Mmm...' The reading, quickly translated into English for Oriane's sake, was brief and to the point but made no mention of Oriane herself and it became clear to her, as Father William read on, that once the property had reverted to the abbey, the business would cease, the contents of the house and shop would be inventoried and passed on to Leo who would then reward each servant, and dispose of the rest however he wished.

'But that means the contents of the shop. Everything!' she whispered. 'He had no need to steal it. It was to be his, anyway.'

'Yes. After Leo, Gerard is to get most of any of the servants.'

'And me? No mention of me?' There was barely enough breath for the words.

The abbot resumed his mock-stern expression at which one caterpillar sought his fringe in alarm. 'This is where we need *your* key, mistress.'

Hurriedly, Oriane delved beneath her mantle to pull forward her leather pouch, producing the golden key that she had once mistaken for a replica of Leo's. She passed it to the abbot. 'It's not the same, Father. It doesn't fit.'

'No, mistress. Help me turn it, Petrus, if you will.'

Between them, they swung the heavy reliquary round so that the opposite gable-end faced them, then, with Oriane's key, he poked down inside the raised edge of the jewelled border into a tiny keyhole that could never have been spotted except in a very detailed search.

'There, this is what he showed me to do.'

The key clicked, sending forward by a hair's breadth the end panel of beaten gold between arches, opening a door on invisible hinges. It was a masterpiece of perfection. Inside the central chamber was a chest-shaped box of polished yew with inlaid bands of chased gold.

The abbot lifted it out and placed it on the table before Oriane, making no secret of the fact that it was heavy. 'For you, mistress. I think you should be seated. Now your treasure is out I think we may safely put St Benedict's digit in, do you think?' His delightful lack of ceremony lessened the tension, but only by a little. 'Will you open it? We're all on tenterhooks.'

The box, as long as her forearm, contained a large and weighty leather pouch, softened with years of handling. This lay on a fitted shelf which, when lifted out, revealed a roll of parchment tied with white tape, and a bundle of folded pieces which she knew instinctively to be letters of a personal nature. She hesitated. 'Do you know what the bag contains, Father?'

'Yes, child. I know it all.'

She had often wondered where the finest jewels for the reliquary had come from, where they were kept, how they had been paid for and to whom. Now she knew. Bills of sale were tucked inside each packet labelled Antwerp, Damascus, Venice, Florence, London, Russe, and within each packet were the largest and most exquisite diamonds, rubies, emeralds and sapphires, pearls, garnets, amethysts and turquoises, cameos of chalcedony, moonstones and topaz. The collection was beyond price, each individual packet worth enough to last her a lifetime. Her heart beat a deep base rhythm. 'But I had the key, so how did he...?'

'He'd finished setting the jewels a half-year ago,' the abbot told her, watching the tears well into her eyes. 'He was well aware of Leo's antagonism towards you, my dear, and placing them separately from the will like this allows your cousin to believe that he is the only one to benefit, thereby removing further cause for conflict. Had he been here today, I should not have opened this. May the abbey keep the key?'

'Of course, Father. But why did Leo wish to keep the will from me? He reads Latin, so he must know by now that all my uncle's possessions are his and that I was to receive none of it.'

'Now that, Mistress Oriane, is a mystery. Perhaps he knows that, once the inventory is made, he will be without a roof over his head, for there is nothing in the will to stipulate that he is to be allowed to stay longer at Silver Street. Perhaps he is stalling for more time, who knows?'

'But, Father, this is a fortune. More than a fortune.'

'You are now an extremely wealthy woman, my dear.' He lifted the roll of parchment and held it out to her. 'Shall you read?'

Barely able to think, she shook her head and sat down. 'Presumably you know what that says, too, Father. Will you tell me first?'

'An excellent notion. It's in English, but it may be easier for you to understand if it comes from me.' He motioned the two men to sit, and what he told them with compassion in that dim and draughty chamber was something that would have been hard to accept from anyone except a friend of long standing. That Oriane was content for Tomas to remain was a sign of her trust in him.

'Your uncle, Oriane, was trained to the goldsmith's craft by his father, but he had always felt his true vocation to be that of a monk. But like many before and since, he discovered that his bodily needs were too strong for him to ignore. Anyway, he left his home here in York to join the Ghilbertine Priory at Watton.'

'A double house?'

'Correct. Monks and nuns on the same site, strictly segregated, of course, but always a problem, these double houses.' He lowered his eyes. 'And in spite of every physical barrier, he fathered a child on one of the nuns. Don't ask me how. No one's yet been able to discover how they managed it.' His revelation, which by its very artlessness would have brought forth some smiles, was received in shocked silence. 'Fortunately for the woman, she was a novice, too. Expelled. It might have been worse. Matthew returned to York, disowned by his father and full of remorse. He turned to us for help, and we agreed to loan him the Silver Street property for his lifetime and to set him up as a goldsmith, since that is the only trade he knew. It was no great risk; we knew his ability. Meanwhile, young Leo was born.'

'Leo? He is Uncle Matthew's natural son?'

'His son, not his stepson as everyone has been led to believe. His mother brought him up in some disgrace with her parents, during which time Matthew coveted the woman his elder brother Mark had betrothed, making her pregnant before their marriage.

'Merciful heavens! Again?'

'Aye, again. But I believe he truly loved her, and she him. Mark, God bless him, took her back and forgave her, knowing the full story.'

'My mother...ah!' Oriane clamped a hand over her mouth.

The abbot continued. 'Your stepfather brought you up as his own daughter.'

The fingers slipped to her chin. 'So Uncle Matthew is my father, and Leo my half-brother.'

'You are shocked, my dear. Forgive me; there is no easy way to tell you this.'

'Yes…no…but this is so unexpected. Please go on, Father.'

'Well, by the time of Mark's marriage to your mother, Leo was a year or so old and, as the price of his silence on the matter, Mark insisted that Matthew should marry Leo's mother and take the responsibility for his son. So he did, calling Leo his stepson to spare your aunt's feelings.'

'To spare her feelings? Not to recognise her son's legitimacy?'

'One cannot have it both ways in these matters, Oriane. Either she could openly acknowledge her part as the mother of an illegitimate child when she married Matthew, or pretend that Leo was the son by a previous marriage. She was from the west country and not known in these parts and, having already sampled the ostracism of those in the know, she preferred to take the latter course. They had no more children, but Mark and your mother went on to have twins and, when your mother died, Oriane, Mark's gesture of condolence was to return you to your true father as a gift of love and reconciliation. It must have cost him dear, for he loves you as his own. A good man, Mark of Scepeton.'

'And that's what my uncle…er…father, tells me in the letter?'

'Yes, he spares nothing. Since then, his life has been exemplary. But what he is also trying to say with the gift of gems is that you are worthy only of the best. Your mother was fortunate to be so loved by two brothers.'

'But how they must all have suffered, Father. Oh, I am quite overcome. I thought my fears and problems were very great, but…' Dazed, she stared at the torches in the wall-brackets and at the grotesque shadows, at the smoke that streamed towards the nearest door; insubstantial, like her fears.

Father Petrus was a pragmatist as well as a doctor. 'Then if this has helped you to see your way more clearly, mistress, the pain it caused has not been in vain, has it? Many of the best medicines are bitter. And perhaps it is young Leo who needs our help now. He was set along the road his father would have travelled but he rebelled even more violently and suffered everyone's displeasure for that. Mercifully, Matthew did not impose on Leo the same fate that his own father had on him. It's a terrible thing when that happens to a man. We've seen nothing of Leo since the funeral.'

Leo had been feverish, his behaviour aggressive. Oriane understood what he was saying. Ill and unhappy people often behaved strangely. 'Have you been paid for my uncle's masses, Father? It will be his month-mind before long.' It was too soon for her to change her habit of address.

The abbot laid his fingers upon the reliquary, pushing the little door closed. 'We have been amply paid, my child, I thank you. Matthew was meticulous about that side of things. Perhaps we might dedicate this at the same mass of remembrance?'

Agreeing to that and to the abbot's offer to have her treasure-chest escorted to Monk Bywater later in the day, Oriane would have taken her leave but, allowing Tomas and Father Petrus to move on ahead, she lingered for one last query. 'Father Abbot, the lease of the Silver Street property. Does it *have* to expire as soon as Leo moves out?'

'That was the agreement: when your father should come to live with us, or when he died, whichever was the sooner. But are you asking me to extend the lease in your name? To continue the business? Start from scratch? Could a woman do that? Would the guild allow it?'

'As a manager only, Father. Yes, I believe so. *Femmes soles*, they call it.'

'But what of your forthcoming marriage? Surely you cannot do two things of such importance at once?'

Having been used to doing at least six important things at once on a daily basis, any less making her feel at a loss, Oriane smiled. 'No, Father. Only as a safeguard, if things should…' She turned her smile downwards.

'As a safeguard? That implies a certain lack of faith, my child. In which case, perhaps you should apply your mind a little more assiduously to the holy estate of matrimony and its implications. You have already seen how these things do not work on hot air, Oriane, nor even on good intentions. They need effort, as does anything worthwhile. But in answer to your request, my dear, yes, of course, I will reconsider the lease, if that's what you decide. I will hold it for you until you have resolved your doubts. Will that do?'

Oriane curtsied and kissed his cheek. 'You are very kind and understanding, Father.'

He was not too old, either, to take some pleasure from a lovely woman's gratitude.

* * *

Looking back on the events of the morning, Oriane appreciated the risk in visiting Silver Street and, at the time, felt it was worth taking. If Leo was really too ill to refuse the abbot's invitation, then he must be very ill indeed. If not, he should be assured of her friendship, at least. With those concerns urging her forward, she ignored further thoughts of danger and made an easy exit from the back entrance of the tapestry-merchant's warehouse on Jubbergate across to the rear courtyard of Silver Street.

Sir Tomas had believed she would be talking of wall-hangings for an hour or so and agreed to return in that time, but when the merchant told him the manner of her leaving, without the horses, he began to understand the reason for Mistress Oriane's urgency to visit York without Fitzhardinge. The minx.

Sending Sir Geffrey D'Azure and Patrick round to the shop entrance and taking Paul with him, Sir Tomas entered the house via the goldsmith's courtyard where a group of sweating horses and a groom warned him of recent arrivals. The servants, huddled at the kitchen end of the hall, were visibly relieved and, in an overlapping babble, told Sir Tomas and Paul of the three who had gone up to the solar a short time ago, not long after Mistress Oriane and Maddie. None of them, they said, dared go near, for Master Gerard, who was not in the shop, had told them to leave well alone and get on with their work, which they were finding difficult to do.

He appeared at that moment, fractionally ahead of Sir Geffrey and Patrick, and would have taken charge of the situation had they not prevented him.

'No, Master Gerard.' Sir Geffrey held him off the stairs by the fullness of his floor-length gown. 'I thank you, but we do not need to be announced. You go back to your customer, if you please. Go, man!' He gave him a shove towards the shop.

Gerard bowed, dignified as ever. 'Of course, but Master Leo is ill. He must not have any excitement.'

'Then we shall take care not to excite him,' Sir Tomas said, closing the door on the man. 'You two,' he said to the twins, 'stay here and see that the guests head for their horses when they come down.'

The door to the upper solar was closed but voices drowned out the sound of the carefully raised latch, and the slow opening was concealed by the large bulk of a man who faced the bed where Leo lay in a dishevelled heap as though attempting to get out. Facing the door, Oriane was the one whose voice was raised against the most recent suggestion. 'Don't be absurd! Why should I go anywhere with you?'

'Leave her alone,' Leo croaked from his bed. 'Oriane, come!'

'Oh, no!' The man nearest the door stepped forward, laughing. 'You stay there, lady. He'll manage without you, unlike ourselves.' He took a step towards her and, beyond the inch-wide gap in the door-frame, a scuffle ensued at the end of which the same man retreated to the accompaniment of raucous laughter from his two friends, holding a hand to his face.

The odour of sweat and stale urine was almost enough to make the two knights cough, but they were disciplined and used to it. Nor would they interfere as long as Oriane was holding her own, for this was a performance that Fitzhardinge would want related in every detail, after all his efforts. Besides that, they knew that Oriane had seen them through the narrow gap, had seen the slow closing of the door. She knew that help was near.

'Bitch!' Tomas heard through the crack. 'You'll come, like it or not. We'll have your saviour begging for you in a day or two, and if he doesn't, we'll have you and her to warm our beds for a while. Eh, lads?'

'Ransom?' Oriane scoffed. 'You're mad if you think that Fitzhardinge would play at that game. He's not so short of women, I assure you.'

The mirthless bark that greeted her brave words almost swallowed up the last of them. 'He'll play, Mistress High and Mighty, when he discovers what we're doing with you, as he will. It's not that you're irreplaceable, lady. It's a matter of pride, you see. We know all about his pride, don't we, lads?'

'Shut your mouth, you blathering fool!'

There was a roar engulfed by a scuffle and, somewhere in the confusion, Leo's weak voice calling to Oriane, 'Get away…quickly…the door…' then a muffled yelp, followed by a thud.

'Leave him…*leave* him! He's ill, damn you. Can't you see?'

'Get her away from that weakling. Come on, bring them.'

Together, Sir Tomas and Sir Geffrey swung the door open with a crack against the wall and stepped across the threshold, their swords drawn. 'We wish you a pleasant journey, my friends,' Sir Geffrey said, 'but you may leave the ladies with us quite safely.'

One man groaned in anger; another spat into the rushes. 'You again,' the third snarled, keeping hold of

Oriane's arm. 'You have an irritating bent for appearing where you're not wanted.'

Tomas smiled at Oriane. 'Yee...e...es,' he drawled. 'Tedious, isn't it?' He flicked the point of his sword towards the door, balancing the hilt delicately between his fingers. 'So? You need persuading, or are you ready to leave now? Whatever you wish.'

'Two against three of us? With those toys?'

As if at a signal, Tomas and Geffrey drew their long daggers and stood poised, a weapon in each hand, the smile in their eyes visibly cooling. 'Count again,' Tomas said. 'Then count those downstairs.'

Irritably, the man who held Oriane pushed her aside. 'I have a score to settle with the Fitzhardinge,' he said, 'but I will choose where and by what method I settle it. Not with his minions, but with him. Come on, you two, there's no hurry. Another day will do just as well.' He barged past Geffrey and down the stairs, followed by his two friends whose contemptuous glances at the corridor of weapons had none of the same noisy bravado.

Tomas sheathed his sword and dagger and Oriane saw that his smile had disappeared with the danger. 'Are you making a habit of this kind of thing, mistress?' he said. 'Mistress Maddie, have you no control over her?'

'Tomas, Geffrey, thank you. I'm sorry. Truly I am. I had meant to be back at the tapestry warehouse long before you, but those three delayed me, though why they should have appeared just now of all times I cannot understand.'

'Could they have known you were coming here?'

'No one knew I was coming here, not even me. It

was only after we'd been to the abbey that I felt I must see how Leo fared. See, they hit him, Tomas. They're vile. Is it only money they want? I thought they were his friends.' Damping the corner of the sheet in the jug of water, she pressed it to Leo's head.

'Money and a place to live, I suppose,' said Tomas. 'I expect they came to pick the carcass clean, like most carrion.'

Oriane continued to dab. 'Poor Leo. I haven't had chance to discuss the will with him; he was barely conscious when I arrived. I *must* stay and care for him, Tomas. You go back now, please, and explain to Sir Euan that I'll return to Monk Bywater when my cousin begins to recover.'

Tell Sir Euan that they had left his betrothed in the lion's den? The two men swapped looks that visualised the guaranteed explosion. They argued, but were forced to compromise. Sir Tomas would stay with Patrick and Paul to guard her against further intrusion.

'Don't look so glum,' she said to Sir Geffrey. 'Tell Sir Euan it was all my fault. He certainly won't disbelieve you.'

The jauntiness of her parting shot deceived none of them; indeed, it was only her strong sense of duty towards the ailing Leo that overcame her fear of Sir Euan's anger. But her cousin had now become her half-brother and shared an illegitimacy that neither of them had suspected. She could not leave him in this state, not for the wrath of a dozen Sir Euans.

While Sir Tomas and her brothers conferred with Master Gerard about domestic arrangements, Oriane sat by Leo to bathe his face and wait for him to wake.

'Leo, it's me, Oriane. Do wake, please. I've so little time.'

His lips moved. 'Oriane.'

'Yes, yes. Can you hear me? Answer my questions, Leo, I beg you.'

'Yes.'

'I bear you no animosity. I've seen the will. I know you've seen it, haven't you?'

'Yes. Have they gone?' The words came more clearly, but the sounds from the street outside did nothing to help.

'They'll not come back. Sir Tomas and the twins are here now. Tell me, Leo, why did you not want anyone to see the will?'

The effort of opening his eyes overcame him. 'It was not *you* I didn't want to know of it, particularly, but I knew that once they discovered I was to receive the contents of the house and shop, they'd make me hand over the lot. So I kept quiet until I could think of what to do.'

Oriane held a cup of wine to his lips. 'They had some hold over you?' she said.

He nodded and turned his face away but was brought back by the cool cloth on his brow. 'Who's been taking care of you since I left, Leo?'

'Gerard. I managed to get out, once, to go and see them in the forest, reason with them, tell them the will was still missing, but it was a waste of time. I was too ill and they ran rings round me. I was lucky to get away in one piece.'

It had been the Sunday of Oriane's visit to Silver Street. 'Well, he's not done you much good, has he? I shall change you myself, and we'll get you better, between us. But trust me, please, and tell me about it. Who are these men and what is this hold they have over you?'

'The Oxford crowd. We were all expelled. Their fathers disowned them. Disgraced. They live in the forest we came through.'

'On the way home from Bridlington?'

He opened his eyes at last to see how she would deduce what he had no need to explain. That they had been the ones to kill Uncle Matthew.

'Oh…Leo!'

'Sorry. Sorry, cousin.'

'You knew it was going to happen?'

'No, it was not my plan, but they knew I recognised them.'

'It was Uncle Matthew they were after? Money?'

'No. It was you they wanted.'

'Me? Whatever for?'

'Ransom. They knew he would pay up.'

'Holy Virgin! But it went wrong. And I believed they were Fitzhardinge's men.'

'Terribly wrong. So then they told me to get you out of the way so that I could sell this place up. Then I learned about the accounts and the missing money. Why did you do it, Oriane? Did you need money, too?'

Oriane's hair rose on her scalp. 'Do it? Leo, I took no money. I made no false accounts. I swear it on my mother's grave. Did you really believe I would do such things? It had been going on since you came home from Oxford, so naturally I thought it was you, but since I assumed you'd eventually inherit, I said nothing. What would have been the point, except to anger my uncle?'

'It wasn't me, Oriane. I swear to you that I know no more about how to falsify accounts than how to fly. And I'd not bite the hand that fed me. If it had not been for Gerard telling me what to look for, I'd have had no idea.'

'Gerard? But he's always helped me with the book-keeping; it was he who kept them before I came. He taught me.'

Outside in the street, the cries of vendors mingled with the tolling of bells, underscoring the inevitable conclusions being drawn in both their minds, conflicting in harmony and rhythm.

Leo's voice was breathless. 'It looks, cousin, as though we are being set up against each other. And I have wronged you. Forgive me, please. I was so afraid.'

'And I thought ill of you, but we're both still alive, Leo. Now we can right the wrongs together, if you will place your trust in me. What was it that you feared from your friends?'

'Not friends. We all behaved badly at Oxford, but I fathered a child on my tutor's daughter and her father would not allow us to marry because of my poor reputation. I loved her, Oriane, and he was a kind man; I thought highly of him. He saw no point in telling my stepfather since I was leaving anyway, but *they* would have told him and he would have disowned me, I'm sure. Then I would have been homeless, like them. That's why I had to co-operate. They believed, as I did, that my father owned the property and that I would inherit it, one day, as the custom is. So you see, cousin, I stood to lose whatever I did. I had no idea, until I saw the will, that it belongs to St Mary's Abbey, nor that he'd made no provision for you. So I stalled because I didn't know what was best to do, and I was too ill to make a sensible decision. All I could see was that they could take everything from me whenever they wished, and those three are the leaders. There are dozens of them.'

'But, Leo, when Uncle Matthew died, how could they have continued to blackmail you? Who was there to tell?'

His eyes, sunk into darkened sockets, closed wearily under heavy lids, and Oriane feared he may be too exhausted to continue. But it seemed that his confession was a release for his tortured mind. 'Blood ties, Oriane. They knew that, in spite of my envy of you, I still did not want any harm to befall you. So they told me that if I didn't get you out of here, they'd take you themselves. They tried once and failed, but they knew that I believed they'd do it. When you returned here this morning, they decided to take you anyway, and hold you to ransom. They believe I'm playing for time, you see. Which is true.'

'But how did they know I was going to be here, Leo? And didn't you play into their hands by not warning us of a possible attack in the forest?'

'I never hated you enough, Oriane, to have planned that, believe me. For one thing, I never told them we were going to Bridlington, so it was as much of a surprise to me as to any of us. I was beating them off as hard as anyone when I was injured. As for you being here this morning, well, who knew of that?'

'No one.'

'Well, they knew about money and jewels missing from the shop. Don't ask me how. The only other person who knew about it was Gerard, at the time, though he didn't speak to me of it until after my stepfather's death. But you knew of it.'

'Yes, of course I knew. How could I not know?'

'They told me to investigate it before the funeral, and accuse you, and then to have you arrested for theft before your father arrived. And by that time I think I was convinced that it must have been you who was responsible. Then there was the missing gold found in your chest, but still I could not bring myself to have you arrested. You did have the key, you see.'

'That's something I cannot explain, Leo. All I can do is to beg you to believe that I had no hand in it.'

'I do believe you, now.'

'But you pursued me with the sheriff's men, even so.'

'No.' He shook his head. 'That morning, when the gold was found in your chest, I realised I had to do something, or they would. I went off to the tavern to contact a couple of travelling players and paid them to act the part of the sheriff's men. It was they who came with me to Clementhorpe where the servants told me you'd gone. I was going to remove you to where that crowd couldn't find you, and even so, I left it as long as I dared. Then, when I arrived at Clementhorpe and you were not there, and I had not seen you on the road as I might have done, I assumed you must be with Lady Faythe and was just about to leave and come back home. Then you arrived and I had to go through with it.'

'But surely, Leo—' Oriane mopped his brow again

'—wasn't the convent the safest place I could have been? Why insist on my going with you?'

'No, it wasn't. I would have taken you to your father, Oriane. I could have told him the whole story at the funeral, I know, but I could not spring a story like that on him at such a time about his own daughter. I intended that he should recompense me, too, for what I believed you'd taken, for I needed every penny I could lay hands on. Instead of that, Fitzhardinge turned up. I can't tell you how relieved I was when he offered to make good the loss and take care of you. Were you really betrothed, Oriane?'

'Not quite. He…er…persuaded me.'

'Blackmail?'

'Bribery.'

'He must have been bewitched to do that.'

'Thank you.'

He smiled and laid a hand on her arm, brotherly rather than gallant. 'Cousin,' he said, 'be careful of what you say to Gerard. I don't think my father took him into his confidence as much as Gerard would have liked, because he's asked me many times where I think the will could be and what I think it could contain, and when the reliquary disappeared to the abbey while he was actually here in the shop at the accounts, he nearly hit the roof.'

'You suspect him, then?'

'I have no proof, but something's very wrong somewhere.'

'Fitzhardinge will discover it.'

'Will he?' His eyes opened, riveting on hers. 'You think so?'

'I'm sure of it. It's his money, too, you know.'

'Of course. And his men's cloaks. I'll tell you how that happened.'

'Later. You've done enough talking. And I'm going to change this bed now. And I shall send for Master Petrus to attend you.'

'Gerard will be furious.'

'He won't be the only one,' she muttered, peeling away the sheets.

Chapter Twelve

Had it not been for the twins, whose penchant for exaggeration had risen to new heights in the last few weeks, Sir Euan's anger might have been less than Master Gerard's instead of greater. And had it not been for the presence of Father Petrus at Silver Street, he would not have been required to contain his anger quite so successfully until he had escorted Oriane and her maid in chilling silence back to Monk Bywater. Her plan to stay had failed.

'Why in heaven's name did you tell him all that?' Oriane had snarled at her brothers. 'Have you no discretion?'

Staring at her in twofold innocence, they defended themselves. 'Because we're bound to tell him everything, Orrie. He's our—'

'I *know* he's your lord, but I'm your sister, dammit! I could have told him what I wanted him to know perfectly well myself, thank you, without your embellishments. I was hardly in any danger with Sir Tomas and Sir Geffrey both there, was I?' The point she had been hoping to make veered off the mark.

Teetering on the brink of a full-scale confrontation, it was some time before Oriane was able to persuade Sir Euan not to leave Leo with only Gerard to care for him but to allow Sir Tomas and the boys to stay at Silver Street for a few days on the pretext of having business in York.

Gerard was clearly uncomfortable with the notion but was in no position to resist, and Oriane's lengthy instructions for her cousin's welfare only delayed the moment when she would have to leave him with the most important part of her news still unspoken. It was partly this ill-humoured haste that made her resolve not to impart the news to anyone else before she could tell Leo, especially not Sir Euan who could think of little else, it seemed, than the danger she had openly encouraged by leaving Tomas's protection.

'I did no such thing,' she had countered, hoping he would not ask her for evidence of this.

But he was in no mind to hear her argument. 'Too bloody impulsive by half, woman,' he said, catching her arm. 'You galloped off to confront my father with accusations before you knew what you were talking about, then you were off to Clementhorpe like a cleg-bitten steer because Monk Bywater didn't suit you. Now you can't wait to get back to Silver Street in case your cousin's moved anything in your absence, can you?'

'I came back here because Father William told me he was ill. You've seen his wound-fever for yourself. It was nothing to do with my not wanting him to move anything. It's his property: why should I care what he moves?'

'His property? Is that what the will says, then?'

She snatched her arm away, angered now by her own slip-up, and strode off towards the waiting horses. 'You know all the answers,' she said, 'so presumably you must know that, too.'

Though their antagonism still brimmed to overflowing, her consolation was that he had come for her and demanded her immediate return. The burning need to establish her worth had been satisfied beyond her wildest dreams, yet what made her heart sing on that hot and dusty ride back to Monk Bywater was the towering figure at her side whose dark glances she could feel on her turned-aside cheek.

About the will she would not tell him and he would rather have burned in hell than ask. It was fortunate, therefore, that the casket of jewels and papers from the reliquary had already reached Monk Bywater and had been placed in Oriane's solar, an unremarkable event which Lady Faythe somehow forgot to mention either to her weakening husband or to her son on his return.

'He's sleeping, Euan,' she whispered in answer to her son's raised eyebrows.

'No, I'm not,' a deep voice emerged from the curtained cavern of the bed. 'Will somebody tell me what's going on around here?'

Lady Faythe's eyebrows responded as she left father and son together.

'How are you, sir?' Euan said.

'Sit down where I can see you, lad. I'm perfectly all right and I've no intention of going anywhere until you and that lass are married. So get on with it.'

'Yes, Father. I will as soon as I can get her to stand still long enough.'

'Hah! Thought you knew all about women, didn't you?' The chest heaved. 'So did I at your age.' The sunken eyes were damp with laughter. 'Still playing you up, is she? Well, try doing what I did, lad.'

'What did you do, sir? I'm told the beating didn't work.'

'Bah! No good at all. Worse, if anything.' His hand flapped on the sheet. 'Sent her back to her father, that's what. That cooled her down a bit. Thought I'd washed my hands of her. She pretended she didn't fancy me, see? Thought I wasn't good enough for her. I knew she did, and so did everyone else. It was a long time ago, Euan, but it worked. She came back to me as meek as a mouse. No...' a fit of coughing delayed his retraction '...no, not a mouse, exactly. You were not born of a mouse, eh? A lioness, perhaps.'

'Oriane is too proud, sir. She'll not say, even though she wants me.'

'Then take it from her, lad. They don't value it until they discover they might lose it. She'll come round soon enough, you'll see. And Mark of Scepeton's on your side, remember. He knows the score.'

There was barely enough time for Oriane to conceal the casket in her clothes chest before Sir Euan entered the solar, holding the door open and staring pointedly at Maddie, who curtsied and left.

Oriane launched into the attack before he did. 'I am aware that you are bursting to give vent to your *deep* disapproval of my actions, but I must point out to you, sir, that I am not yet your wife and I am not bound to obtain your permission to conduct my own business in my own manner. Now, if you will excuse me, I need to change.' She turned away, twisting to unlace the side-opening of her figure-hugging cote-hardie.

Sir Euan sauntered into the room and lounged, facing her, on the bed. 'You are right about one thing only, lady; that you need to change. However, I am not optimistic about that. As far as the rest is concerned, do rid yourself of the idea that you are as free now as you were before our betrothal. You are not. Words of consent cannot be unsaid, whatever you may wish.'

'I can...' Oriane stopped unlacing to contradict him.

'No, you cannot, unfortunately. It's too late. Remember?'

Oriane blushed. 'We could pretend that never happened,' she said.

His scornful tone made her blush even deeper. 'Oh, I do agree. The occasion made no lasting impression on me, either. But it did happen, I recall, and who would believe otherwise, knowing my reputation? No, lady, our wedding cannot be cancelled. Only postponed.'

'Postponed?'

'Certainly. I'm in no more of a desperate hurry to repeat the performance than you. I'm sending you back to your father. He'll need help with his wedding preparations, I dare say, and you'll be able to attend the celebrations without the embarrassment of having me by your side. You can always tell them I was thinking of your safety, if you prefer, but I dare say the truth might be more convincing. You are silent. Surely you cannot…'

'No, indeed, they will welcome an extra hand, I know. I am perfectly happy to go and stay with my father indefinitely, but I would have preferred to go at a time of my own choosing, sir.'

'Then perhaps you will remember that I too would prefer to choose when and how to be dragged away from my father's side to go chasing after you, lady.'

'Ah, so that's what this is about. No one asked you to, I was perfectly safe.'

'Yes. As safe as houses with your maid, an unconscious relative, and three thugs intent on abducting you.'

With the lacing of her dress undone, there was no more she could do before an audience of one, and the gaping hole was now an invitation to further inquisitiveness. But to her surprise, he showed no particular interest. Unsettled, she looked across at the parched field to the ribbon of silver water. 'What of Sir Tomas and my brothers?' she said.

He walked towards the door. 'They'll stay with their duties,' he said. 'Is there some reason you need Tomas?'

'No. None at all.'

'Then begin your packing, Oriane of York. You can leave tomorrow at first light. I'll send a message to St Aelfled's and to your father.'

'Yes. Thank you.'

'Then I bid you a safe journey, lady.'

'You won't be there to say farewell?'

'I doubt it. I have things to attend to.'

'What things?'

He had his hand on the latch of the door. 'Do you care?' he said, and disappeared without another glance.

Unable to move on feet as heavy as lead, Oriane's thudding heart sent an ache into her chest and a ball of fire into her throat. His anger she could have borne and given back in good measure but his coldness was that of a practised soldier who knew how to wound with skill and precision. She had no defence against that, nor had she used what womanly advantages she possessed to pacify, comfort, reassure and heal wounds. She had let pass every chance and now, when she had taken the decision not to follow in her mother's faithless footsteps with the nightly charade, Sir Euan himself had removed the initiative into his own hands, rendering her more helpless than ever.

Wealth or no wealth, she could not go back on the vows they had spoken nor, despite her protests, did she wish to. But, defying the calls of her heart to go to him, to explain what she knew, offer him her submission, she remained silent so that, by dawn, her pride was still intact while the resurgence of fears concerning his reputation had grown like mushrooms in the night.

She would rather have stayed at Ketils Ing, of course, but that option had not been offered to her for, although a mere two miles away, it was now closed up with only the village bailiff and reeve to keep an eye on the workmen who still repaired the outer walls.

'Ho, my lass!' Her father engulfed her in a hug that

was blind to whether her wan smile indicated fatigue or something more basic. 'Come on, we'll allow you a quick bite and then you'll have to earn your keep with advice till your head sings. I never knew a wedding took all this preparation.' It would have made no difference; he was enjoying every minute of it, being far from the same man Oriane had pitied two days ago as the one who had married the woman his own brother had made pregnant.

Mistress Cherry and Jane joined them that evening, and then the talk intensified around the church decorations, the guests and their accommodation, the drinks and food, the minstrels and mummers, the dancing, the gowns and the order of the day, subjects on which Oriane's views were asked, given and accepted as if she were an authority. It was not long before her father's prediction came true; the only time in which she was able to entertain the desolate thoughts of her heart was in the huge bed shared with Maddie from well after midnight until dawn, which came early.

Four more days of hectic preparations passed, four more nights of sticky discomfort and nagging fears that the one who had shared her nights at Monk Bywater might now be sharing them with another. No tears were shed, but disquiet and longing washed over her in waves of sickly dread, and though the remembrance that she was now wealthy came forward to balance her unhappiness, the thought had no substance. Her love for him was beyond wealth and had been there from the start, stifled in pride, and she was now suffering for it. She could offer him her wealth, every last gem of it, but he had wanted her without that and the only thanks she had given him in return had been a quick, loveless coupling. She had been prepared to offer Tomas more than that, and had done, in her intention. What man would not feel anger and resentment at that insult?

Her father's old shepherd had predicted rain that morning but few had taken him seriously, nor had they paid any attention to the bank of blue-black clouds over the farthest hills. With no breeze to move them on, the wedding day would surely be undisturbed, the distant rumbles adding no more than a breathy base to the cymbals and pipes and the yelps of the rowdier guests.

Unseen, Oriane had slipped away from the oppressive heat, from the clinging smells of roasting ox and boar, the clamour and nonsensical chatter of the young men who had pushed and shoved like bullocks to be near her. She had done her part and now felt no further need to hold back the encroaching tide of misery. Euan had not appeared as she had hoped he might: the signs could not have been more serious.

First thing in the morning, she told herself, she would begin her return to Monk Bywater. Then the imaginings began of how he would be taken unawares, be closeted with that cheeky-faced lass or the other one with the hat. Soundlessly, her feet thudded on the springy turf, pounding out the catalogue of forebodings and chastising her with dread until their weight bent her double and she came to rest on a lichen-covered rock, her head on her arms, in every sense miles from anywhere.

The light breeze tapped her shoulder with the first heavy splashes of rain, warning her to move on and seek shelter even though she risked a soaking in the process. A crack of thunder added its voice, darkening the sky with its frown. Oriane moved aimlessly back in the direction she had come, expecting that the cluster of oaks she had passed would give her as good protection as anything. Then, as a streak of lightning bleached the landscape, she saw the shepherd's hut dug securely into the face of a limestone crag, a thatched roof stuck like a limpet over its head. She ran like a hare.

Mercifully, the door opened at a first push as the full force of the storm made its first assault upon her back, soaking her in an instant, and she found herself in a small windowless room that smelled of sheep, tallow and wood-smoke. The latter was still rising gently from a mound in the centre of the floor and escaping through a small hole in the thatch above. She wedged the door almost closed and piled logs upon the lazy fire, blowing at the embers and applauding the shepherd's foresight.

Pulling up a three-legged joint-stool, she watched how the little room darkened by the second, how the door shuddered against the strengthening wind and how, illuminated by each vivid flash of light, she was able to see a neat pile of sheepskins over by the far wall, two stools, a lamp, two wicker baskets, a table and a shepherd's crook. On the table lay a dead rabbit and a knife and so, rather than monitor the storm's progress, Oriane proceeded to skin it, working as expertly in the dimness as in the daylight. If the storm lasted all night, she might have to eat it.

The task completed, she carried the knife and small table out into the sheeting rain to be washed clean of blood and entrails, and was about to dash back under the low-hanging thatch when a man's figure, grey and shining, ran from the roaring arms of the oaks as she had done a while earlier. With no thoughts except for her personal safety, she held the knife at the ready and watched him approach, hardly able to believe the familiar movements, the shoulders, the long legs. She forgot her body, her stance, the knife.

He came to a halt just beyond her reach, gasping at the rain. 'Put that bloody knife down!' he yelled. 'It's me!' And when she did not obey promptly enough, he reached her in one stride, took her immobile arm to remove the weapon, and pushed her bodily into the hut where they both stood, soaked and blackened with hair plastered over scowling faces.

'Well?' His greeting coincided with a shattering thunderclap. 'Are there not duties a wife's supposed to perform?' Already a pool of water formed around his feet over the hard earth.

Still speechless, her numbed fingers tangling with his, Oriane tore at his sodden clothes and flung them aside, breaking the ties that wetness had stuck together and peeling him like willow-bark for rushlights, heaving at his braes and shoes in one move until he stood, naked and glistening before the crackling fire. Steam hung around him like mist, and she smelled the sweat of his exertions. He had been running for some time.

'At last!' he shouted above the din, shaking his wet hair into the fire.

Already defensive, Oriane yelled back. 'At last what?'

'You're doing what a wife's supposed to do.'

'How do I know what a wife's supposed to do? I've never been one.'

'Time I taught you, then. Come here.'

Whatever it was she had hoped for from his appearance in this unlikely place, whatever joy had surged through her out there in the merciless rain, the old fear, the antagonism and unsureness of his manner towards her maintained a barrier against her longing to set matter straight. The removal of his clothes had not diminished by one whit the aura of power that clung to him, and his sharp command to come to him for instruction made no gentle inroads into her heart. That his terseness was due to the relief of finding her did not occur to her.

He held out a hand.

'I can manage,' she said, turning away.

The sound of his exasperation was swamped by the noise outside, but his hands on her upper arms were not so easy to miss as she turned sideways-on to the glow, his deft fingers doing for her what she had just done for him, his touch on her back sending her no signals except urgency and efficiency.

'You're soaked to the skin, lass. Is that the rabbit you've just been skinning?'

She nodded, shivering at the clammy wetness.

'I'll cut it up for thee. We'll have it for supper.'

'You're staying?' It was a foolish thing to say, she

knew, but she blamed her teeth for chattering so. Perhaps he wouldn't hear.

But he had. Swinging her round to face him, his fingers peeled away the wet fabric from her shoulders and pulled it downwards, skimming her arms, one by one, as she had done to the helpless rabbit only a half-hour before. 'Aye, woman. I'm staying. And so are you.'

The fabric fell onto her hips and stuck there with his thumbs tucked into it, waiting for her co-operation, his chest and throat at eye-level, like his familiar smell, the steady rise and fall of his warm breath on her forehead. Her hands, hanging by her sides, had almost flown to her breasts to cover them but now stayed, kept away by some compulsion to savour, if only for a second or two, his overpowering nearness. And by the time she had breathed in the wish-fulfillment of the last few days it was too late for reversals.

She sensed his waiting, felt the weight of his hands over her hips, his head tipped to watch her face, his stillness. Never once, throughout their brief and ambiguous relationship had they faced each other so with the path ahead so clearly marked and with the initiative so clearly designated. He was a man above men. He was proud. He had done as much as any man could be expected to do, and more. The rest was up to her.

The need was already upon her; her eyes half closed. Opening her lips, she leaned forward and placed them upon the damp skin of his chest, barely controlling her breathing as she moved from hill to valley to hill again, bringing her arms up to hold him under her mouth as he had often done to her.

She felt the tremors of his body and the breath whoosh from his lungs, the tight contraction of his stomach below the massive ribcage. Her arms crept on upwards to encircle his head, skimming over his wet hair.

'Forgive me, beloved. It was ever you. No one else.' She would not even mention the other by name. 'From the moment you carried me home, my heart has been yours. You have carried me ever since and have had nothing from me but resentment and whining. And deceit. Forgive me.'

'Not deceit. You had every reason.' His face came round to hers, bathing in her kisses and the exploring hands that had not until now been allowed to roam unchecked over his face.

'You must let me say it,' she said, her fingers on his lips.

'No need.'

'Yes, let me. I want you to hear it from me, first. I love you, Euan. Have always loved you, unable to stop what I had started and wanting you more than I could bear.'

'I came here…'

'…to bring me back?'

'…because I could not eat, or sleep, or think without you.'

'Truly?'

'Why are you standing in this wet stuff?' he said into her ear over the noise of the thunderous applause. He slid his hands over her hips.

'I don't know.' She placed her hands over his and pushed, heaving the sodden cloth over the curves until it fell to her ankles. Then, reaching up to him again, she pressed herself along his length, taking in his warmth on her front and the fire's warmth on her back. 'You asked for more packaging,' she said, laughing and kissing at the same time. 'Will this do?'

His hands tightened over her buttocks and she felt herself being lifted, carried in two strides across to the pallet of dried heather and sheepskins heavy with white fleece that received them both like thistledown.

'You offered me a gift and I was too churlish to unwrap it. Forgive me,' he said, drawing her into his arms. 'Will you offer it to me again now, and pretend it's for the first time?'

'With words? And caresses?'

'And love, and respect, and admiration.'

'You have no cause to admire me, beloved.'

He kissed her and fanned out her damp hair over the fleece. 'Wrong. I tried to force you to come to me, and you resisted, fighting like a wildcat. I admired you then for your courage and your determination and your beauty, and every day since you barged into the middle of my courtyard to challenge me. I could not keep away from you, even though we made each other angry. You had reason to fear me, for I offered you no gentleness, did I?'

'I knew you were angry with me.'

'And with myself for falling in love when the last thing I needed was another excuse to keep me longer at home. It was channelled towards you, sweetheart, because I am a fool, a churlish and pigheaded fool.

But I love you, Oriane of York. Ah, I love you, woman. Marry me, Oriane. Marry me?'

'You know I will. But you're not angry at my deceit?'

'Tomas told me all, sweetheart, and made me understand your reasoning. I could hardly blame you. He didn't.' He smiled. 'Mercifully, he's a true and loyal friend, and our deception offered me the chance I needed.'

'To make good your intentions?'

He kissed her frown away. 'No, sweetheart, not that. There was no revenge intended on my part. The chance I needed was to get close to you, for you wouldn't let me get within striking-distance, would you? Eh?'

'Come close to me now then, beloved. Show me the things you might have done had we not been blinded by anger and fear.' She held out her arms and drew him down to her again. 'I told you once that I had no wish to learn how to please my husband-to-be. Now I do. Will you show me?'

Carefully, as if she had been a virgin, he led her once again through every move, receiving each deep sigh as a sign to proceed gracefully, slowly, using his hand to prepare the way as he had done for the first time, but prolonging the delight until her wail reached him over the thunder-roll. He entered her again, using the same words, hearing the same responses, until neither of them could recall or control the direction of the avalanche that overtook them.

Above them, the storm rumbled off into the far hills, its audience preoccupied. Oriane snuggled deeply into the crook of his arm. 'I can hardly believe it,' she whispered. But when her fingers reached his face, she changed her mind. 'Yes, I can: your hair needs cutting. I'll do it for you. I can, you know.'

Euan's chest heaved in silent laughter. 'Your skills with a knife, woman, were never in question, but how are they with rabbit and a pile of damp clothes?'

Wrapped in sheep-pelts, they sat by the fire eating well-cooked rabbit-joints and drinking fresh rainwater from the barrel outside the door. Later, in the darkened stone hut draped with steaming clothes, they lay again in each other's arms, sure that the shepherd would be making as good use of Mark of Scepeton's hospitality as they were of his. And there they talked of Euan's activities while Oriane had been away with her far-from-accurate imaginings, activities which, she discovered, had centred entirely around herself.

The arrest of Master Gerard caused her no great surprise, more a satisfying but sad verification of her own growing suspicions. Looking back, she saw how easy it had been for Matthew le Seler's old friend to manipulate events from his position of trust in a way that none of the other servants could have done.

'The accounts? The thefts? Are you saying he did that to make me believe it was Leo?'

'And to make Leo believe it was you, sweetheart. The sheriff found a massive hoard beneath the planks of his bed, jewels, gold, you'd not believe it.'

'A week ago I wouldn't. I believed him to be an ally. My uncle relied heavily on him, you know. He was glad for Gerard to do the accounts and leave him free to do the goldsmithing. Gerard must have been ill pleased when Uncle Matthew asked me to manage the shop after my aunt died. I believe he hoped he'd have been given the task.'

'And when he wasn't, he did his best to make you disappear.'

'Those men? Did Gerard know them, then?'

'He knew them all right. It was he, not them, who bought the cloaks from two of my men while I was away and passed them on to that crowd.'

'Knowing that, if they left the badges on, the attention would be diverted from the outlaws to Fitzhardinge men.'

'My men told Gerard they were my father's badges and that he was in no position to care where his men's cloaks went. Then Gerard encouraged their connection with your cousin and let them make a nuisance of themselves.'

'Why that?'

Euan's arm tightened around her. 'With a view to getting you to leave, sweetheart. Make you go home to Scepeton. Abduct you. Whatever. A ransom would do for a start.'

Oriane sat up, leaning over him. 'So it was Gerard who told them of our trip to Bridlington?'

'That's right. He was not injured, remember, but your cousin recognised them and helped to beat them off.' Again he drew her close, pushing the hair from her face. 'Even so, he had not intended to have your uncle injured.'

'Wouldn't that have solved his problem? To have him killed?'

'No. He understood that his friend Matthew intended Leo to inherit the contents of the house and shop. He *assumed* that you would inherit the building and that you would therefore stay at Silver Street. So he stole what he could to fill his own coffers, tried to discredit and remove you, place Leo in the grip of his erstwhile friends and make him poorer than he might have been, thereby getting more than whatever his friend Matthew had set aside for him. He had no idea that the property belonged to St Mary's.'

Oriane sat up again, sidling over his limbs until she lay on top of him, nose to nose. His laughing almost dislodged her. 'You *know*,' she accused him. 'You know, don't you? How did you find out, Fitzhardinge? Tell me, or I shall beat you black and blue. Come on, tell me!'

His arms enclosed her, and he rolled, reversing their position and kissing her protests into silence. 'Do not let it enter your head for one moment, woman, that I desire one penny of your fortune. When we marry, it will be mine, I know, but you shall do with it whatever you wish except to distance yourself from me. Do you understand?'

'Yes.'

'And to forestall your next question, I had a long conversation with Fathers William and Petrus who now know the whole story.'

'The whole story?'

'Everything.'

'And they advised you…?'

'No, they didn't. I need no one's advice. I know my own heart. Always did. It was yours I was not sure of.'

'Oh, Euan, we've wasted precious time. I loved you from the beginning.'

'I handled you poorly. You were already distressed.'

If somewhat breathlessly, the conversation resumed after an interval. 'Euan, Gerard didn't know what Uncle Matthew left to me, did he?'

'No, sweetheart. No one knows of that except you, me and Tomas, and the two fathers. Nor would they discuss with me what else was in your casket. They said that that was for you to tell me when you were ready.'

'But Tomas knows.'

'Then he has kept it to himself, as I would expect him to. Nor have I asked him to tell me.'

'Then I shall tell you myself, beloved.'

The two bedraggled but happy lovers who approached the gatehouse of Ketils Ing Manor through the mists of early morning drew forth little more than a nod of greeting from the gatekeeper's wife. By midmorning, in time for the main meal of the day at Mark of Scepeton's manor, their damp clothes had been exchanged for an interesting assortment of borrowed pieces, and the welcome they received from the crowd in the courtyard echoed around the high walls. Almost pulled from their horses, they were dragged indoors to a hall still decked with yesterday's garlands, their happy smiles wider at the joy their reconciliation was causing.

'Shepherd's cott, eh? D'ye hear that, Edwin old friend? They used your cott and ate your rabbit, man. You should be honoured.'

Sheepishly, Edwin showed his pleasure with a declaration that the rain would continue until Sunday when the twins were expected to arrive with Sir Tomas and Sir Geffrey. He took his leave, bestowing upon Oriane an exceedingly slow and meaningful wink of one rheumy eye.

Over a feast composed of leftovers more plentiful than the loaves and fishes, Euan was pressed for more details of his crusade to clear Oriane's name, an operation of which she had been ashamedly unaware.

She joined in the questioning. 'So how were those bags of gold pieces removed from Uncle Matthew's chest when Maddie slept with the key and I was there, in the room? It wasn't Leo. He told me so.'

'It was Gerard, sweetheart. Master Johannes left Leo a sleeping-draught which Master Gerard introduced into your ale which you and Maddie both sampled, apparently, before you went to sit with your uncle.'

'I did, indeed. That's why I slept so soundly.'

'And Gerard didn't need the keys from beneath Maddie's pillow because he had duplicates.'

'Which accounts for his remark about needing another set of keys, to put me off the scent. He already had one.'

'To every chest in the house. We found them.'

'Even to my clothes chest where he hid the stolen gold. But why did he not have a duplicate key to the reliquary, I wonder?'

'Because he never thought he'd need one, simple as that. The only time he knew he'd want to get into that was when Matthew was dead, and he knew how to get at the key. Unfortunately, it was hidden during your excursion to Bridlington and Leo found it first. He'd been lacing Leo's medication with too much of the stuff Master Johannes left, too. Master Petrus discovered that. The foolish man should never have left such a quantity.'

'No wonder the poor lad could scarce stand.'

Mark of Scepeton, clutching his new bride's hand, could not understand how the outlaws had arrived so timely at Silver Street after Oriane's arrival there. 'Was it Gerard who sent for them, d'ye think?' he said.

'Yes, sir,' Euan replied. 'It's not so far from Silver Street to the forest, you know. It was stupid of him to think I'd allow her to go unescorted to York, but it suited him to grasp at the chance while it was there. He was sure that the house must have been left to her, though he must have known she'd not be allowed to carry on a goldsmith's business alone, even with Leo there.'

'*Femmes soles,*' Oriane said, pertly. 'Women alone. It's law.'

'Er...no,' Euan replied. 'Widows, not unmarried women.'

'Wrong!' Mistress Katherine called, gleefully. 'As long as the woman's been apprenticed for the right length of time or assisted her husband in the business as an equal, then a woman may carry on alone. I could have carried on my late husband's business, but I chose not to. Oriane is quite correct.'

Euan turned to Oriane. 'But you were not apprenticed, were you?' He struggled to sound impartial.

Oriane remained silent. It was her father who spoke. 'No,' he said, quietly. 'She was not. Matthew believed that his daughter had no legal need to be apprenticed but, like everything else he's ever done in his life, he got it wrong, didn't he? Every bloody thing he touched, he made a botch of. Like his son.'

'Father…' Oriane stretched out a hand to cover his. 'I can't stop calling you that now, for my father you have always been and always will be, but this talk takes us nowhere. Uncle Matthew didn't botch the reliquary; he was an outstanding goldsmith. Nor was his care of me less than careful. He may not have understood the law too well—who does?—but even the wealth he left me doesn't persuade me to start the goldsmith's business again. I believe we should let it cease with Matthew le Seler and allow the property to return to the abbey. They'll have good use for it.'

Mark nodded. 'I'm relieved to hear you say that, love.'

'So am I, sir,' Sir Euan said, with feeling.

But Oriane prevented any more banter by keeping hold of her father. 'What pleases me most about the bequest is that now I can repay you both for…'

Mark of Scepeton shook his daughter's hand on the table as if to wake her from a dream. 'What foolishness, lass. Once Gerard's case has been dealt with, and the outlaws, the money will be returned to Leo and he'll pay us back with interest.'

She frowned. 'Are you sure?'

'As sure as you're sitting there, love. What's more, he's told Sir Euan that he wants to come up here and try his hand at the wool business, so it's in his own interests to behave himself, isn't it? With the right handling and a few lungsful of fresh air, we'll soon put new life into him. Eh, love?' He smiled at his new wife. 'I'll be more of a father to him than Matthew ever was.'

'Father, you are truly a good man.'

'Hah!' He leaned back, scowling.

'Father William and Father Petrus both say so.'

'Eh? Ohh…oh, well then. They know best, I suppose.' His laugh had something in it of self-deprecation, relief and acceptance; a delicious brew. It bellowed around the hall and ended in a muffled hug from Mistress Katherine.

'Leo's being cared for, is he?'

'Up and about already, sweetheart. Father Petrus.'

'And your father?'

'He's promised not to go anywhere until we're married. Will you marry me, sweetheart? To please my father?'

'Could you persuade me, Euan? Just a little?'

'Is there anywhere private in this noisy place? Come, where's your room?'

Their departure was noticed but not remarked upon, and in the small room which she had shared with Maddie, Euan held her with a man's fierce grip, his eyes as grim as they had been at their first meeting.

'I cannot be gentle with you this time, Oriane of York. I cannot be persuasive. God, woman! I've never felt such desire.'

Her laugh came in a gasp, her reply cut short by his mouth on hers.

Naked, except for a sprinkling of black hair that littered his shoulders, knees and feet, Sir Euan blew upwards at the last clipping on his nose. 'Enough, woman. Leave me some, I beg you.'

'It's summer, my lord. This may cool you down.' She blew on his neck.

'Tell me, if you will, what you know of the wager between the sun and the north wind.'

'You don't remember? Did your nurse never...?'

'Just tell me.'

'Very well. The sun and the north wind argued about which of them was the stronger, and they wagered that whoever could remove the coat of the man who walked on the road below them would be the winner. The north wind blew, in a rage, but the man only held his coat more tightly around him. Then the sun turned on his warmth and, eventually, the man removed his coat. That's all. Why did you want to know that?'

Euan smiled, declining to answer directly. 'A gap in my education,' he said. He took her wrist and pulled her on to his knees. 'Let go of the shears, woman. Must I be forever disarming you?'

'Come and count out the sows and heifers with me, Euan.'

'Indeed I will. Every last one. Later.'